A PILEAUS ANTHOLOGY

Edited by
Scott Colby

SYMPHONY NO.1: A PILEAUS ANTHOLOGY

Published by Outland Entertainment LLC
3119 Gillham Road
Kansas City, MO 64109

Founder/Creative Director: Jeremy D. Mohler
Editor-in-Chief: Alana Joli Abbott

ISBN: 978-1-954255-19-7
EBOOK ISBN: 978-1-954255-20-3
Worldwide Rights
Created in the United States of America

Editor: Scott Colby
Cover Illustration: Chris Yarbrough
Cover Design: Jeremy D. Mohler
Interior Layout: Mikael Brodu

Printed and bound in the United States of America.

— TABLE OF CONTENTS —

— INTRODUCTION —

Max Gladstone

We share stories.

When a joke gets us, we look for someone who hasn't heard it before, someone to whom we can tell it. When a tale shapes us, we're drawn to tell it again to others, or we tell new tales in response. We share books we love with the people we love. Myth cycles and legends gather this way, layer by layer: knights accumulate around King Arthur's table like rings in a tree, as successive storytellers take up the legend, and with successive tellings the legend gains the intricate simplicity called elegance.

The process is a little more complicated now, in the early 21st century, than it used to be. Modern copyright regimes have changed the conditions under which stories are told, by giving one teller (or—more worrying, to my mind—one multinational corporation) the legal power to say what the "real" story is. Of course, writers have been asserting creative control over their work in one form or another for a long time—my favorite example is how dedicated Miguel de Cervantes is, throughout Part 2 of Don Quixote, to read for trash what we might now describe as a "fan-authored sequel" to Part 1. But if I want to write a story starring Raymond Chandler's detective Phillip Marlowe, I can't—barring the permission of the Chandler estate or the slow entry of the Marlowe stories into public domain.

There are a few possible responses to this challenge. One is the modern invention of the "subgenre": I can write a story that's *practically* a Phillip Marlowe story, or *practically* The Lord of the Rings, in terms of style, structure, affect architecture, as long as I don't use any of the same names or plagiarize the literal text. Another strategy is fan fiction: write what you want to write, even if it stars Luke Skywalker and Captain Kirk, but don't sell it in the general marketplace, and recognize that your work is unlikely to become part of the story that's passed on in the mainstream culture.

One of my favorite responses to this pressure is the joint project. An idea comes together, a world, a concept—but it's more than one person's vision, one person's story, and that's the point. The initial creative impulse builds room for others to engage with and enlarge not just the fictional setting—the collection of things present in the world of the story—but its creative and emotional possibilities. Joint projects can have many different modes of organization and many different relationships to copyright, but when they do function, they create something uniquely shared and, as a result, uniquely welcoming to readers. Rather than a single tree growing outward ring by ring, you have a banyan, prop roots and vines spreading around and through.

Which brings us to Pileaus and the stories you'll find in this volume. When I first encountered the world of Pileaus, I was struck by how much room it offered for invention, mystery, and strangeness. Joint fantasy worlds so often take their cues from Dungeons and Dragons, not necessarily in terms of their world building, but in terms of their main interaction metaphors—the things characters *do* on a moment to moment basis. They go on adventures. They hit spiky critters with sharp sticks. They cast spells and gather gold pieces to fund their next adventure. It's a fun model, but it limits itself to certain kinds of stories.

Under the moons of Pileaus, music is magic, fae hunt violinists, and bards weave plots as well as spells. Empires tighten their grip and rebels resist, while in the dreamworld, faerie lords and ladies cavort and scheme. Certainly, there are adventurers here, as there are in real life. But just as striking to me are the people—a desperate musician, a half-fae child, a failed rebel, a skyship pilot haunted by a strange discordant song—trying to live, to find a place for themselves in a world that obeys fairy-tale logic more than the logic of adventure fantasy: a world in which the hero is not the hawk but the mouse, the small and clever and scared being trying to survive, to grow, to remember, to carry on, and, occasionally, to sing. A world, in that respect, not unlike our own.

Under a single author's pen, no matter how expansive the initial vision, all these stories would tend to circle back around to a single coherent theme—even the wildest of us tends to feel the gravity of meaning and significance. But while the stories in this volume are guided by a unified editorial vision, Pileaus is flexible and mysterious enough to be shaped to its authors' many interests and obsessions. It can be a hard-bitten barfight, it can be the lonely and the lost banding together against impossible odds, it can be a broken man desperate to make amends, it can be an explorer's obsession. When I was first introduced to Pileaus, it felt like something I'd dreamed—and, rarer still, it felt like someplace big enough to dream in. A place, in short, to share.

Go slowly here. Pileaus is a world of multitudes—moons, species, curses, societies, magics, languages. It may help to follow a single thread, as when we listen to a single instrument in a symphony: a single character or concept or even author can be your compass. Music is an excellent starting place. Listen to the many forms of music, here—music as flight, as dream, revelation, music as vision, as drug, music as liberation and as an instrument of control.

It twists, surprises, conceals, and reveals. And you might find yourself humming a few bars—or walking over to a friend with your headphones out: "Hey. You've *got* to hear this."

These are old stories: not by the standards of *stories,* by which they were practically written yesterday, but by the standards of the internet world in which they took root and in which they have grown. The authors—including me—are older and we would hope wiser now than they were when they first dreamed these characters and wrote these words. But there's a bright freshness to the work, of leaves not yet unfurled, of bright clear notes drawn from a new-strung fiddle. Hear it. Take it in. I hope you find something here to pass along.

NO MATTER
— HOW YOU HIDE HER —

Alana Joli Abbott

Rhia shrugged further into her cloak. The moment the sun sank, the air turned cold, and she could see her breath hovering on the fog in the air.

"Fair Dilys, I saw smiling," sang the girl behind her shoulder, breath catching much like Rhia's had, but then dancing through the fog, almost in time with the notes. Rhia hummed quietly along, allowing the music to calm her, which was certainly what Dilys had intended. The girl's hand slipped into Rhia's below her cloak, and Rhia squeezed back.

Neither of them wanted to be here.

Rhia's gaze cast about, trying to make the shapes in the fog become the people she'd been sent to identify. If they were people the Lady was interested in, Rhia was fairly sure she didn't actually want to know them. It was safer to stay in the shadows, out of the Lady's attention, but it was far too late for safety. If only she'd never caught the Lady's eye—but it was too late for that, too. Now, she was what she was, and Dilys was with her.

"I see them," Dilys said, the girl's long and graceful arm extending through the fog, parting it like a shroud.

There were four shapes: three man-shaped, though one was by far shorter than the others, and one woman shape that appeared to be carrying a light or lantern of some kind. Or perhaps she just glowed. Rhia fingered the beads on her bracelet, hanging into her palms beneath her cloak, and murmured a charm against evil.

"What do you see?" she asked quietly.

"Five, like fingers, the little one's the thumb," Dilys sing-songed. She gripped Rhia's hand, starting to pull forward, but Rhia held back.

"Where's the fifth?" she whispered, squinting against the fog.

Dilys' arm dipped, and Rhia saw a small shape, no more than a child, between the tallest man and the glowing woman. But the fog shifted, and Rhia couldn't make out the shape any more than she'd been able to when she first saw the group.

Then they stopped, the tall man giving instructions to the others, and they separated, forms drifting into abstraction as the fog covered them. Rhia bit the tip of her tongue, wanting to avoid the leader, because surely that was who the Lady was really interested in. Better to do the job simply, get enough information to please the Lady without actually complying. There was little enough she could do to rebel, not like the old days.

Dilys started off after the tall man, but Rhia yanked her back, and they followed the short man instead.

From his seat at the bar, Llew watched the short man enter, the smile on his face too broad for him to be up to any good. They'd been in town for a few days already, looking for something, and Llew was as curious as anyone to know what it might be.

No less because there were apparently folk willing to pay good coin for the information.

Beads clattered around his ears, tumbling forward with his hair, as he slammed his mug down, barking for another, despite the fact that he'd slopped most of the last one on the bar's surface. The bartender—a Pilean import as much as his whiskey—took the pay without noticing, and Llew's eyes wandered over the crowd. Few of them wore their colors anymore and not openly. The beads that had once decorated the hair of every man and woman there had now been relegated to smaller decoration—a bracelet here, an embroidery there. The people of Norrington were hiding amongst themselves, waiting. All except Llew, who'd never bothered to hide from anyone.

He ordered an additional second drink, the same slew that the short man with the axe had just ordered, and waited for the opportunity to offer it to the fellow. If habits from the previous night continued, the short man would begin telling stories of his own glorious exploits, which practically begged for people to buy him drinks. Llew would be ready.

And then Rhia came in, and his plans flitted off. The girl came in behind her, a waif of a thing in a too-big cloak, nearly thirteen but still slender as a reed. People rarely noticed Dilys in Rhia's shadow, and Llew would hardly have seen her himself if he hadn't known to look. But he'd learned that watching Rhia was a danger of its own, and so he kept his eyes locked on Dilys as Rhia let her cloak fall down around her shoulders, showcasing her slim figure and amplifying her curves through a gauzy dress in the Mana'Olai style.

Llew saw the way Dilys looked around, searching for familiar faces, waving with a grin as she saw people who recognized her and faltering when she noticed they were too busy staring at Rhia to make eye contact. Dilys almost resigned herself into a pout until she seemed to feel his gaze—Llew watching her so he could ignore the way that Rhia tossed her hair, the way she searched the room for her mark. Llew mirrored Dilys' shy wave, and she giggled.

Rhia's face broke out into a dazzling smile that even Llew could not manage to ignore, and she approached the bar, Dilys in tow.

But they did not approach Llew—instead, they made their way toward the short man with the axe. Dilys tried to heft herself onto the too-tall barstool while Rhia touched the short man's shoulder lightly. The bartender, enchanted by Rhia as much as the next man, called for music without her so much as asking.

Llew cursed as Rhia and the short man made their way out onto the dance floor.

"Bad words do not a good man make," Dilys' voice lilted at his side. He swallowed a second curse for not having noticed her sneaking up on him, then offered her a hand.

"What does the fair Dilys wish to drink this evening?" Llew asked quietly, darting his attention between the girl and the man he'd hoped to be the source of his coin.

"Apples and sky, all mixed together," she giggled.

Llew reached out and touched the beads the girl had woven into her braid. They weren't family colors—they were a myriad of blues and oranges and golds that echoed the hues in the girl's eyes. "You're too young for cider," he warned her.

"You're too old for wine," she countered. "No matter how you hide her—"

"She's never hard to find," Llew intoned along with her. He barked at the bartender again, ordering the weakest cider in the house. It was cleaner and safer than the water had been since they'd lost Mydess to the Pilean invaders and hardly enough to give her more than a warm feeling in her stomach. Rhia would still kill him. "You be good, Dilys. Keep your eyes open."

She wrapped her small hands around the cup, those blue and orange and gold eyes looking up at him, sparkling. "I see more when they're closed."

He pushed away from the bar, affecting a stumble, and Dilys giggled. It didn't take long to spot Rhia and the short man on the dance floor—as usual, all attention was on Rhia, her tumble of auburn hair, her too-well-revealed figure. From the barmaids to the singer to the patrons, everyone watched her, some with animosity born of jealousy, others with unseemly interest. As Llew staggered through the crowd, spilling the drink he'd brought with him, he thought of what she'd looked like as a child, not so long ago, when they'd run messages together under the noses of the same Pilean soldiers who now policed them: mud-covered, freckled, lanky Rhia whose legs were too long for her body. If he could see that image, he could ignore whatever spell it was she wove around herself—true magic or not.

As she spun, laughing, in the short man's arms, Llew lurched into them, sending all of them tumbling off balance. Llew's mug flew and clattered on the ground.

"Sorry! Sorry!" Llew said, slowly and loudly enough to maintain his appearance. He offered a hand to help up the short man, but Rhia took his arm instead, pulling herself up too close to his chest to be coincidental.

"No trouble," said the short man, making his way back out of the crowd, looking at both of them with suspicion. He patted his purse casually, quickly enough that a common passerby wouldn't have noticed, and kept watching as he started back toward the bar.

"Aw, let me 'least buy you a drink!" Llew tried, hiding his desperation, but Rhia had grabbed his hands, wrapping one around her waist as she closed the other around her fingers.

"Dance," she commanded, and he did as he was told, watching his fortune walk away.

Rhia was tall enough that her mouth buzzed right next to his ear, her warm breath tickling as they swayed to the music. "Who are you working for this time?" she murmured.

"Freelance," he grumbled back into her hair, remembering to stumble. She compensated, spinning away before pulling herself back into his arms. "You?"

She had the good manners to blanch. "I don't know what you're talking about."

That meant she was working for her, Losa, the Black Queen, the one who had taken their freedom, their nation, out from under their feet. "I wish you didn't," Llew growled, pinching her fingers in his hand. The beads she wore on a bracelet, identifying her family line, her heritage, her place among their people, clattered against his wrist. "What does she want with them?"

He thought for a moment she wouldn't answer. The tempo picked up, and he staggered through the steps again, but she held on, her chin resting on his shoulder despite his jerky motions.

"Same as everyone else, I imagine," she whispered. "I only have to learn a little."

There was an "or" hanging after the sentence, but both of them knew what the "or" meant. Rhia had had the bad luck of being noticed by the Black Queen and there was no way for her to avoid that scrutiny now.

"What if these are the type of people we need?" he said into a crescendo in the music. They both stamped along with the drum beat, he a bare moment off the heavy rhythm. "There's something about them, Rhia. What if they could help us?"

The music stopped and she smiled with only her lips, an expression that still captured those who had been watching them, despite the sadness that Llew saw lurking behind it. "It's over, Llew," she whispered, her body language implying that she was telling him something far more secret, something full of promise. "We lost."

He couldn't stand to look at her, and he turned, pushing through the crowd as another patron asked her to dance. The music started up again as he reached his seat and ordered another drink with the intention of actually drinking this one. He looked over to the seat the short man with the axe had occupied for the past two nights, and then glared at its emptiness.

As his drink arrived, he noticed the empty cider glass on the bar. The seat next to him had been abandoned. Ignoring the new mug and forgetting his pretense of being drunk, he searched the crowd openly, looking for Dilys, knowing that she'd be nowhere inside. Rhia saw him and he jerked his head over his shoulder, without anger, and headed out into the night.

The air was cool and full of fog; his breath caught in the chill and hung in front of him. The street lamps glowed in small rings, balls of lit moisture rather than useful illumination. But they were enough to show him two figures walking away: the short man with the axe, hand in hand with a slight girl, skipping in the darkness.

Rhia pushed out the door behind him, wrapping her cloak around her hurriedly. "Where is she?"

Llew pointed. "Looks like she's better at this job than either of us," he said. Rhia pushed forward but he held her shoulder. "Let's see what she can find out."

Rhia snarled a curse and clawed at Llew's hand on her shoulder. "She's just a little girl," she said, practically begging.

"We'll follow," he offered, pulling his hand into his jacket, suspecting she'd grabbed at him hard enough to draw blood. "We'll keep an eye on her, so she won't get hurt. We'll keep her safe."

"But we'll let her do our work," Rhia said tersely. "I don't like it."

Yet as they followed, keeping the shapes in sight without giving away their positions, she didn't object again.

Dilys felt through her hand that the short man with the axe was a good man somewhere deep inside, but he had trouble with being good. He liked gold and women, but he was taking her to the blue man, because he was loyal too, and she wasn't supposed to know about the letters on the blue man's arms. She wasn't sure why. They were so pretty that she'd had to ask about them.

"What do they call you?" she asked him.

He looked down at her, and she felt the novelty of the action in his expression.

"Pile," he said, his voice flat, like he was waiting for her to bite him.

"It must be hard to have to look up to the whole world, Pile," she said.

He stopped, blinked at her twice, and then laughed. "Boruin's going to like you," he said, and she could feel his fear go away, though she hadn't meant what she said as a joke.

They went into another tavern, this one with many rooms, and a sad old man playing an over-large fiddle in the corner watched the door. She waggled her fingers at him, breathing in the way he felt like the Fae. He'd danced with them long ago, but their scent on him was acrid, and she knew all at once that they had taken something that belonged to him. Pile led her over to him.

"What have you got there?" he growled. His beads, blue and orange and white like the sunset, hid at the collar of his shirt in the gray wisps of his chest hair.

"Girl who sees things," Pile said shortly. "Where are they?"

"Upstairs," the sad man answered.

"I'm sorry they stole from you," Dilys said.

The fiddler looked at her and his jaw clenched, his bony fingers tightening on his instrument. She cowered behind Pile.

"I'll get them," the sad man said, and left.

She continued hiding as a woman came down the stairs. Sin Eater, her mind whispered, and images of darkness and suffering filled it. She almost cried out with pain as the woman touched her hair. Pile crouched next to her, making himself shorter again, and she clutched his shirt tightly. "I just want to see the blue man," she said.

The woman looked at her again and turned away. It wasn't until she moved that Dilys could see the blue man and the boy at the foot of the tavern stairs.

She waggled her fingers at the boy. He waved back.

The blue man came over finally, and now she could see that the patterns weren't blue, just black, each symbol a word, a meaning, an image, a possibility. She reached out, letting go of Pile, to trace the marks up and down his arm. He almost pulled away, she could sense it, but he let her run her fingers along his skin. She closed her eyes, seeing the images more clearly now, as the potential behind them danced along her lids. Information flooded into her, and she knew more than she thought her brain could hold, words rushing on top of words too fast for her to understand.

Her eyes snapped open again and she looked into his, crystal blue, clearer than sky and water.

"I'd like to visit your library," she said. "But it's yours to keep."

"Tell me what you saw," the blue man said.

And she did.

The short man found them, hovering behind the window, in part because their breath spiraled up like smoke, giving them away. Rhia pulled her cloak more tightly around her, feeling Llew coil, ready to spring forward in their defense—or run. With him, she was never sure.

"I thought you two were on the grift," the short man said with a smirk.

"It isn't like that," Rhia said, before Llew could answer.

"No," the short man agreed, surprising her. "I can tell it's not. My friends say your girl's part Fae. Is that true?"

Rhia's heart clenched as she automatically shook her head in protest, but Llew grabbed her arm.

"What if she is?" Llew demanded, and the short man shrugged.

"No difference to me," he said. "I'd like to know who's interested in us, though. In case either of you should know."

Rhia wondered for an instant if that was a threat, but dismissed it when Dilys came out, dancing, then wrapped her arms around the short man's waist from behind in a hug. He patted her head, but never stopped looking at Rhia and Llew, waiting for an answer.

"The Black Queen," Rhia said, her fingers automatically touching the beads on her wrist, and she made the sign against evil. "She's curious about you."

"Well, we're curious about her, too." The short man pulled out a small purse and handed it to Dilys, along with a piece of parchment, sealed. "The payment is so you see this gets delivered to her."

She could almost hear Llew growl behind her. "And what about Norrington?" he said, too quietly, and the tension in his words was palpable. "What if you could help us out from under her?"

It was open dissention, and Rhia made the sign against evil again.

But the short man only shrugged. "We're just travelers here."

Dilys danced over and tugged Rhia's hand. "Time to go."

The short man nodded curtly and went back into the inn. Llew stormed off into the darkness, and Rhia felt the weight of the coins in her hand as heavily as she felt the Lady's orders on her heart.

"Time to go," she echoed.

— SHE'S NEVER HARD TO FIND —

Alana Joli Abbott

Bowens Pont Road had been renamed something-or-the-other having to do with Yuin when the Pileans made it plain they were staying. Yuin's Glory? Yuin's Peace? Rhia never could remember. It would always be Bowens Pont Road. The bridge had been named after her great-grandfather, who had built it. He'd been particularly proud of the stone trees, the way they mimicked their living cousins. It wasn't just a road; it was art. It was something that showed the spirit of Norrington, the soul of her people.

Rhia's hand felt numb around Dilys' fingers. Tentacles lashed out from the trees, reaching for the crowd now shying away from the bridge's edge. The center dipped downward, spiraling just out of her sight. She was smarter than to get too close to either the mob or the monsters that had once been her family's pride. Dilys pulled forward, but Rhia held on, even though she could barely feel the girl's skin against hers.

"Trees and vines, stone blooms," Dilys said petulantly. "The boy danced in them and came to no harm." But when the girl looked up at her she grew quiet and still, the way that meant she was seeing something Rhia would rather she didn't. Dilys wrapped her free arm around Rhia's waist, and Rhia freed her other hand so the girl could cling to her, keeping the ground from falling out from under her. "The Blue Man saw it in his library and the colors are still flowing on the wind, twisting in and out of the branches."

Bowens Pont tumbled downward, touching the avenue below, while the mob of rioters tried to keep the tentacles from reaching too closely, batting them away with torches and clubs.

"Are they Pileans?" she asked Dilys, knowing the girl would be able to tell.

"The Emperor is gone," Dilys said. "Hidden away. All taken apart. They want him back together."

One of the vines snaked into the crowd and yanked, pulling a man onto the remains of the bridge. He slammed his torch into the vine, and it let him go. The man stumbled to regain his balance and slid in the rubble, sending him over the edge and tumbling down the twisted spiral. Dilys hid her face in Rhia's belly.

"The Emperor is dead," Rhia said, feeling years of bitterness catch up with her. "Long live the Queen."

Howell the Fiddler leaned against the side of an empty shop, pressing his back against the wall. Glass shattered in the streets as Pilean immigrants and their Norrington sympathizers took out their grief on the property of local merchants. He'd stopped trying to keep up with the lynch mob—even at his peak, his skills wouldn't have been able to calm that. Instead, he found himself trailing after stragglers, waiting until the crowds were small enough that he could do something to keep the peace.

He was too old for this.

About half of the group charged down the street, leaving a group of looters across the street from the shop providing Howell with cover. He closed his eyes, touched the tips of his fingers to the beads at his neck, and let out a deep breath. Then he lifted his fiddle and his bow and began to play.

The chaos of the looters' emotions rolled over him. Their will—their grief, their desire to destroy and cause harm to echo their own pain—rushed through him. He controlled his breathing, feeding his own will into the quiet tune, a song of home and family. It was a traditional Norrington ballad, something that would have resonated with audiences in the old days, and he hoped that it carried enough of him along with it that, even though the Pileans would not know the words, they would feel the emotion. Their violence battled with his calm, and he struggled to keep his focus. He breathed in the music, drew on the power that lingered there, and sent out waves of magic on the notes.

The looters began to approach, drawn by the notes, and their rage slowed. One man at the edge of the group seemed to come to himself—he dropped the armful of stolen goods he'd gathered and headed off away from the rest. Many of them had homes to go to, and the song reminded them of the places they belonged, homes with beds waiting, the sweetness of a lover's arms, the laughter of children who would miss them if anything happened in the madness of their grief.

Without exchanging words, the looters wandered away as the last notes of his song played.

Howell sighed, feeling the drain in his bones. He wouldn't be able to do this much longer. He shouldn't have been doing it at all. But Mydess wouldn't burn on his watch. The Fae had taken his youth from him, and the Pilean invaders had taken much of his livelihood, but the Emperor would not take his city from him by dying.

He heard the roar of another crowd, slowed his breathing, and gathered his strength. He hobbled down the road, keeping close to the buildings and hiding in the mists, trying to keep well out of sight until he knew whether or not he stood a chance of ordering the chaos.

A fist crunched into Llew's jaw, and he swung back, connecting with something he didn't actually see. He stumbled back into the arms of a waiting audience, who thrust him back into the center of the fight. If it could be called that. There were at least four men on him and another three on the other Norrington who'd dared to wear his beads out in the open on a night like tonight.

They'd taken his knives right at the very beginning, then dared him to fight his way out of the throng. It wasn't going well.

But at least it was going better for him than for poor Matho. The older man had dropped a few moments before, and the way they were kicking his ribs in, Llew doubted his friend would be getting up again. He pushed forward, trying to push through to the other Norrington, but arms grabbed him from behind, holding him so the others could hit him. He kicked as they approached then stomped hard on his captor's foot and twisted. The Pilean lost his balance and tumbled into his peers, while Llew darted toward Matho again. One of the fighters was aiming a savage kick toward Matho's head, and Llew rolled in front of it, foot connecting hard against his stomach.

He looked up into the fog that hovered above them, wishing he could see the moon. He thought he saw an airship flying overhead, but a splash of light and it was gone, and then he was buried in other people's limbs, each one creating a new hurt on top of old scars.

It should have been different, now that the self-proclaimed god was dead. They should have gotten their country back. The heroes that could have saved them should have stayed, not been accused of murder and forced to flee.

He almost hoped that the lynch mob would catch up with them. Almost. But he was in too much pain to wish his hurts on anyone but the people giving them to him. He flailed blindly, trying to keep Matho covered, even though it was likely that the other man was already dead.

Just like the Emperor.

They headed toward home, trying to stay away from the crowds, making themselves small in the fog. Being small was easy enough. Dilys wrapped the fog around them, convinced it to keep them hidden. She knew Rhia wouldn't notice. Rhia never noticed those things, and she was even more distracted tonight.

Dilys could almost understand. There was so much sadness and anger flying around. It tasted different from Rhia's, though. Tasted different from Llew's.

She gasped when she felt it, then pulled on Rhia's arm. Rhia's fingers slipped away for only a moment, but it was all Dilys needed. She sprinted ahead through the fog, feeling the mist cling to her skin as she moved.

"Dilys!" Rhia cried, and footsteps came from behind.

Dilys thought of the Blue Man's library, tried to remember the words in the books, but they floated in and out of her mind too quickly for her to hold onto them. It wasn't her library, and they weren't her words. She gritted her teeth. The mist was hers, and the songs, and the colors that floated on the wind that were named Aiemer. The city was hers, too, and the magic that flowed through it in trickles, Aiemer in strands, in flavors and shapes. She could see it, feel it in her bones, and she knew she belonged to it just as much as it belonged to her.

The fight was just yards ahead of them. The fiddler, the one who had been with the Blue Man, stood in a shadow, watching. He was afraid, mostly that he wouldn't be able to do anything and would have to watch two men die.

"Play!" she ordered him.

He looked at her blankly, and she wove Aiemer around her, around them both, drew it along the strings of his fiddle. She watched him realize what she'd done, watched as the wax of his bow began to vibrate along the strings.

And then she began to dance.

"You're too young for cider," she sang, too bright and loud for the chaos. Her voice was a knife that cut and sliced.

The watchers skittered away, like pebbles faced with a rush of water. Dilys danced closer.

"You're too old for wine."

Notes lifted behind her, drawing on her will and amplifying as it combined with the fiddler's. This had to end. The violence had to stop. No one else would die tonight, so help them all.

More watchers peeled away, and two of the fighters paused, flexing their fingers. They weren't yet prepared to give in. She whirled mist around them, blinding them.

"No matter how you hide her, she's never hard to find."

She danced into the fray, her skinny legs amplified by the song, by the Aiemer she wove around herself like armor. She kicked out, sending one of the fighters off balance and tumbling into his friends.

"Fair Dilys I saw smiling, nearby the riverside."

Four of the fighters dashed away. She felt herself changing as she pulled in the Aiemer. She'd never drawn on this much before, and she wondered if she should stop. But as she began to draw back, it flooded into her more firmly, and she let it seep into her skin.

The remaining fighters were approaching her, looking at her with the same expression of hate she'd felt on them when they'd been striking Llew and the other man. One of them said something, and she thought it was probably crude, but the Aiemer roared in her ears, and the music filled her to the toes, and she could not hear what he said.

"Her beauty was beguiling; for her song, men have died."

The mist drew around the men like blankets, like pillows, filling their noses and mouths until they choked. She eased back, wanting their slumber but not their end. They dropped, one, two, three.

The fiddler's bow scraped against the strings. The song wasn't over, but she could feel his exhaustion. If he continued, he would die.

She knelt down beside Llew, who groaned as she touched his cheek, and she placed one hand on his chest and another hand on the shoulder of the man he had draped himself over.

"'My mother was a bard,' she sang. "'My father was a sage.'"

The Aiemer dripped out of her, touching the beads of life in the beaten man. It glided over Llew's skin, pausing at each hurt, bunching over bruises and washing them clean.

The last words caught on her breath, and she whispered them. "'And I shall have my cider, regardless of my age.'"

The tune left her body, and with it, the flood of Aiemer vanished. Her lips tasted like cherry cordial and her fingers tingled. She collapsed, but Llew caught her, holding her in his arms so tightly she thought she might burst. Rhia rushed over to them and put her arms around them both. The pair of them held her together, though she thought she might fly apart without the Aiemer, might shatter into tiny pieces, like leaves and colors and bubbles in the air—like the Aiemer itself. She wondered if the Blue Man felt the same when he touched it, when he'd used it to twist the bridge. She wondered if he was somewhere between the Aiemer and the land, like she was. But the thought broke and fluttered as soon as she had it.

She felt Rhia brush her hair back over her ear, heard her gasp and then murmur words that were meant to be a comfort, but Dilys could not hear them. They were nonsense, not even a language anymore—her brain spoke only in melodies, words long forgotten.

They were at the same tavern where Howell had taken Boruin when that crew had needed a guide. It was far enough away from the center of things that the violence hadn't reached this part of the city. Leading them here had exhausted most of the energy that Howell had left. Rhia and Llew looked at him, as though he'd know the answers, as though he'd be able to help them.

"She shouldn't have been able to do what she did," he said finally. He could hear the age in his voice, and he felt every one of his years in his bones.

Rhia shook her head. "I still don't understand what happened. Not at all." The young woman brushed her fingers through the Fae girl's hair, stroking it as the girl slept.

"Magic, that's certain," said Llew. He jerked his chin toward Howell, beads in his hair crashing into a jaw that had been broken not an hour before. "You've got it, too."

"I'm Guild," Howell admitted. "Retired, more or less."

"More or less?" Rhia echoed.

Howell just shrugged. "It wasn't bardic. Not in the song she sang, at any rate." He rubbed his hands together, as though warding off a chill. "If she is what I think she is, it wouldn't be in the music. Must have been something in the movement. In the way of her dance."

"Whatever she did, I'm glad of it," Llew said. "Matho wouldn't have made it, and I..." He shook the thought away, sending his beads clacking again. "I'm glad of it."

Rhia looked at Howell, and again he felt as though she was searching him for answers. "What can I do with her now?"

The girl's fingers had elongated, and her toes poked out through holes in the tips of her shoes. Her head had lengthened into a deeper oval shape, her hair taking on a texture like fine silk, spun so thin it almost floated. Howell had seen this sort of thing before, but not since he danced at the edge of the Dreaming. Not since they took his love through their Gate. Elora had been their blood, and he'd watched as she held their magic inside her, let it change her form. He watched as she left to learn their ways, and though she'd promised to dance with him again, she'd never returned.

"She'll want to wander, I've heard," Howell admitted. "And some say that wandering's best for her kind. Half one thing, half another...Stay in one place too long, she might run into trouble."

Rhia brushed the floating silk of hair off of the girl's now exaggerated forehead and tucked it behind her ear.

"I'll go."

Llew didn't look up to meet either Howell's gaze or Rhia's, but continued staring at the table.

"She saved my life," he said. "You were right, Rhia. We've lost. The war's done. I'll go with her where she needs to go."

"That makes three of us, then," Rhia said, her tone far lighter than her expression.

"But..."

"Bowens Pont is gone," she said, and her voice warbled. "Maybe someday I can come back, but now...Mydess isn't home any more. Maybe it hasn't been for a long time."

Howell sighed. "If we leave tonight, we're not likely to be stopped. Losa's men have plenty on their hands. We could be halfway to Ommany by dawn."

The two young people looked at him in surprise, but he stood, bracing himself on the table because he couldn't quite trust his knees to hold him. "I have a cart. And a horse. She's slow, but she'll get us where we need to go."

Llew stood, and Howell thought it might have been out of respect. "I don't..." The younger man sighed. "You hardly know us."

Howell looked at Llew, wearing his beads openly, just as he had when he was that age. He looked at Rhia, frightened but determined, so protective of the young girl who was the same race as his love had been. He'd been nothing but a musician then, and he had little enough to offer now. But it was enough.

"There's no reason for me to stay," he said, reaching down to touch the silk of Dilys' hair. "I'll be taking what's left of Norrington with me."

Dilys' eyes opened, her irises blue now, like cornflower, bright as a clear sky.

"Time to go," she said.

— MY KIND OF PLACE —

Robert Lee Beers

The air in this pub smells like it could have been bottled and shipped to all the joints throughout Pileaus' domain. Each one smells like the other: a mix of sweat, blood, crap, and overcooked sausage. My kind of place.

I'm Lieutenant Sanctim Dosadi. I've seen it all, done it all, and managed to kill most of it. I was with Roderick Smallmuss from the first. Now, I'm about the only one left. The Emperor has given me plenty of work since then.

The pubkeep eyes me. It's expected. The claymore strapped across my back isn't just a showpiece. Nor is the hammer at my hip, and I'm not the prettiest of men.

The light's dim, so I move through the sawdust on the floor with care. Nothing like a dropped tankard or bottle to trip you—or an outstretched boot—when all you want is a quiet drink.

I have to duck a bit. The heavy beams in the ceiling drop about to where my ears hang. Off to my left is a man, nearly my size, but the hair down his back is red, not gray like mine. His snores sound more musical than the duet off in the corner. The singer is not too bad looking, for a slip. Pity she can't sing.

The pubkeep grunts as I reach the bar. The rag he's holding is too dirty to clean anything—it just moves the filth around. Like I said, my kind of place.

One of the whores wriggles her way through the tables and blocks my path to the bar. She has to be a couple of wars younger than me. Firm enough to be interesting, but too young to be worth it.

She takes in the whole package with one appraising glance. She has some experience, at least. "Mmm," she purrs, "looks like we've got a real man here at last."

I reach out and put a hand on her shoulder.

She reads me wrong. "Oh, and he likes it rough."

I shove her into the drunken sleeper, and she proceeds to prove that she also has a decent vocabulary. Must've learned some of those words from the sailors.

"Ale," I say as I reach the bar.

The pubkeep grunts and grabs a tankard. As he pumps the handle, he turns a yellowed eyeball my way. "She don't like being turned down," he mutters.

"She'll live," I reply.

The tankard slides to a stop in front of me. Foam dribbles down its side.

"She ain't the one what needs to worry."

Instinct is a wonderful thing. It kept my hide mostly intact during those years I spent with Smallmuss. You develop a knack for sensing danger. I step to the side and turn, whipping my fist around as I move. The sleeper's chin meets my fist. The chin loses.

I finish the turn with the claymore's hilt in my other hand. No one else has moved. The whore glares at me from the sleeper's chair.

"Thanks for the warning." I turn back to the bar and reach out for the tankard as I put the claymore back.

"You ain't paid yet."

I like a man who has his priorities right. I slap a copper coin onto the bar. The ale tastes good enough, so I down most of it after the first sip.

As I work on the second pint, a little fellow with the look of a mouse sidles up to my left. "Umm..." he begins.

I sip. The pubkeep goes back to pushing the grime around.

"Uhh..."

"You want something?" I ask.

"Umm..."

"Don't waste your whole vocabulary in one go." I finish the pint, slapping another copper onto the bar. What the hell. It's only money.

"Uhh, you in the army, right?"

"What, you want to join up?" The refilled tankard slides into place.

"Uh, heh," my new neighbor laughs. It's a nervous, tittering laugh. "No, no. Just making conversation," he continues. I feel him looking at me. If he moves wrong, he'll find out what my left hand can do, but I doubt a mouse like him will do more than talk. "Those are lieutenant's pips, right?"

I nod. The mouse has eyes.

"How come a man as old as you is only a lieutenant?"

I shake my head. Always the same old tired questions.

"Wrong family background." The mouse wouldn't understand. I like the action. Captains and above...it just wouldn't be the same.

"Oh."

"You gonna yack or drink, Pridget?" asks the pubkeep.

So, the mouse has a name. He's also got a lot more guts than size, or I'm reading him wrong.

Pridget reaches into his purse and pulls out a couple of coins about half the size of mine. He drops them onto the bar and watches as the pubkeep picks one of them up.

The pubkeep grunts and sweeps the other coin into his hands. Pridget gets a half pint.

I turn around and watch the band for a while. The singer continues to mangle whatever song the musicians are attempting to play. A marii or two would have been better.

Pridget tries again. "Uhh, what's wrong with your family?"

I turn around real slow and stare down the mouse. I have to give the little guy credit; he doesn't back away. A lot of others have. I smile. Some say it's worse than my stare. "Don't have one."

The sleeper groans and begins to stir from his place in the sawdust. The whore bends down to check on him. Nice jugs. Better than the pair the singer hauls around.

The pubkeep mutters, "He's wakin' up."

I nod, leaning back, resting my elbows against the bar. A few of the men and a couple of the women gathered about the tables glance my way. Most are involved in their own conversations or are busy watching the band.

"Umm..."

"What?" I ask. Maybe Pridget's question would prove diverting.

"Why don't you have a family?"

I look down at him. Pridget twitches, just like the rodent he favors. "They were killed by shuen," I say.

"Why?"

"They didn't take well to a few of Smallmuss' tricks."

"Roderick Smallmuss, as in Emperor Pileaus?"

So, the mouse knows his history. I don't feel the need to explain that I declined several commissions so I could stay on the front lines and do to the shuen what they did to my family. I grunt in reply.

The whore keeps her eyes on me as the sleeper staggers from the pub. I smile. She doesn't.

A couple comes up to the bar and orders drinks. The man watches me out of the corner of his eye. The woman watches the band.

Pridget coughs.

"What now?"

"The way you put down that man..."

"What about it?" I growl.

I could hear the mouse swallow. He doesn't say anything else.

The door to the pub opens and six men come through. A couple of them wear gang sashes I'd seen near Deos' docks. All of them carry long knives of shuen make—the hardened jawbones of fierce sea creatures ground down at the joint to provide a good grip, the razor-sharp teeth still intact. Those'll make a nasty wound. Some sailors like them, but for another reason: it shows you fought a shuen and survived. Some of the newcomers bear scars. I've heard a few soldiers say a scar or two makes a man look tough. To me it says there was at least one other man tougher.

Two of the shady crew stand out. One is nearly as big as me and another is nearer to Pridget in size, but where Pridget resembles a mouse, this one is pure rat to the bone. Under a shock of red hair, his shifty eyes take in everything in the room. I can tell he has already noticed where the escape routes are and who in the pub is trouble. He looks at me...twice. The second time he smiles. He's filed his teeth to points so they look like a shuen's. I smile back. The rat doesn't like that. He nudges the big one and says something. The rest of the gang looks in my direction, and the rat says something else. They all laugh, too loudly and too quickly. I widen my smile, nod, and then turn my back on them.

"Seablades," Pridget breathes.

I grunt and raise a finger for another refill.

"Killers, especially when they're dusted," he adds.

I sip. Pommin dust is nasty stuff. It turns off the pain response. A dusted man will keep coming, even if he's mortally wounded. I'd seen a commander use it once on his men to keep them fighting as the battle was pitching downhill. Turns out dust is a real problem in sea battles. A dusted sailor won't even try to swim. He'll just sink and watch the pretty bubbles as he floats down.

"Oy, Sergeant!" Laughter follows the shout.

Pridget edges his way over to the far wall of the pub. I finish my ale and set the empty onto the bar. The pubkeep's eyes are fixed on the gang. I watch their movement as I wipe foam from my mouth.

"What's the matter, Sergeant? Shuen take your tongue as a trophy?"

I don't know what's more irritating: the nasal tones of the redhead's voice or the phony laughter. Getting my rank wrong doesn't irritate. I like sergeants—they've earned my respect. This twerp hasn't.

"I'm talking to you, Sergeant!"

The twerp makes his first real mistake: he puts a hand on my left shoulder and tries to pull me around. I don't move. He tries harder, so I move with him, bringing my hand around and grabbing him by the back of the neck. I bounce his forehead off the bar.

There's no laughter now. A tense silence follows the dull thud of the twerp hitting the sawdust. It doesn't last long. The big one roars like a pricked bear and charges, hands held high. He folds nicely around the toe of my boot. The twerp is staying down. So, they're not dusted. No problem there.

Two down, four to go. The others aren't as rash. They've got their knives out. Good, I like a bit of a challenge. The claymore's got more reach and I've got a lot more experience. Four to one…seems about right.

They spread out, flanking to my right and left. The serrated teeth on the shuen knives glitter in the dimness of the pub. I pull out my war hammer and bounce it in my hand. "Come on," I murmur. "I don't have all day here."

The idiots listen. They rush in from both sides. I step left and give the nearest one a tap on his funny bone with the hammer as I pink the neck of his neighbor with the claymore. Stepping past, I spin and catch the one I pinked with my heel. He flies into the arms of his mates. That gives me a few free seconds with the first fellow. His right arm is useless and he has no idea how to use a knife with his left hand. An uppercut with the hammer breaks his neck. I hear the bones snap as I turn back towards the remaining three.

The big one is on his hands and knees, puking. The twerp continues to nap in the sawdust.

"I'm gonna gut you, graybeard." The one in the middle grins at me as he juggles his knife back and forth.

It's an impressive move when you really know how to handle a blade. I slap the knife out of the air in mid-toss and he's left holding nothing.

The juggler is even dumber than his little show led me to believe. He rushes me, grabbing for the claymore. He finishes his rush screaming and clutching the stump where his hand used to be. I imagine juggling will be a problem now.

The remaining two don't look as convinced of their invincibility as they used to. "Well, boys," I say with a grin, "How about a dance?"

In this case, the grin works. They begin edging back, glancing over their shoulders at the door.

I lunge toward the two punks left standing. "Boo!"

One throws his knife. I duck to the side and move forward. The other panics and runs out the door. His partner gasps and follows his buddy at even greater speed.

I turn and see the reason. The big one is still on his knees, but now he's staring at the hilt of a knife sticking out of his chest. He plucks at the hilt, but the action is weak. His eyes roll back, and he topples forward.

That leaves the twerp. I hang the hammer back onto its hook and slip the claymore back into its scabbard as I cross the floor over to where he lays. I kneel down and pull the twerp's knife from its sheath. It's a real shuen blade alright; the gang must have waylaid a sailor or three.

The twerp groans and moves his head.

"Ale," I say to the pubkeep.

He nods and grabs a tankard.

The twerp tries to push himself onto his hands and knees but I place my boot into the middle of his back and force him back down. "Stay down, boy. You'll live longer."

Mumbling comes from the sawdust. Part of it sounds like, "...kill...you."

"You're about fifty years and several wars too late, lad."

Pridget joins me at the bar and says, "Wow."

I grab the tankard as it's pushed toward me and, I take a drink. I notice the whore looking at me in a different way now. I salute her and drink again, then I slap a couple of coppers onto the bar in front of the mouse. Like I said, my kind of place.

— DEBT —

Scott Colby

Darin watched in contented wonder as the soft somber tones of his battered violin put his new wife to sleep. Arica looked so beautiful, so peaceful, her petite curves making a soft line against the worn linens. All in all, Darin thought, this was the perfect end to the perfect wedding day.

He pulled the old bow across the strings slowly to draw out the final note, savoring the melancholy sound. Although he'd been using them for nearly a year now, he was always amazed at the power of the melodies he'd bargained from Old Man Grastow.

"You're a natural with that thing, kid," Grastow told him once. "Your playing touches something deep inside of people, but it could do oh so much more."

Darin set his violin and bow down on the windowsill and snuck quietly out of his tiny house. Arica didn't so much as stir at his passing. He gently closed the door behind him and took a few steps out into his tiny flower garden.

"The right melody can move a mountain," Grastow had said mischievously. "A sonata in the proper key can turn water to wine. A dirge played slightly askew can kill."

Darin turned to examine his home in Diun's pale silver glow. The quaint, one-room shack had been in his family for generations, with not one of his ancestors monetarily equipped to make it into something more. It languished as dull local stone while houses in the town proper were trimmed with northern marble and rare redwoods. He and Arica already had plans for a new cooking and eating area and a nursery for their children, all to be financed with her hefty dowry.

"But can music make someone fall in love?" he'd asked Old Man Grastow tentatively in response.

He shoved his hands into his pockets and wandered around the house to examine his meager field. Six measly rows of sickly potatoes greeted him. His tomatoes had died a few months back, and his corn hadn't even sprouted. His stomach rumbled at the thought.

There was plenty of room on his land for more, to be sure, and soon he'd be able to buy a proper horse, plow, fresh seeds, and good fertilizer, and he could give up trapping in Easlinder's dangerous forests and settle down to farm. Then, he'd go to the tailor for a new pair of pants—no, three new pairs of pants—and a set of sandals that didn't squeak mightily with every step. Maybe he'd splurge on a new hat. He sighed heavily, pleased that all of the things he'd ever wanted were finally within his grasp.

Suddenly, a familiar voice creaked through the night and destroyed his fantasy. "Just as easy as I said it would be, eh?"

Darin balled his hands into fists and closed his eyes, but he didn't turn around. "You're supposed to be dead."

"Ha!" Old Man Grastow cackled. "Don't believe everything you hear, boy! I'll tell you one thing, though: the supposedly deceased have a much easier time of things than the known-to-be-living!"

"So, you're back to collect your favor, then?" Darin asked.

"Aye, that's the gist of it. Seeing as how I helped you make the prettiest, richest girl fall in love with you—"

"There was no 'making!'" Darin shouted, spinning on his heel to finally face Old Man Grastow. "The music helped Arica get to know me—but she came to love me on her own!"

The bent old man leaned heavily on his thick cane, just an arm's length away. Grastow was a disgusting creature; his teeth were caked with years of rot, his left eye shrunken, yellowed, and useless. The tattered shreds of colorful robes hung from his spare frame like feathers from a Thilan woman's extravagant hat. He stroked his long white beard and shrugged. "Believe what you want and justify what you will. The truth is that I helped you, and now it's time for you to help me."

"'A lifetime of servitude, but infinite knowledge.'" Darin quoted Grastow's offer from long ago. "You've come to collect."

"To collect, yes," Grastow said with a heavy nod of his wrinkled head. "But also to further instruct. You'll be a valuable piece, Darin. Whether you play or not, people are inclined to trust you. Not many of our number can pull that off."

"You sound as if you speak from experience," Darin replied irritably.

"Blonde, blue-eyed whippersnappers like yourself tend to be more popular than old coots like me," Grastow replied. "And since I am an old coot, I must insist we move this bit of drama along. Can't stay out as late as I used to, you know."

Darin shook his head. His worst fear was finally manifesting. Grastow was a terrible individual rumored to be responsible for all manner of ills in the area, from the death of the mayor's infant son to the failure of Doc Luden's prized roses. The thought of doing Grastow's dirty work, whatever it turned out to be, was absolutely repulsive.

And any association with the local villain would destroy the social standing he'd earned in the community by marrying Arica.

"Your first task awaits, my student," Grastow crowed. "There lives in this area an individual deeply in debt to my superiors. A brilliant trader with connections in the richest markets of Nefazo and Mana'Olai, and a man who may or may not have discovered an efficient route to the riches of the north."

"Jales Elanick," Darin said sadly, naming his new father-in-law. "How much?"

"Hmmm..." Grastow mused. "All of it. Every...last...coin. You've three days to make him sign his entire estate over to me—and doom Elanick to a lifetime of knowing his fortune was taken from him by the man his daughter loves."

Darin's heart sank. All of it included Arica's dowry, and without that...

"You've a choice to make, Darin. The type of knowledge I've given you does not come cheap. Dedicate your music to the service of my cause, or I take it away completely."

"You can't do that," he muttered, his voice cracking.

"Ha!" the old man cackled. "You're not the first to tell me such a lie, and all of 'em that didn't fall in line can't hum so much as a bar. Either you're with the Guild, or we make sure you can't possibly hurt us."

In spite of himself, Darin took a step backwards and away from his antagonist. He didn't doubt that Grastow would make good on his promises, or worse. His imagination wandered further than he would've liked in that regard.

"Don't you dare threaten Arica."

Instead of a cackle, Old Man Grastow responded with a deep, menacing chuckle. "Frankly, my boy, I don't give a damn about your wife—mainly because I think you'd cut your losses and run off to con another without a second thought."

"That's not true!" Or, at least, Darin wanted to believe it wasn't.

Grastow smiled wickedly. "You've seen how she reacts to the songs I've given you. You've watched her pupils dilate, her breathing and heart rate hasten, and no doubt you've attempted conversation during such times that she's merely brushed away so that you'd focus on playing. Music can be a religious experience. Without the music, then, how long do you think it will take Arica to realize this was all a mistake?"

Though he tried to deny it, Darin could sense a hint of truth in Grastow's words. The songs the old man had taught him certainly were powerful.

"You're going to run, aren't you?" Grastow asked. "It's great sport when your kind try to get away."

At that point, Darin decided his best chance would be to catch his opponent off guard. He stood silent and still, pretending to brood as he waited for Grastow to continue his verbal assault. Just as Grastow opened his mouth to speak, Darin lunged forward to tackle the old man and beat him down. But all he caught was air, a mouthful of grass, and a sharp blow across his lower back from Grastow's cane.

"Runners usually try that first," Grastow said casually as Darin spat out a wad of soil and pulled himself back to his feet. "Apparently I'm quicker than I look."

And with that, Darin was off. It wasn't far to the dense northern Easlinder forest that surrounded his property, and he'd soon torn through the first layer of brush and into the woods proper. He knew the area well, but the dark forest would confuse Grastow, and Darin was sure he could take him from behind.

When not plying his trade as a musician, Darin made a living as a trapper, and thus he was a more than competent woodsman. After his initial haste had put enough distance between himself and his enemy, he slowed to a more deliberate pace. He slipped in between the hulking trees as silently and stealthily as any predator on the hunt, leaving little evidence of his passing. He'd given Grastow an initial trail to follow; the Old Man would be well within Darin's domain when that trail suddenly ended.

He swung to the east and down a sharp gulley, his heart beating in his throat as he tried to keep himself calm. The dry riverbed made travel easy, and the walls of the gulley would hide him from sight. He quickly reached the game path that would take him back around to the point where he'd started hiding his tracks—and with any luck, directly behind Old Man Grastow. He paused at the start of the trail, knowing better than to rush things. He wanted to give his enemy ample time to reach the ambush point.

"He's going to get you, you know," hissed a low, squeaky voice from behind Darin. "He's a clever one."

Darin whirled, wishing he'd thought to grab a weapon of some sort. A scrawny man half Darin's height sat on the opposite bank, smiling down at him benevolently. The fine silver buttons of his expensive-looking vest and pants glittered in Diun's waning light. Bright green eyes stared back at Darin from under a fine black hat trimmed with a long, green feather.

"What do you know of our business?" Darin whispered sharply.

"Of the specifics? Nothing," the little man replied confidently. "But I've seen this plot play out before. The master gives his student a few tidbits of the power that could be his. Just a taste, mind you. The student takes advantage of what he's been taught, building his own personal empire, however large or small. Then the master comes for his due, and the student refuses to pay up. The inevitable conflict ensues..."

"Enough!" Darin snarled in annoyance. The little man had hit too close to home. "What exactly do you want?"

"In such situations, I've yet to see said student get the better of said master. And because of that, certain economic opportunities present themselves..."

"No more deals!" Darin said a little louder than he'd intended. He turned and stalked up the game trail.

"As if you'll have a choice," the little man called after him. "Huffnaggle will be waiting for you! Just call my name!"

Darin traveled through the woods as quickly as he dared, wanting to put as much distance between himself and the strange little man as he could without alerting his quarry. The incident in the gully had left him unsettled. Something about Huffnagle wasn't right, and Darin did his best to try to forget the name.

The soft tones of a simple flute wove through the forest, setting Darin's nerves further on edge. The trees around him seemed to move in time with the herky-jerky tune. He picked up his pace, hoping to catch Grastow before he could finish whatever musical incantation he was readying.

He soon came upon his chosen point of ambush, and he peered cautiously around a gently swaying oak. Old Man Grastow sat on the forest floor, his back to Darin, playing a slender flute that curled under his left arm and around his back. He gave no indication that he knew he was being watched.

Darin reached down and plucked a heavy rock from the forest floor. He hefted it a few times, testing its weight. Finally satisfied, he took a deep breath and sprung at the back of his enemy's head.

A heavy tree limb caught him across the chest in mid-leap, knocking the wind out of Darin and sending him sprawling. Grastow played a quick scale on his flute, and four nearby trees bent their trunks at impossible angles to pin Darin to the ground with their massive girth. The young man struggled mightily against the weight, but he couldn't free himself.

"Let me go, you crazy old bastard!" Darin shouted in panic.

"You'll live," Grastow said ominously. Darin couldn't see him, but he could hear the old man rise and start toward him.

"I swear, I'll track you down and kill you!"

Grastow leaned over Darin and cackled mightily. His breath was hot and rank. "Many have tried, my boy. Too many. Now—have you reconsidered your position, or do you still refuse to honor our bargain?"

"I'll never work for a creature as foul as you!" Darin spat.

"If you only knew," Grastow replied sadly.

He reached into his pocket and produced a small black box with a tiny key sticking from its side. Grastow gave the key a few cranks, then he opened the box's lid with a quick flick of his wrist. Inside, a miniature ballerina spun slowly on a silver pedestal covered with unintelligible runes. It looked like a music box, but it didn't make any sound.

The pain began in Darin's chest, a slight burning sensation around his heart. It quickly spread to his lungs and his stomach, then outward and onward until it had enveloped his fingers and toes. Every nerve in Darin's body cried out, and he bit back a groan of pain.

He watched in utter horror as a twinkling blue gas trickled from his mouth and nostrils, heading inexorably toward the little ballerina, where it disappeared.

He could feel the music being torn from him. Notes from songs he knew by heart were disappearing from his memory. He tried to flex his fingers into position around an imaginary violin, but he couldn't find the right strings. Old Man Grastow was making good on his promise, and Darin had only one chance to escape.

"Huffnagle!" he screamed.

The strange little man strode out of the forest to his left, carrying a golden measure in his left hand. On one side of the scale, three eerie clefs danced around each other in midair. On the opposite side stood a ghostly miniature of Darin, violin in hand.

"Few appreciate fine music more than my master," Huffnagle chirped. "For three years in his orchestra, I'll spare you from this horrible fate."

Grastow started at the sound of Huffnagle's voice. "How did you...you...you're one of the Fae!"

Darin didn't know what the term "Fae" meant, but three years in an orchestra sounded extremely reasonable—and he was sure he could find his way out of the deal, if he really wanted to. "Your master's got himself a new violinist!" he shouted.

"No, Darin!" Grastow shouted. "He's the one responsible for—"

A flash of intense red light cut off Grastow's warning, and Darin's world went black.

When he came to, the first thing he noticed was the cold. It was sharp and piercing and wet and coming from all around. The ground beneath him was hard and unforgiving.

He opened his eyes and found himself in a dark cell built of dense black stone. The only light was a single beam piercing through a tiny window lined with iron bars. The beam of light fell upon the far corner where a beautiful violin rested against a music stand supporting a heavy book.

Strange music echoed into his cell through the tiny spaces around a thick iron door. He could hear all manner of instruments and voices echoing through the hallway beyond, the various tones and pitches combining into an evil melody that sent a chill up Darin's spine.

A small window in the door slid aside, revealing a frightening pair of crimson eyes. The terrible gaze lingered on Darin for a moment, and then the window shut once more.

"How'd you get this one?" asked a deep voice from out in the hall.

"Just like the rest," came Huffnagle's familiar voice. "Couldn't pay his debts."

— DREAMS AND NIGHTMARES —

Scott Colby

May I present to you Mistress Obata, the Lady Dream, ruler and conduit of fantasy and desire."

Dream stormed haughtily into her brother's throne room. His terse summons the day before had infuriated her and sent her attendants diving for cover. Who did he think he was, demanding her attendance? Sometimes his lack of gratitude for all she'd done for him was absolutely disgusting.

And why did he choose to live in such a dreary pit of a palace? Dream's bare feet prickled against the hard stone floor, and she fought the urge to shiver. Her sheer gown, woven from the strands of joyous visions and carefree daydreams, wasn't much help against the chill, and its lustrous shimmer was lost without a light source to reflect, but she refused to give her brother the satisfaction of causing her to change her wardrobe. She supposed it was better that she couldn't see much of anything, if only because the darkness hid whatever vile, twisted things lurked in the corners of her brother's lair.

Like Dream, her brother was Nai'Oigher, the elite of the Bragheayn nobles. Anything he'd asked for could've been his: the richest clothing, the finest foods, the most luxurious home. Yet he chose to live in a hole, far from the Dreaming Land's sole city, Maeda Criacao, indulging in whatever despicable desire struck his fancy. He could've been someone worth her time, rather than being a nobody she barely tolerated.

Then again, she supposed such abhorrent behavior was likely part of a day's work for anyone named Nightmare.

Dream waited impatiently for a response to her herald's announcement. Just as she was about to clear her throat in annoyance, a quick scale from a violin wafted through the dank air and sent a tingle through her bones. She shook off the feeling before it could take hold of her.

"It is typically considered good form to return a guest's greeting with respect and courtesy," she snarled to the surrounding darkness. "It is also common practice to light a torch or two when one knows company is on its way."

Another quick scale screeched across the violin, and the sconces lining the walls exploded to life. Dream held her composure and didn't so much as blink.

Nightmare's throne room was a massive space, larger even than her own, Dream noticed with dismay. The walls were all sharp, abrupt angles. In the flickering firelight, they almost seemed alive and in motion—and slightly frightening.

Far across the throne room, a young man sat sprawled in a dilapidated chair perched across a crooked dais. His hair was long and unkempt, his clothing little more than tattered rags hanging loosely from his emaciated body. He was dirty and exceptionally pale, as if he hadn't seen the world beyond Nightmare's catacombs in quite a while.

His violin, on the other hand, looked good as new. Oiled to a lustrous shine, it gleamed in the strange shadows cast across the room.

Dream clicked her tongue and put her hands on her hips. "My idiot brother had best have a good reason to leave a mortal to greet me."

"That he does," the young man crooned as he swung himself down to the floor and strode toward her. She could tell by the slight twitch in his leg that he was doing well to hide his dread. It was shameful how her brother always felt the need to frighten people into doing his bidding. Dream herself was above such tactics, as well as such persuasions. "He knew it would make your blood boil."

She smiled and sauntered forward. "My brother has always known how to get a rise out of me. A singular talent, that."

The man sneered and played a sharp set of chords on his violin. In spite of herself, Dream shivered a bit. His parlor tricks were becoming annoying.

"Perhaps not so much," he said tauntingly. He stopped ten paces away, trying to leave a careful separation between them.

But Dream kept on walking. "If it's talent you want..."

She spun her fingers in front of his face with a quick flick of her wrist and sent him a little mental shove, rendering him asleep instantly. The man's eyes rolled back in his head ever so briefly, then they flicked shut and he collapsed to the floor.

"Let's see what hold my waste of a brother has over you."

Dream reached a thin tendril into the prone man's subconscious. Her brother's handiwork was everywhere: fear, doubt, sorrow, and a host of other negative emotions she found positively repulsive. She knew it was his life's responsibility, but she couldn't fathom how her brother could do such things to people. Such scenes always made her glad she'd had the foresight to make sure her brother had been around to take on the dirtier side of the job when she'd killed her father.

As she'd expected, all of the damage focused on a single subject: a young woman with a shimmering smile and long, golden hair. For a mortal, she was quite striking.

But the horrors Nightmare had created around her were another matter entirely. Dream saw the young woman die a thousand different ways. She saw her raped and beaten by bandits, wasted by disease, incinerated in a fire—but none of these images was as heartbreaking as the pain that each caused to the poor young man at Dream's feet.

She couldn't take those images away, but she could give him something wonderful to which he could cling, a shining beacon to light his way through the dark. A little hope would make him so much more useful.

Though there was no music in Nightmare's throne room, Dream began to dance. She focused on the woman, and she imagined her returning the young man's love sevenfold. The soles of Dream's feet grew warm as she pirouetted across the smooth floor, keeping perfect time to a tune she could remember but which was lost when song was taken from the Fae long ago.

A smile spread across the young man's lips, and Dream slowly spiraled to a stop. She snapped her fingers, and his eyes jerked open. He looked around in panicked confusion for a quick second, and then his smile returned.

"Thank you for that," he said, a hint of embarrassment quivering through his voice.

Dream nodded. She'd always found that she could catch more flies with honey than with vinegar. "Your name?"

"Darin," he whispered.

"Nice to meet you, Darin. Now tell me—just what is my dear brother up to today?"

Without standing, Darin searched the floor frantically for his violin and his bow. When he found both, he scooped them up and played a low, somber scale. The room rumbled and the floor quaked as portions of stone twisted into doors, one in the wall to Dream's left, the other to her right.

"He said if I take you through that one, the two of you will sit and drink tea and reminisce about the good old days," Darin explained, pointing his bow to the left. "Through the other, he says you'll get what you deserve."

Dream hid her irritation behind a giggle. Her brother had always amused himself by presenting people with strange and difficult choices. She couldn't understand the base pleasures he let dictate his behavior. "And which door would you have me take?"

Darin looked at the floor, seemingly embarrassed. "Had he told me you were his sister..."

Dream clicked her tongue and shook her head. "I shall save you the unease with which my dear brother intends to entertain himself. I admit, I've always found tea a bit too formal."

She felt his eyes follow her as she stalked toward the door to her right. She knew that he was smitten, that his beloved was but a leper in comparison, that he was worried for her safety. Though his affections made perfect sense, his concern did not; Nightmare neither could nor would do her any harm. Whatever awaited her on the other side would be another one of his silly games. She'd enjoy putting him in his place again.

A cool breeze rustled through Dream's hair as she defiantly yanked the door open. The next room was shrouded in darkness, but the pleasant air and the scent of sweet things within called to her. Had she not known her brother to be up to no good, she might have actually expected to find something pleasurable inside.

She felt Darin creeping up behind her as she strode through the portal. She paused and let him come, amused as always by the attentions of others. She heard a slight snick as his stone blade cleaved free a long lock of her golden hair—the indignant little toad had taken a souvenir! She was about to whirl upon him indignantly when the door slammed shut behind her and twisted itself back into solid rock.

"I know you're here, Nungisa," she called out calmly. "I hope you didn't summon me all this way just to ruin my coif."

She was answered by the thunderous tone of a mighty gong. The instrument tolled twice more, then a swarm of drums joined into a deep, dark harmony. Dream felt her skin prickle and her heart flutter.

"I'll have none of your nonsense, brother. Face me like a Nai'Oigher, or I'll leave you to your ridiculous mortal friend back there."

A clash of cymbals joined in, soon accompanied by a thick, melancholy bass. Dream tried to fight the urge to keep time with the haunting rhythm, but she couldn't keep her foot from tapping in time.

"Nightmare! Stop being a fool!"

A towering crescendo shook Dream to her very core, adding violins, harpsichords, organs, flutes, and a bevy of instruments she didn't recognize to the mix. She gasped as the music jerked her into an ungainly pirouette. No ordinary song could've affected a Nai'Oigher so; her brother had taught his pets things he shouldn't have.

An oboe solo lit the massive fire pit in the center of the room, bathing the great amphitheater in sharp firelight. Dream found herself at the bottom of the intimidating space, staring upward at tier after tier after tier of musicians and their instruments. Her brother had assembled an orchestra consisting of hundreds of mortals, each seemingly more downtrodden than the last—and each poised to fill the room with the intoxicating sounds of his or her own instrument.

Dream gasped, realizing the power Nightmare had gathered there. Such collections were forbidden for a good reason.

Her brother was beside her then, a tangle of torn finery hanging loosely from a deathly spare frame. His tired yellow eyes peered out at her from under a slick tangle of hair that concealed most of his face and neck. His hands, though, told her all she needed to know about his condition. Deep purple notes and clefs scarred his alabaster skin, laying his addiction to the Duine music bare.

"This is what it's come to, then," Dream muttered, allowing her voice to crack ever so slightly. He'd always been a sucker for a damsel in distress.

"We've played at godliness for long enough, Obata," he replied, slow and sad. "We'll soon be giving the job back."

The oboe screeched anew, and the fire died for a split second. When it flared back to life, Nightmare was gone.

The orchestra didn't even give her time to curse at him. Nightmare's musicians sprang into a roiling dirge, pulling every fiber of Dream's being into a terrible dance she couldn't stop or control.

Nightmare himself couldn't have touched her, but his lackeys knew just how to exploit the weakness in her blood.

— BALLASTS OF MAGIC —

Gwendolyn N. Nix

This is the worst decision I have ever made, Lera thought as her skyship fishtailed out of control. A cresting wave of Aiemer crashed around her, coating her world in a stream of ghostly impressions drawn in mist. Her nictitating membranes blinked and blinked, trying to clear away the ever-shifting shapes so she could see what truly existed beyond it.

The boughs of the Imorin wood under her feet creaked and groaned under the pressure. The channels accepting the Aiemer embedded in the living wood had broadened to take in as much of the magic stream as possible. Yet still, the Aiemer storm battered the skyship.

I need a marii to sing, she thought. I need an azh'rei to guide. Why did I think I could do this alone?

Another wave ripped her from the steering wheel and sent her sprawling across the ship. She slammed into the side with a gasp.

I might not make it.

She grappled for a note of the songs the marii sang to appease the oyster-shelled a'shen that stabilized the skyship, but her voice came out as a breathy gasp. The brassy golden trill that had haunted her from the first day she'd stepped on a skyship seemed to be in control of everything—from the Aiemer stream she needed to navigate to the very materials crafting the skyship itself. Lera gritted her teeth and stumbled upwards to grab the wheel and steady it.

The final cyclone of the storm came when she wasn't expecting it. The Aiemer rose around her in a pale wispy wall, curling around the hull of her ship. Lera cried out and shifted her direction even as the channels in the wood flared open, taking on more Aiemer and sending the ship thrashing from side to side, caught between two competing Aiemer streams. Lera slid across the wood, her feet scrambling for purchase, barely holding onto the wheel with a curse. The membrane between her shoulders quivered, as if eager to flare open and let her fly.

A strange new ache thrummed in her body, something that felt like the odd tickling scrape of a knife against her long, claw-tipped foot. It pared with the vibrato of the growling noise in her head—the strange music that had brought her here in the first place—making her feel off-kilter.

Had her crewmates been right? Was she losing her mind?

An invisible friction of the two Aiemer streams finally sent the ship spinning out of control. The pale wall of the magical flow dispersed for a bare moment, and Lera looked over the edge. A scream built in her throat.

"No, no, no!" She spun the skyship's wheel hard, sang the song to bring the ship up and out of the storm, but instead the Aiemer streams shoved her downward.

The ocean sat as a flat expanse of blue rushing up in front of her.

The dread inside her welled up. Tears streamed from her eyes, caught in the wind and flown away as if they were raindrops. Long ago, her ancestors had been cursed from the water and now made the skies their home. Even though she had the remnants of the ocean-born in her bloodline, she'd never swam a day in her life. This pain she felt was her people's banishment from the sea and now, an eashue was going to crash straight into shuen territory.

In all honesty, she'd drown before meeting her long-lost brethren. If she somehow survived that, she'd be executed.

There was a lot to regret these days, but following the music—music only she could hear—had to be the worst mistake of her life.

The skyship shot out of the Aiemer stream to be caught by a gust of wind, angling her off the trajectory heading into the horizon where shades of blue met each other. Now, she was directed towards a sea mount of black lava rock sticking out of the water like a knife.

It was too close. It was too close. She was going to hit.

A stray Aiemer flow spiraled the ship further into the air. Lera told herself she was a Windrider, a Child of Heaven, and she would not fall from the skies. The sky was her home.

The lava rock had other ideas. It scraped against the bottom of her skyship like fingernails on a chalkboard. Lera cursed her foolish heart and her hot-headed ways as the harmonious yet hard-edged music that had driven her here nearly encapsulated all her senses in song.

The sound of breaking wood against rock brought a surge of terror into the screaming blankness to the front of her brain. The ship shuddered to a halt. Lera was thrown forward. The ship teetered and then began to slide down the rock outcropping toward the ocean.

Lera closed her eyes with her breath suspended in her chest with no escape. She'd ruined the ship. The boughs beneath her hemorrhaged magic and cried out in pain. The wind deafened her, all except for that sour timbre want of the song that had brought her to her doom.

The first time Lera heard the song, she was convinced the marii had gotten an arrow in the throat. The song magic to make the vessel fly normally wasn't that bad.

The ghastly, trembling warble had her slapping her hand flat on the skyship's floor-boughs, imagining the Aiemer flowing over and around them suddenly dropping away, leaving them in freefall.

That cursed azh'rei had better not have led them astray.

Lera sang her own song into the supple wood, now cleaned of boot tracks by her labor, in terror that her maiden voyage would suddenly end in a dirge.

When the ship stayed afloat, she let out a shaky laugh until the uncanny song reached her again. It sounded like something created with a reed and mouthpiece, something metallic and grungy, so different to the lilting tunes that floated from the marii navigator and floated around Lera like tulle and silk. The marii song would melt, sweetness in her mouth, unlike this raw, brassy pitch that haunted her now. Lera clapped her hands over her ears, but the dark tone did not leave. She squinted her round eyes and tried to match the brassy cry with her own voice as if that would make it better. Finally, she let the unresolved chord sit heavy in her belly; this strange, melancholy climbing scale.

One of the crew touched her tentatively on the shoulder and asked if she was ill. Asked if it was the Aiemer affecting her in this way, rubbed her back, and telling her it was hard for all new crew. When she didn't answer, that touch slipped away.

Soon, so did the song.

Beneath her, the skyship rocked as if displeased.

"Well, same to you," she shot back when she could catch her breath and left new dirty boot prints on the wood.

The hundredth time she'd heard the song, she'd since earned nicknames that ached like old bruises. She was still a grunt at the bottom of the social chain, still scrubbing the decks. She lathered sap into the broad boughs of the Imorin to keep them supple and gleaming. Even though the trees had agreed to be shaped into a hull and deck and mast, they still needed care. Everything living would be scraped and worn by time—immortal or not—and the trees from the Imorin forests were no different. Lera looked longingly at the captain at the helm, a tall marii, who was in deep conversation with the ship's azh'rei. Together, they tested notes and songs. The marii sang a snippet that rang as if it came directly from the World Song itself and the azh-rei's head tipped back in laughter as he pointed upwards. The captain adjusted and Lera felt the ship lift and catch an Aiemer stream, catapulting them forward.

One day, Lera daydreamed she would captain a ship. She would stand at the tip and look down at the world as the wind streamed past her. She would cruise through the floating trees of the Imorin forest and sip from the hidden crystal lakes of a newfound island buoyed up by the magical Aiemer. Her life would be a gleaming gem that others would speak of in awe. Her adventures would be told during bedtime to children, who would dream of being her in turn. Her voice would lift and join the World Song like the marii as she steered her majestic skyship into the sun.

She promised herself that one day she would see the sea, just to understand what all the fuss was about.

The dark growl of the unknown song that haunted her days and nights reached her ears as if renewed in spirit. She sighed and threw her cleaning materials down. No one else heard this. No one but her.

She slipped to the edge of the ship and slung her long legs over the edge, balanced on the banister and the emptiness of the sky above. The stretch of loose flesh between her shoulder blades prickled as if aware that she could be in empty air at any moment. The quills along her elbows bristled like paddles sensing the currents of air and magic. She wondered if she could spread her arms and that membrane would catch a thermal and let her float.

The noise—because that fluttering, wailing rumble could not be music—took on a breathy tone. The ship angled upward even more into a thick stream of Aiemer and it seemed as if the skyship sighed with pleasure. Sometimes, when the noise in her ears was loud and the Aiemer was abundant, Lera could see it as ghostly wisps floating by her. It would dance and twist, spiraling into curls, pointing her in a direction she could never follow.

"Do you hear it now?" the azh'rei asked, sliding up to her on one side. He gazed out at the Aiemer, and she knew he saw so much more than she did.

Lera's nictitating eyelids flickered. "Yes," she said and then swiftly looked away from his feral profile with just a hint of lij, an indication that both types of blood ran in his veins. "Don't poke fun at me. I'm not in the mood."

"I would never," he said gently and then looked over the edge, studying something completely different. Some days, she wondered what it was like to see through eyes like his. "But when we return to port, you should see a physician. This song you speak of could be a bad reaction to the Aiemer."

"The Aiemer changes everyone!" Lera cried out in frustration. This was something she had also feared, but hearing it out loud made her dig in her heels. Yet, the azh'rei's words were more command than advice. It broke her heart to be seen as unworthy of the skyship, marked by a song no one else could hear. Somehow, it made her feel broken inside.

"The Aiemer has changed you too," she added. "It's a sign of being part of the ship. It's supposed to be an honor."

"Yes, but if it is affecting what you see and how you perceive the world, it might be doing worse to you than you think." He tapped his forehead and gave her a knowing look. "If it is deteriorating something inside of you, dying scrubbing the deck is not worth the change of who you are at your core."

Lera looked sharply away, tears prickling her eyes. Before her, the Aiemer swirled and became a beckoning hand. She looked down at her turquoise skin, muted but still so rich in the growing dusk. She wondered what it said about her as an eashue. Her people had been exiled from the ocean to find solace in the winds, and now she was no longer fit for the skies. Her legacy was to become a Wind Shepherd, and now that hope was disintegrating on the breeze.

"Trust me," the ship's azh'rei said, and clapped her on the back. "There are more paths than this."

But as if in disagreement, the song took up again—a sharp punctuating squall. Lera knew better than to ask the azh'rei if he heard it, too. She already knew what his answer would be.

And still the Aiemer beckoned.

Landing in a port meant cheerful families, meant waiting lovers, meant lingering in the shadows until the lively hum of the skyship's crew was gone before wrapping fingers around the navigational wheel and taking it for her own. Ever since she realized her loud mouth and honesty would soon lead her to being kicked off the crew, Lera kept her head down and, when asked, made promises to her concerned fellows that she was going to take a break. That she was going to spend some time landbound to test if the sharp, soulful song she heard would disappear. That she would learn through care to her mind and body if the Aiemer-exposure was too much for her to continue as a windrider.

Lera was going to do none of those things.

She'd planned it out in her mind and repeated it as she unhooked the ropes keeping the ship still, as she nudged it into a gentle, reliable Aiemer stream that allowed the skyships to come and go into port. The ship was small, manageable by a crew of one. She could see the strongest of the Aiemer streams with her eyesight. If she just stayed where the Aiemer was densest—if she just stayed in the thick mist—she would be able to point the skyship in the direction of the melody that haunted her and see if it got louder. See if it led her anywhere. See if the Aeimer would guide her where she needed to go.

She would not be landbound. She would float on the thermals of the ship like her ancestors once rode the waves of the sea. She would not lose this, too.

And if it was true? That the song was nothing but a lie by her brain? Well.

Well.

She stole the ship in the dead of night when the moons were at their highest. The ship's ballasts were round with Aiemer. Her eyelids rapidly blinked as she warbled out a bare song that she'd heard others on board sing when the skyship lifted off. The ship hummed beneath her feet. The oyster-shelled a'shen responded, opening up the channels within the Imorin wood, flooding it with the Aiemer that flowed throughout the universe. The skyship creaked and groaned. Lera sang to it, but this time she matched the sad lonely trill echoing in her mind.

Her heart stuttered when the ship lifted and pushed away from its dock. She heard cries from below, shouts to halt, but Lera's ears were attuned to keeping the World Song in her mind's eye, imagining the notes floating around her. She smiled into the wind and felt a sensation of both freedom and aloneness as she'd never felt before.

The vessel cut through the sky easily. Hours passed with Lera at the helm, navigating as if she were born to it, as if the stars could tell her where to go. Thermal currents guided her deeper into unknown territory. When the Imorin timber rumbled, warning her the Aiemer was too thin, she sang to the a'shen attached to the wood, hungrily eating the enzymes from the Imorin and regulating the Aiemer, sending them higher until the thin air made Lera sway on her feet in dizziness.

The floating forests fell away. The noise in her mind didn't so much increase in frequency, but elongated, giving her not just squawks and snippets, but rushed scales full of lowered thirds that had her heart aching in an unknown way. Now that she was alone, it was as though she could finally hear what the song was telling her—and it was such a lonely call.

"I'm coming," she told it and sang until her own voice was raw. "I know you're not in my head. I know you're real. You have to be."

After the crash, Lera woke to the taste of sea salt on her mouth. She gagged and coughed, scrabbling away from the foamy spray of the surf before it could touch her. The scent of mulched algae with the aftertaste of scales and fish sat unusual in the back of her throat. Her body ached and a series of dark purple bruises covered her turquoise skin. The barbs along her elbow had been ripped out, leaving blood to drip down her onto the rocky sand. Another kind of ache settled in her, an uneasiness that made her want to pace and flee all at once. For the first time, she realized how hollow her bones were.

Her beautiful stolen ship perched on a cradle of lava rocks. A gouge had been torn along the side of the Imorin wood. Lera couldn't see it, but she knew that the stored Aiemer spilled from that wound, emptying the ballasts of magic. The uneasiness in her bones sharpened to a prickling discomfort. She eyed the creeping ocean.

It was only then that she realized that the music in her head had stopped. She inhaled a shaky breath, listening intently. Nothing. Only the unnerving sound of lapping water filled her ears. A smile broke across her lips. She tried to stand, only to feel the sharp cut of a blade against the nape of her neck.

"Listen, shuen," a low raspy voice said from behind her. The blade pressed to a point of pain, threatening to break skin. "I may have only a few moments left on this rock before you take me. But I won't let that end come one breath earlier."

Lera's mouth opened in shock. Slowly, she raised her hands to show she meant no danger to her captor. "I'm not a shuen," she said.

Behind her, the voice snorted and said, "Sound like a shuen. Look like a shuen. You think those big violet eyes are reserved for lij?" She laughed darkly and eased around Lera. Her eyes flickered with an uneasy recognition before hardening further. "I'm making every second of my time in this realm count before I move onto whatever awaits me after death."

Lera eyed her captor from her long legs to her golden-colored eyes, shiny as coins. The same odd melancholy that had infused the haunting music seeped from the newcomer. It seemed fresh and raw within her alto voice. Even so—even with a knife to her throat—Lera was full of a mixture of wild hope. "You're azh'rei?" she asked.

If she was azh'rei, Lera might have a sliver of a chance to survive this barren, rocky outpost. Skyships thrived when under the gentle azh'rei touch, directing Aiemer streams to fill their Imorin wood to the brim with magic.

"I'm not just some half-breed." The azh'rei looked offended. "I have a name. Aeolia." Her mouth curved into a snarl as if to continue with her indignation that Lera had disturbed her final moments.

Lera wasn't in the mood to be reamed with such quibbles, not when the seawater was starting to climb closer. The white and gray waves lapped at the front of her skyship. "Are you the one projecting that dreadful music?"

Aeolia paled. A bright blush colored her high cheekbones. "I sing. Sometimes."

"Sing now."

The blush darkened from embarrassed pink to reddened anger. "I will do no such thing, eashue."

"So you do know that I'm not a shuen," Lera said.

"I can deduce facts based on my surroundings."

"Well, know this, Aeolia. I am not just a Wind Shepard. I'm not just an eashue. I am Lera." She worried the azh'rei didn't understand her humor, but forged on regardless. "Please, sing." She paused and softened, knowing she sounded mad. "It's important."

Aeolia shook her head. "This sea mount will be consumed by the ocean in minutes, and you want me to spend my final moments serenading you? I will do no such thing."

Lera took a step forward. Her fragile bones twinged from both the crash and the mysterious repelling force the surrounding ocean had on her. "Please. You must. Everyone thinks I've gone mad with Aiemer. Now that I've stolen and crashed my ship, they'll definitely believe it. They'll landbind me. I have to prove, to myself if no one else, that everything I've done has been for a reason. That is has a purpose. I'm begging you. Please sing."

"You stole a skyship?" Aeolia sounded suspicious.

Lera raised her eyebrows. "So you know what a skyship is, too, then?"

The blush deepened. "It's a boat. It floated. On the air. I'm only making assumptions."

"Sure," Lera said and gave the azh'rei a weak grin.

"I can deduce facts based on my surroundings."

"Sure, so you've implied," Lera said, "but that isn't the point, azh'rei. The point is that you must sing."

Aeolia bit her thin lower lip and peered at Lera as if trying to absorb every facet about her. As if she sought to locate the lie in

Lera's words. Lera put her hands together, palm-to-palm, and wished. Behind the azh'rei, the waterline inched closer.

Finally, after what seemed an age, Aeolia's soft mouth parted. Out flowed a verbal magic that wrapped around Lera's heart and infused it with an addictive blues ache. "That's it," she said breathlessly and grabbed the azh'rei's hand, gripping it tightly. "You're it. I'm not mad. I've heard that song over so much distance." She chuckled. "It was always terrible."

Aeolia's pink blush was back. "Is that why you slammed a skyship into this island?"

Lera paused, hearing the grief underneath Aeolia's question. Sadness crawled within the timbre of her song, mixed with shame and that eagerness when a certain longed-for end was near. Aeolia's golden eyes flashed and met Lera's, trading glare for glare, when Lera didn't answer right away.

Lera had met many azh'rei in her young days, but she'd never met someone that looked like Aeolia. Most of the azh'rei that crossed Lera's path were half-marii, but Aeolia wasn't so easily pinned down. She held her hand up. "Help me stand. I need to assess the damage. If this piece of rock is going under like you say, I need to get off of it."

The azh'rei looked at her curiously, but put her knife away and took the offered hand. "Are you with the Empire?"

Lera shook her head, not really knowing much about the machinations of lij, nor the boundaries drawn on maps or their hunger for magical knowledge. She said what she'd heard a million times from her friends and companions. "Lij always want what the eashue won't give," she said with a shrug.

The ocean roared as if in response. The strange scraping pain at the bottom of her feet flared. She inched further back and watched in distress as the water surged closer around her ship. She realized that if the water rose high enough to fill the Aiemer ballasts she would be well and truly stranded. She wouldn't be able to make the ship rise on the Aiemer streams when it was full of ocean.

Her heart pounded and her nictitating eyelid flickered with stress. The membrane spanning her shoulder blades quivered. Yet, she knew what she had to do. This azh'rei might have a death wish, but Lera needed her to get them off this rock before they both drowned.

"The ballast has been ruined," she said, "but the ship will still float if a skillful navigator can pivot her into an Aiemer stream long enough for the Imorin to get enough lift. We only need the ballasts to keep us afloat in Aiemer-thin air. You're azh'rei. You can see the Aiemer. I'm eashue. I can tap into a song to lift the Imorin's spirits. We can escape if we work together. We can live!"

Aeolia seemed to shrink inside herself. "I can't."

"You can," Lera said as she put her hands on her sharp hips and hoped she didn't look as lanky and disjointed as she felt. "I'm here to rescue you. Coincidentally, you're going to rescue me. No debts between us. No ties. Once we're airborne, I'll take you wherever you want to go."

The azh'rei looked at her and folded her arms. "No."

"No? What do you mean no?" Lera knew she sounded frantic, but the water was rising even faster than before and the pain in her feet slid into a constant ache.

"This is my execution that you've stumbled upon, eashue. I've accepted that fate. I've come to terms with it."

"But you don't have to! Don't you understand? You may be the strangest azh'rei I've ever seen, but if your music called me all the way from the floating forests, you've got to be one powerful being. So, why don't you help me help you help me to get us off this forsaken rock!"

"Because," Aeolia said and her chin quivered as if she were trying to hold back tears. "I sold eashue designs to the Empire. I wrote down eashue secrets and gave them to the Imperials. And I'm going to die for it. I'm going to die for what I've done."

Lera's heart stuttered in her chest. Whispered boat-tales rushed through her mind—of eashue gone missing, of lij capturing skyships and taking them apart to understand them, of retrofitted monstrosities flying with both black plumed fuel and Aiemer, rushed through her mind. But an azh'rei who had become an enemy of the Wind Shepherds? That had never been told.

"I sold out my crew," Aeolia said, as if confessing a well-rehearsed story to Lera. "I gave lij the eashue to experiment on. I gave them what design features I could for one of the Imorin ships. But it was damaged, and they suspected a double cross. They put me on trial. They exposed me to everyone. Then, when they deemed me no longer useful, they brought me out here for the water to take me and the shuen to drown me." She let out a deep breath and Lera heard that exhausted melancholy music embedded in her story. This sadness filled up the azh'rei's own internal ballasts until she seemed to burst with it.

And perhaps she had. Perhaps it was that sadness that had called out for Lera to help Aeolia when Aeolia wouldn't help herself.

"Why would you do such a thing?" Lera demanded.

A tear slipped down Aeolia's cheek. "The Empire promised they'd be able to tell me where I came from. I'm azh'rei and by nature I'm a half-breed, but a half-breed of what? Who are my people? I have to choose a side soon, pick my true name, but what if there are no known sides to choose from?"

"How would the Empire know this?" Lera asked. "Why would you trust them?"

Aeolia looked agonized. "They proved themselves before, but they lied to me on this most important point. I've given up everything for nothing. I deserve the fate that's coming for me."

Lera blinked furiously. She felt as if her hollow bones were being heated and solidifying into brittle glass. She glanced at her ship and saw that the water was rising faster now. Close behind the ship, a monstrous creature broke the surface in a plume of sea spray that caught the light. The azh'rei was right. The shuen were coming. Most likely, this outcropping was in their territory and now the two of them were stomping over it as if they owned it.

And the shuen did not like trespassers.

Lera put her hand on the azh'rei's shoulder. Aeolia's golden eyes widened, tears brimming along them in a luminous sheen. "Listen to me," Lera said. "We do not know each other, you and I. But I'm probably one of the few people in this world that knows your true story, now."

Aeolia swallowed hard and nodded as if she'd lost her voice.

"I am here, and I am helpless. I will die without your help. I will be another lost soul on your conscience. If you help me, I promise I will allow you your judgement. I'll bring you to the Empire. I'll drop you off on a deserted island. Or I will help you find your lost crew. We can save them." Her grip on Aeolia tightened. "I do not want to die this day. Do you hear me? I do not want to die."

The water crept ever closer to the gouge in the skyship. Aeolia was silent.

"My ship is going underwater," Lera said. "It is our one chance. You called to me, Aeolia. I heard your mournful music across the winds and Aiemer. I came all the way out here to prove you were real. If you don't want to save yourself, save me. Come with me. Make what you've done right."

"I don't even know you," Aeolia whispered brokenly.

"But I've been listening to your songs for a hundred days," Lera said.

The water rushed forward, licking the rocky sand close to Lera's feet. The ache in her limbs increased like the twist of a knife. The presence of the ocean somehow hurt her from the inside out.

Aeolia took a deep breath, her eyes flickering from the ship, to the huge taishu coming closer and closer, and back to Lera. In one swift motion, she bent down and swept Lera up into her arms. Lena squawked and wrapped her arms tight around the azh'rei's neck. Aeolia splashed through the ocean toward the boat. Lera glanced back and saw lithe shapes diving from the taishu and rippling beneath the ocean surface.

"Hurry!" Lera urged as Aeolia stumbled through the water to the ship. Lera reached up high, catching the edge of the ballast gouge, and hauled herself up so she could clamber over the deck. She reached down, clasped hands with Aeolia, and hauled the azh'rei up.

Finally on the deck, the two of them scrambled to the front. Lera wrapped her hands around the navigational wheel like a lifeline. Aeolia's eyes scanned around them, seeming to catch sight of things that Lera couldn't. "I see a stream above us," she said and lifted her hands up into the air as if calling the Aiemer directly to her.

A sudden sharp impact rattled the ship. Lera dodged forward to look over the side and saw a shuen—looking so similar to her—beginning to climb the wood. They met eyes and shock rattled throughout them both. Lera wrenched back as the shuen began to climb faster. Lera ran back to Aeolia and took the knife from the azh'rei's pockets, before running back to defend the ship.

Lera had to trust Aeolia completely. Even though she could only see the Aiemer at its thickest, she had to believe that Aeolia was pulling the Aiemer towards them instead of letting Lera believe salvation was at hand. Lera started to sing, her fearful warbles making the a'shen connected to the Imorin wood tremble with want. The channels along the wood flared open, ready to take on Aeimer and fly.

Below, the water had nearly reached the gouge.

With our songs, we can fly again, Lera thought and put everything she wanted into her words.

The ship groaned and then swayed. Lera's heart soared. The shuen reached the top of the ship. In a surge of terror, Lera ran at him with the knife, trying to push him off. The shuen grappled with her, attempting to keep a hand on the boat and defend against her clumsy stabs, when the ship suddenly lifted and broke free.

Lera let out a cry of victory when the shuen dropped from the ship and landed back into the water with a splash. The ship wobbled, swaying side to side, before floating in an off-kilter angle upwards and into the clouds.

A whoop of joy erupted from Lera's throat. She jumped up and down as the pain in her bones melted away the farther they got from the ocean. Around her, ghostly shapes of a thick Aiemer stream surrounded her. She refused to look back and kept her eyes forward on the sun, the bright blue crest of sky, the slow, shy smile that emerged from Aeolia's lips.

"We did it!" she cried to the azh'rei. "You called the Aiemer to us! We did it!"

"We did," Aeolia said, sounding dazed. Lera engulfed her in a crushing hug. When she pulled back, the azh'rei's cheeks were flushed with pink again, as rosy and beautiful as a breaking dawn. "We really did," she said.

Lera grinned wide enough to split her face open and took the helm. She pointed upwards, to the open and waiting expanse of sky. Adventure lay before them. The rush of survival made her want to dance, sing, and leap to celebrate their lives.

"Angle the ship to the right," Aeolia said, her flush still bright and high. Her golden eyes glimmered with pride and something new. Hope.

Lera winked at her and obeyed, sending them catapulting upwards and into the clouds, free.

— DUTY TO EXTREMES —

Dylan Birtolo

Morann watched in silence as the two Duine—humans both—attempted to cross the bridge. He sat on a small pile of rocks next to the edge of the chasm spanned by the rope and wooden catwalk. The couple was making their way towards him very slowly. The wind howled through the ravine, making the bridge sway and the lij clutch the ropes in tight fists. They walked along an inch at a time, tucking their faces against their chests to hide from the wind.

The wind eased briefly, encouraging the lij to use only one hand for balance on the ropes. They picked up their pace, attempting to finish the crossing while it was less precarious. However, the lull in the gusts was brief, and it soon picked up with renewed intensity. The bridge swayed far to the side, and the two people fell over the edge, clutching the rope in desperation.

Morann stood up from his rocky seat and walked onto the wooden planks. Even though they swayed just as much as before, he walked as if he were on solid ground. He stood over the two women and looked down at them. One looked up at him with wide eyes.

"Please, help us!"

Morann reached out and clasped the speaker's wrist. With a smooth motion, he lifted her up onto the bridge. As soon as he let go of her wrist, she dropped to her knees and clutched the wooden boards with both hands. Morann turned to the other woman. She reached out with her hand, the same pleading look on her face. He grabbed her wrist and lifted her up as easily as the first. Without uttering a single word, he released his hold. The woman screamed as she fell into the chasm. Morann turned to walk back where he came from.

"Why did you let her go?" the survivor shrieked as he passed her. Morann twisted, looking down at the human still on her hands and knees and holding onto the rocking bridge. "There must be balance," he said.

"You killed her!"

"One life saved, one life taken." Morann continued his journey as if that explanation was enough.

Several days later, Morann sat on the edge of a floating island, trees towering overhead behind him. He looked at the other islands, feeling the large civilization that was hidden in the trees. He could sense thousands of people going about their lives and the airships circling, awaiting their chance to dock and complete their journeys. These Duine were a curious folk—they were as busy as some of the most fastidious Fae, but they accomplished so little over their short lives.

Yet there was something captivating about them. Morann opened his eyes and watched for several minutes, barely moving as he did so. It was hypnotic in a way—watching the marii and eashue carry on as if their tasks were of critical importance. He might not ever agree with the Sidhe'Lien, but he had to admit that the Duine at least served well as a source of entertainment.

As he watched, one of the airships circling over the islands began to lose altitude. It dropped suddenly from its regular pattern, clearly an indication that something was wrong. The world seemed to slow down as the large machine plummeted towards one of the central islands, headed on a collision course with a densely populated part of the city. Morann continued to watch, intrigued and curious to see how things would play out. Smoke trailed from one side of the airship, leaving a streak of gray against the otherwise clear sky.

Slowly, the angle of the ship changed. The trail of smoke curved; it was no longer a straight line pointed directly at the densely packed civilization. The ship's decent slowed as well, leveling out so that it looked as if it might manage to clear the tops of the trees and safely soar past the islands. The crew banked the ship hard to miss the last of the floating woods and level out for a rough landing on the ground far below.

Morann's eyes narrowed. The disaster was inevitable. While heroic deeds might have saved thousands of lives, those must be balanced. Those lives saved by noble actions needed to be weighed against the lives of others lost through malice. Morann knew what had to be done. The balance needed to be restored.

With a start, Morann jumped to his feet. His entire body tensed as he scanned the sky for an airship of approximately the same size as the one that was just saved. It needed to be a passenger vessel, otherwise the balance would be skewed. He settled on a target, reaching out with his hand as if to grasp it in his palm. And then he began to dance.

The Fae twisted and turned on the edge of the landmass to a tune that was ancient by any creature's standards, even the immortal ones. The tension eased from his body as he danced, his movements becoming more liquid and less rigid with each beat. The dirt on the ground shifted and rolled with him, reverberating from the song without words or tune. All the while, Morann kept his gaze locked on the airship he had designated as his victim, often twisting his neck halfway around to keep it in view as he spun.

His feet came dangerously close to the edge, but it did not give him pause. More than once dust and small stones skittered out into the open air, but Morann only picked up his pace. The wind began to respond in kind, making the trees creak as it rushed past and followed the path laid out by his outstretched hands. As the gust struck the airship, the flying monstrosity tilted in the air and shifted far off course.

Morann adjusted his dance, keeping the vessel trapped between his hands. The air itself heeded his commands and continued its assault. The vessel dropped suddenly, the bow of it pointed straight down for a moment.

"Morann! Cease your dance!"

Morann froze. After a second, he twisted his head to face the voice which commanded him to stop. He kept his hands outstretched and the wind continued to push past him. He saw another man standing behind him—at least he looked like a man on the surface. But Morann knew he was no Duine. He wore simple clothes and carried a dagger with an ornate handle on his belt.

"Dorhanin. It has been years."

"Morann, I beg you to stop." Dorhanin's voice was softer as he pleaded.

"I cannot. The balance must be maintained." Morann began to dance again, ignoring the other Fae behind him.

"You must cease—it is not our place to interfere."

Morann continued to move and direct the wind at the airship. It once again turned into a dive, plummeting towards the city.

Dorhanin took several strides forward and reached out to grab Morann's wrist. He jerked on it, forcing Morann to turn and face him. Morann spun around and brought his other arm across his body in a punch. It connected with Dorhanin's jaw, dropping him to the ground and making him let go of Morann's arm. The other Fae continued to his dance, ignoring his companion.

"This is madness!" Dorhanin cried as he stood up and moved to grab Morann again.

"This is my purpose!" Morann screamed to the sky as he summoned more wind with his movements. "I am Ainghid Fas!"

Dorhanin reached out with both hands, trying to grab Morann and force him to stop. Morann twisted away, avoiding the other Fae's grasp. He continued to keep his arms pointed towards the falling airship but split his attention between his adversary and his target. Dorhanin scrambled forward, launching himself into a headlong dive. He wrapped his arm around Morann just before his shoulder collided with Morann's ribs. The two of them hit the ground with a crack. The wind died down immediately, but the ship continued to accelerate toward the city.

Morann growled as he tried to pry himself free from the other Fae. He wedged his foot against Dorhanin's hip. He pushed through his leg as strongly as he could and the two opponents slid away from each other. Morann scrambled to his feet first. He took two quick steps and kicked out, catching Dorhanin in the jaw and forcing him to roll onto his back.

Looking up at the sky, Morann saw the airship correcting its course. It had managed to avert disaster and was already on the rise back into the relative safety of the open air. With a wordless scream, Morann began his dance again, this time with renewed intensity. The wind howled in response, immediately picking up to a frenzy that made his clothes snap as they whipped around his body. With a snarl, he directed the raw energy of the wind towards the escaping airship.

Dorhanin shook his head to clear it, and then reached down to his dagger. He curled his fingers around the handle and slowly drew it from its sheath. Dorhanin gathered his feet underneath him and charged into the center of the building gale, straight at Morann. The force of the wind threatened to push him off balance, but Dorhanin reached out and grabbed his companion's shoulder. He dug in his fingers and pulled, yanking Morann off balance. Morann fell backwards, straight on Dorhanin's outstretched dagger. The mystical blade sank up to the hilt in Morann's back. He gasped once and froze as the weapon pierced his lung.

The wind died down to a gentle breeze as Dorhanin eased his kin to the ground.

The airship managed to right itself once again, pulling itself out of a maddening spin. Morann gasped, each attempt ending in a wet gurgle. Dorhanin wiped his blade clean and tucked it away with a slow motion. Then he reached out and grabbed one of Morann's hands in both of his. He gave a reassuring squeeze. The gesture was returned, but significantly weaker.

"Thank you," Morann whispered, so quiet that Dorhanin needed to lean forward in order to hear it. "I no longer need to carry the sins of our people. This, too, is balance." As he spoke, a smile spread across Morann's face.

"Rest well, my friend. Allow another to carry the weight of our clan." As he spoke, Dorhanin reached out and gently closed Morann's eyes. He hung his head low with his chin against his chest and began to utter a prayer.

— OCEANS OF THE HEART —

Emma Melville

"What is it?" Nikos asked Akahli. His friend knelt beside the figure sprawled across the path, forcing his two companions to halt.

"Shuen," Akahli replied.

"Shuen?" Nikos's voice rose in amazement.

Akahli sat back on his heels and looked up at the bard. "Definitely."

"Never seen one," Nikos admitted. "Never been that close to the sea."

Akahli nodded vaguely, his eyes troubled. "Journeyed north a couple of years back. You can't miss them when you have to cross the water."

They both studied the sprawled figure lying beside the path. It was wearing very little, and its bone structure showed clearly through its bronzed skin. Its eyes were abnormally large, the face strangely empty without a nose. A slight bruise on its smooth head betrayed the part of its body that landed first when it finally collapsed.

"So what is it doing here?" Shuen lived at sea, rarely venturing ashore and never out of sight of the water.

"It's cursed," Gwynhaefar had been standing silently behind them while they examined the shuen.

Nikos shuddered. The word sent echoes through the music in his soul, struck chords of memory.

Akahli sighed. Understanding glimmered in his brown eyes, which, more often now, were blue.

"Shall we leave it?" Nikos already knew the sorrow this would cause the Ainghid Fas.

"No," Gwyn said as she touched Nikos's hand briefly in thanks for his unspoken concern. Her words were firm. "The shuen needs help. Bring him."

Her two companions exchanged nervous glances. Nikos bent to help Akahli lift the unconscious figure—not a simple task, as it easily dwarfed both of them. Luckily, it showed no signs of rousing as they manhandled it towards the inn.

The Bear's Head was small and relatively empty. This close to the Suricles Mountains, villages were few and sparsely populated. The Thilans did not care to live so close to the double threat of bandit and giant, not to mention the recent tales seeping from nearby Burnaumen.

The innkeeper's eyes lingered on the distinctive shape of Nikos's harp case as he entered. The bard could expect a demanding crowd tonight. The prospect of harp music and the old tales would bring most out, however dark the night.

"Can we have a room?" Gwyn asked. "We have a friend who needs rest."

The innkeeper rose from his crouch before the fireplace, wiping his hands on an already dirty apron. He was almost as wide as he was tall, with what was left of his white hair close cropped to match his short beard. His eyes widened at the slim features of the Fae woman. "Yes, out the back," he said with a quick nod. Nikos couldn't miss the disappointment in the man's voice, though the jovial features retained most of their smile.

"I will play for you once I have eaten," he assured their host, who regained his humor, "but we would like to help our…friend first." He wished—a frequent regret—that Gwyn's heart was smaller, her compassion not so immediate.

The few individuals already seated at the short bar watched the strange procession with mild interest. Most seemed more interested in the bard's harp than the unconscious shuen. Nikos wondered briefly whether the tales of strange events from Burnaumen would be added to retellings of that evening—stories of a giant, unconscious sea-man being found in the mountains.

They were shown past the end of the bar and a door which obviously led to the kitchen. Mouth-watering smells of roasting meat wafted out to them as they passed, reminding Nikos that it had been a long day of walking on an early breakfast. The innkeeper pushed open the next door along and ushered them in, then scurried off to arrange food and—most probably—spread the news of the bard's arrival.

They laid the shuen on one of the beds in the large room at the rear of the inn. He showed no signs of recovery, his copper skin muddy and dull. Nikos stared at the still form in concern.

"Should we try to wake…" he paused, "him or her?"

"Him." Akahli joined Nikos by the bed. "Leave him to rest. Let us eat and play, and then we can see."

"The music?"

"May help. Try later."

The inn filled to hear a young, white-haired harper sing the ancient tales of Baeg Tobar. Nikos sang alone. Akahli stayed with the unconscious shuen, and Gwyn rarely came to hear him play when he performed for others these days. He gave them tales of eastern Thila and its defiance against the threats from the Pilean Empire and, later, tales of romance and hope from those who'd built new lives in the south end of the continent.

At the end of a long evening, Nikos closed with the Ballad of Kivid's Rest. It was the tale of the eashue, a group of shuen forever banished from the sea and left to search for a new home among the land dwellers. It seemed appropriate after having found the shuen. Its sorrow touched the listeners with deep longing, filling their hearts with the dream of a place to belong in all the wild, oceanless spaces of the world. The harp twined in mournful harmony about the softly spoken words, but it was the music in Nikos' voice that spoke to the heart and drew forth tears.

"Gifted by the marii," said one listener.

"A note on the World Song," agreed another.

Neither knew how close they came to truth. Nikos was gifted indeed, but his was a prize hard won—a ballad written by the songless Fae.

Nikos let it finish with sorrow, sending them home on a tale of loss so that they might better value the joy of their lives. And if some were caught by the deeper pain and found, upon looking, that they also had no place of the heart, then a bard could not answer for the questions his stories raised in another's soul.

The shuen stirred when the harper returned from the bar. The creature sat up on the bed, his arms hugging his knees. He glanced at Nikos with curiosity as the bard placed his harp back in its case.

"You enhanced the last one," Akahli said with a slight smile—not a question.

"I hoped it would get through."

"It did." Gwynhaefar sat on another of the single beds, her cloak wrapped tightly around her despite the warmth of the fire. She had drawn her knees up to her chest, mirroring the shuen's sad, nervous pose.

Nikos perched on the edge of the shuen's bed. "I am Nikos. This is Akahli, and that's Gwyn," he explained gently, the music still soft in his voice. "Would you give us your name?" He kept himself still and confident, as if dealing with a frightened animal.

"I have no name." The words were stiff and mangled.

"Ushu," Gwyn said, also speaking softly. "The shuen speak Ushu."

Nikos sighed but Akahli disagreed. "They learn enough of the local tongues to trade. He should be able to tell us his name."

"I have no name," the shuen reiterated harshly, his voice slightly clearer. "I am Riku Chou now. I deserve no name."

The three companions exchanged concerned glances.

"We need to call you something," Nikos said.

"Kivid," Akahli suggested, his thoughts doubtless on the lament Nikos had so recently finished.

"All right," Nikos said with a nod, "Kivid. Can we call you that for now?"

The shuen's dark green eyes stared back at him without emotion. "I will answer to it," he said a few moments later. "I care not."

"Can you tell us what happened to you, Kivid?" Nikos wasn't sure the shuen had enough language to explain.

"I am Riku Chou," he said impatiently. The soul-numbing despair in that simple sentence wasn't something the harper knew how to encompass without music.

"Cursed to be land-locked," Gwyn said, her voice barely a whisper. "Removed from the sea, marooned upon land."

"The fate of the eashue," Akahli agreed. "You sang more truly than you knew."

The shuen flinched at Akahli's words as if from a blow and turned his head to the wall.

Early the next morning, Nikos and Akahli took a stroll through the village to check their path south. It had been a year since either of them had travelled the central regions, and the journey was not without its dangers—even for a bard and a man with Akahli's mah'saiid heritage.

"What do we do about the shuen?" Nikos had been pondering the problem all night.

"Kivid," Akahli reminded him—names mattered.

"Mmm, why has he come so far? There are places on the Ururo Bay which would take him in, where he could find others who have left the sea."

"Sometimes the curses of the Osei Xio can be harsh indeed," Akahli warned. "The hex placed upon the eashue is not used without cause. He could be dangerous." Akahli spoke with the certainty of one who had travelled the sea and seen the floating cities first hand.

"Equally, he may not be." Nikos stopped walking and turned to his friend. "I sing the tales of the Osei Xio priests and their sea worship. I know what they can do."

"So, what would you have us do?"

Nikos walked on in silence for a while then stopped again and sighed. "Gwyn? This is something she shouldn't handle."

Akahli shook his head. "I agree, my friend. Here she cannot help."

"She will try."

"She will."

They began to retrace their steps, neither of them happy or resolved upon a course, neither willing to commit to the shuen's strange request.

"I need to come south with you," he had explained haltingly in the deep watches of the night when it became clear to him where they were going. "You have to make sure I continue. I cannot do it alone."

He had not explained where he needed to go so desperately, so far from the sea.

Kivid had recovered some of his composure when they returned. Gwyn sat holding his hand as they talked, offering sympathy and release.

"What have you done?" Nikos' voice came out harsher than he intended, but his love for her ran deep.

Akahli touched his friend's shoulder, but the Ainghid'Fas woman took no offense. "I took some of his pain, nothing more."

"The curse?" Nikos asked quickly.

"I need his agreement, Nikos, you know that." She was gently amused by his concern. It was an old argument—an old grief. "Besides, I would not do anything here."

"I feel better," the shuen said. "Able to continue."

"Continue where?" Akahli asked. "Where do you need to go?"

Kivid's green eyes darkened in concern. "But I thought you knew. You sang of it for me—I saw it in your words."

"Sang?" Nikos suddenly realized what he meant. "Kivid's Rest? You want to go there?"

"There is nowhere else."

"But I sang the legend, not..." Nikos looked to Akahli for support, but the shuen would not be dissuaded.

"You can take me there," he said firmly. "I know this."

"You have no idea what you ask." Nikos sat opposite the shuen. "The distances from here are impossible."

"I have to go. There I can find a home."

"There are other places, closer. The lakes of the Shoro or Bazul. There is much water inland."

Nothing they could say would shake his faith or turn him aside. With a hunger born of desperation, his soul thirsted after Kivid's Rest and a home for one left homeless. The best they could get was a compromise; that they would take him to the nearest water they knew and he could rest there.

So they departed the village, four where there had been three, and grief a constant companion. They would journey inland, each step an extra burden along the way.

— DISCORD —

Emma Melville

Nikos held his harp protectively in front of him as he sat, nervous and alone, in the grandeur of the Bards' Guild Great Hall. He recited the words of a few well-known songs under his breath, but it did little to calm his nerves and the words echoed oddly. He wanted to play, to hide in music, but he wasn't sure that would be acceptable. The demand for his attendance had been blunt and unpleasant, and their welcome was cold.

Glimpses of people scurrying past stirred up the memory of his last visit to the Great Hall when he'd played his graduation piece before the guild to obtain membership. Five years ago, every musician and servant had stopped to wish him well. Today, not one of them took the few short paces needed to greet him.

Nikos regretted his decision to come alone. He was a Thilan, and this was enemy territory. The guild had taught him that nationality came second to the music, but today, with the Thilan defiance more than a decade old and Pileaus' dream of dominion stalled at their wall, Nikos was less sure of his welcome here.

"Nikos!" The man who confronted him was a singer of exceptional skill. He'd been one of Nikos' teachers, a master of harmony and resonance. His voice rang through the hall, carrying its rich timbre to every corner.

Nikos relaxed his firm clasp on the harp and tried a smile. "Master Karos, how good to see you again." He was ignored.

Karos resolutely fixed his gaze on a point two inches to the left of Nikos' head in a most disconcerting manner. "Welcome," he said, his voice lacking any warmth or sincerity. "Do come with me."

The tall singer strode off across the marble floor without a backward glance. Nikos briefly considered staying where he was or even leaving, but it wasn't every day a bard was summoned—however rudely—to the guild. Failure to respond to such a summons was simply unacceptable.

With a heavy heart, he hurried to catch Karos and fell into step beside him.

"I wondered why—"

"You'll be told." Karos still refused to look straight at him.

"You're obviously not happy about it," Nikos said. "Can't you tell me something?"

"No."

They walked a few steps further. Nikos hoped there would be more, but Karos continued in silence.

"How about if I leave now?" Nikos suggested.

Karos finally look him in the eye. "Don't be an idiot, Nikos. You're right; I don't like this one bit, but we're saving the guild, so..." He turned away and walked on.

"Saving the guild?"

"Enough. You'll be told. Through here." He led the way into the testing chamber at the back of the Great Hall.

Nikos remembered the room from his very first visit. Here was where all musicians were judged by their skills. The small chamber was perfectly round, its acoustics faultless. The floor tiles with their central circle of pale green were occupied by a single chair, placed in the very center. Here the applicant would sit to play while those assessing could view him from every angle.

Two guild members stood in the room today. They turned to face the door as Karos pushed it open. Nikos recognized both of them. Thera had tutored him on the harp and assured Nikos on graduation that his playing would one day surpass even hers. It had been the greatest compliment he had ever received. Today, like Karos, she couldn't meet his gaze. The third bard, standing perfectly still and watching Nikos with hard eyes, was the head of the guild. Gylmyn Mor was as grim-faced as ever, forbidding lines etched in each side of his long, thin nose. Karos stepped away from Nikos and joined his colleagues, indicating that Nikos should take the chair.

Judgment—the word ran circles round Nikos' head. This was a place of judgment, of testing. But he was already a member of the guild, and he knew he had done nothing wrong.

Such a thought, and with the silent judges, made the cold room even worse. "I'm a Thilan," he thought. "It must be that. I'm going to pay for Pileaus' failures."

"We have heard the paths of the future," Gylmyn announced, disregarding all introductory courtesies. "They are strident with discord, and the tunes of some we love will be silenced forever."

Nikos blinked in surprise. This was nothing like he'd expected.

"It is clear," Gylmyn continued, glancing at his companions who stood either side of him. "Is it not?"

"Clear," Karos agreed, staring again at the wall beyond Nikos.

"It saddens me that it is so," Thera said.

"It is clear," Gylmyn repeated, "that all disharmony to the guild spreads from your tune in the world."

"Me?" Nikos half-stood and then sat back, stunned. "I've done nothing against the guild."

"As yet."

"But what—tell me how to avoid—"

"Your music rips the threads of everything the guild weaves." Gylmyn leaned forward, his brows creased in an angry frown. "If we allow you to proceed, then you will destroy us."

"I would never—"

"Really?" Gylmyn straightened, his dark eyes never flinching from Nikos's face. "Would you spread word for the guild against Aetos?"

Nikos pressed his lips together to prevent his first angry words. This was a test, then, and of course it came back to who he was: foster brother of the Thilan king. All this talk of his future actions was just nonsense designed to shock him. They were here to test his loyalty to Aetos. Controlling his fluttering thoughts, he forced himself to relax.

"The guild is above politics and nationality. That's what I was taught—what you taught me." And yet he knew Pileaus used bards as spies because of that very reason; they could go anywhere and were above suspicion. Perhaps they were going to ask him to spy on Aetos. Then they might be justified in their fears about him because he would never betray his brother.

"We want peace, Nikos," Gylmyn said, "and sometimes we must involve ourselves in politics to further that. We lay the most careful of plans to ensure the guild's survival and patronage. I'm sure you understand."

Nikos nodded; here it came. He took a deep breath. "Of course," he hesitated, unwilling to commit himself to the words which would surely have him stripped of guild membership.

"But?" Karos said gently.

"I will not betray my king." Aetos was the closest he had to family. Some bonds could never be broken.

"And so you introduce discord—" Gylmyn began.

"We do not know whether the problem springs from Aetos or from Thila," Thera argued.

"We have had this argument," Gylmyn rounded on his colleague. She stood her ground, her head raised. Gylmyn paused and then sighed. "At least grant that we know Nikos is the cause."

Thera nodded and dropped her gaze. "We do. I'm sorry, Nikos. You could have been one of the greatest."

Her regret sounded genuine. Nikos hugged his harp tighter. Could have been? If they really intended to expel him from the guild because of Aetos, then he would start his own guild in Thila. He would be one of the greatest, and his guild would rival theirs. Strengthened by the thought, Nikos sat up straight and glared at Gylmyn.

"You mean you're throwing me out of the guild because something I may do in the future will be bad for you?" He made it a challenge; growing up in a king's court had taught him something of hostile negotiation. "Surely treating me in a way I feel is unjust is the best way to turn me against you. There must be another way."

"It is your music which is the greatest threat," Gylmyn said. "In the echoes of the future, your song drowns ours out."

"Of course, if you throw me out then I will—"

"You are not just here to be expelled from the guild. You are here to have your music taken away. We shall perform a full silencing, and you will no longer be a threat."

Nikos felt the blood drain from his face. His knees trembled, and he barely managed to stay upright. "Silencing," he whispered, "you can't...you can't take my music from me." He'd seen it done—the guild using a small music box to take song from a musician rather than give it to the world. An unlicensed flautist in Thila had been silenced before the court for attempting to raise sedition with his tales.

"It has been agreed," Gylmyn said.

"I haven't agreed."

"That is not necessary."

"But—"

"The safety of the guild—"

"You can't!" Nikos stumbled to his feet, clutching his precious harp to his chest. "Music is my life!"

"Now, I think." Gylmyn stood, Karos and Thera following his lead. For the first time, all three looked straight at him, the weight of their stare almost overpowering.

"I...but...you..." Nikos' thoughts ran wild, his heart hammering. They couldn't mean it. A silencing was never used, not on guild members, not a full one.

The three bards moved to surround the circle Nikos occupied the center of. Each reached into inner pockets and withdrew small crystal flutes, not the small music box he'd seen before.

They put them to their lips and blew. Three slightly discordant notes, pure and sweet, rang in the chamber. The green tiles of the floor began to shimmer, and Nikos thought he could almost see the notes bouncing from the floor and twisting towards him. The sound became light, streaming in multicolored beams to enmesh Nikos. Each new note brought a new color to life, weaving a rainbow net around him.

The notes rang on, more beautiful and terrible than any he'd heard before. They reverberated within him, pulling a response where he willed none.

He fought to keep his mouth closed, but it opened against his will and answering notes poured from him, dragged from deep inside. As each sound struck the colored net, it died and the color faded to black.

Each note of the crystal flutes pulled forth an answering one from Nikos that was swallowed and hidden from him.

What had been beauty became discordant chaos to his ears. Nikos reached out, desperate to catch back the stream of sound. His harp slipped from his arms. He grabbed at it too late, watching the precious instrument tumble to the floor. All the while notes scraped from a throat raw with the effort of attempting to hold them back.

The mesh was nearly all black now, looming around him, beginning to spin.

Something inside Nikos broke. He fell to his knees, sobs clamouring against the noise.

The notes his tormentors played spun faster, hammering inside in jagged bursts, ripping to shreds all the lyrics he held dear, scattering them to be lost in the whirling dark.

The pain of his loss was unbearable. Nikos screamed aloud, the anguish adding violence to the cacophony he heard until blessed unconsciousness descended.

He awoke to a hard bed, cobblestones cold beneath him in the early morning light. His harp was gone, and a weight sat in his pocket. Nikos sat up gingerly; his body felt bruised and battered, though there were no marks on any parts he could see. The weight in his pocket was a purse, full of coins and a note from Thera wishing him well in the future. It was obviously meant as a kindness, but no gold in the world could compensate him for a silencing.

He sat up straighter. They would not silence him; he would show the world. Taking a deep breath, he opened his mouth—and there was nothing, just a rolling nausea. The note had to be there, just a note, a scale, exercises he'd done every day for years.

Forcing himself to calm, he tried again. He decided to sing something easy, one of the first things he'd learned. There was one about a maiden—how did that go? Her love had been a prince, and they...Nikos frowned; the story was there, and he could probably tell it, but he couldn't quite remember how the verse started. How about the shoemaker and...no, the words slipped from him.

"No, you can't do this!" he shouted, not caring who heard. "You'll not beat me! I'll find someone to sing with—that's it! I will learn again!"

He leapt up and looked round. There had to be an inn close by—every other street corner was home to one. And where there was an inn, there would be a musician of some description earning his trade.

He strode down the street, taking corners randomly until he found an inn, 'The Pipes'—a good omen if ever there was one. He hammered on the door until a bleary-eyed barmaid answered.

"We're not open," she insisted as he pushed his way past her.

"I need a musician, now."

"A what?"

"A player. Someone must play here!"

"You mean Tam. Plays the fiddle a bit of an evening, stays upstairs and helps with pulling the barrels up and—"

"Yes, I mean Tam. Go get him!"

She stomped upstairs, muttering under her breath, while Nikos tried to control the pounding in his head. No matter how hard he tried, the words simply weren't there.

Tam was an older, wiry fellow who looked remarkably bright considering he had just been pulled from his bed. "You look awful," he said cheerfully, throwing himself into a seat beside Nikos. "Bad night?"

"The worst. I need you to sing for me."

Tam blinked and sat up straight. "Sing what?"

"Do you know 'The Jolly Shoemaker?'"

"Of course. Thought everyone did."

"So did I, but the words—they're gone. They're just—" Nikos gritted his teeth to keep the pain inside. "Please, just sing it for me, so I can learn it again."

"You have a knock on the head, then?"

"No. Please."

"All right, all right."

Tam opened his mouth and began to sing—at least, Nikos assumed he did, but the noise that reached his ears was a cacophony, a sickening wail that clenched his stomach into knots and pounded inside his head. He could make out no words or notes. After a short while he realized the noise had stopped and that he was curled on the floor in a tight ball with his hands clamped over his head.

"Not a reaction I normally get," Tam said dryly. "Only saw it once before, up north, and nothing like as bad. You've been silenced."

Nikos nodded, rocking himself back and forwards.

"You can't get it back, you know."

"I'll die. Music is everything."

"Not anymore." Tam reached out to help him up. "You have to let go now, move on."

"I can't."

"Then you're right: you'll die or go mad chasing something you can't have."

"There must be somewhere I can find—"

"There isn't."

Nikos stood up and headed for the door. "There has to be. I'll try another inn, someone who can sing better and—"

"Try the marii," Tam said as he opened the door, "if you're set on this madness."

Nikos looked back at the thin fiddler and managed a wan smile of thanks. The marii, of course! The singers of the World Song! They could give him his music back.

Without a backward glance, Nikos headed south.

Refrain

Nikos staggered through the trees, his feet catching obscured roots and sudden hollows as he plunged along. Leafy branches snagged his tattered clothes and slapped his already bruised and battered flesh.

"Marii," he muttered, "must get to the marii." It had become a mantra, the only thing keeping his legs going and holding his fragile sanity together. For mile after mile he'd driven himself south, far beyond the reach of civilization and into the inner continent. He'd bypassed any place in Thila where he might be known. He wasn't strong enough to take Aetos's pity or face the truth of his loss. The hope that the marii, with their link to the World Song, could restore his music was all that kept him moving. He ate little and slept less; the deep void where his talent had been was present even in dreams, a hunger gnawing at his soul.

"Marii," he said again, the words slurred, "must get—" His foot twisted out from under him, sending him sprawling. Ignoring the pain and the tears, Nikos dragged himself back to his feet. "Marii," barely a breath.

There seemed to be a red light through the trees, a sharp contrast to Diun's silver twilight. Nikos stumbled towards it, his twisted ankle depositing him in a heap every few paces until he resorted to crawling.

"Music..."

Dragging himself into a small clearing, he registered two forms leaping up in surprise at his arrival before he crashed onto his face beside their fire.

"What is it, Fale?" The first voice was soft and feminine.

"A man, and a badly injured one at that." The second voice had the peculiar lilt of the marii, somehow heard inside one's soul as well as through one's ears. The guild taught that it was a by-product of their music and the magic in it.

"Marii!" Nikos struggled to rise, but the last of his strength had seeped away.

"It's all right," the woman said, misunderstanding him. She came to kneel at his side. "Can we help? Can I help?"

"Leave him, Gwyn. You don't know him."

"But I can help."

Nikos shook his head as best he could. "No, marii—music. I need music!"

The marii knelt at his other side. "Do you indeed?" she asked.

The two of them helped him up and moved him to sit beside the fire. They sat opposite, side by side, staring intently at him. One was indeed a marii, its animalistic features more wolf than human, its eyes wary. The other surprised Nikos.

"Fae? You are not mortal."

"I am Fae. My name is Gwynhaefar and this is Fale. Who are you?"

"Nikos."

"You said you needed music," Fale said.

"Mine has...was...it's gone." Fresh anguish left him trembling.

"Gone?"

"Taken."

"How can someone—" Gwyn began, but Fale laid a hand on her arm.

"Silenced?" the marii asked.

Nikos flinched away from the word, his hands covering his ears.

"Who would do such a thing?" Gwyn said.

"Bards," Fale snapped, spitting the word like something distasteful and sour.

"Why would they silence someone? I thought they—"

"Why?" Fale demanded, cutting her off. "What did you do?"

"Nothing!" The word was screamed from a torn soul. Nikos slumped and he repeated softly. "Nothing. They said I caused disharmony in perceived futures."

"No!"

"What is it?" Gwyn demanded. "What have they done to him?"

"Cursed him. Taken all his music from him. Silencing leaves a man devoid of all ability, all hearing, all—" The marii stood, obviously agitated. "It is evil beyond any words of mine. To sever anyone's path to the World Song—how dare they?"

"I hoped the marii—" Nikos whispered.

Sad realization dawned in Fale's luminous eyes. "Oh, child, I am sorry. Our music has not such power to heal."

Nikos's last hope crumbled, and he felt his tenuous grip on sanity slip. "Please, you've got to help me!"

"Truly, I cannot. I wish I could."

"I can," Gwyn said firmly. "This is something I can do."

"This is a destiny you came here to escape," Fale said. "You turned your back on your own kin because they asked—"

"He didn't ask."

"Semantics. What difference—"

"You cannot take what someone is away from them like this. It's killing him." Gwyn came around the fire to kneel in front of him. She was taller than Nikos and very slim. He noticed that her long chestnut curls were flecked with green and marred by a single black streak. "I can take this curse from you," she said. "It is what I am."

"How?" He looked to the marii, who was obviously unhappy with Gwyn's offer.

"You were right: she is Fae, but she is more than that. She is Ainghad Fas, one of those who takes in the darkness of others in order to maintain the paths of light upon which the world rests. She can take your curse upon herself."

Nikos' heart leapt. He would be able to play again! But what would this kind woman suffer? He drew back slightly. "This is killing me," he said, knowing it to be true. "I cannot ask you to die for me." With the effort such a denial took, he gripped the log he sat on so tightly that his nails tore and bled.

"I will not die. I am Fae. It would take many hundred such curses to kill me." Gwyn took his hand. "Though I may sorrow over the loss of the delight in a song, I am no musician. Losing a gift I never had will do me little harm."

He could see that she meant what she said, but his heart told him she would suffer all the same.

Fale, beyond the fire, shook her head but kept silent.

"I...I—" But he could only be strong so far. A second refusal might kill him. "Please, help me."

"Wait." Fale joined them. "You say the guild saw you as a threat."

"But I'm not, I—"

"That's not what I meant. You must be a great bard to worry them so."

"Thera said I would be."

"Then you will do something for Gwyn in return."

"Anything."

"I was going to attempt to help her, but I think this link you are about to forge will give you greater access to her than I can ever have. I am going to show you how to reach the World Song, and you are going to use it to mitigate the effects of her calling. Do you understand?"

"No, but I will do anything to help her as she is helping me."

Fale nodded, her features relaxing slightly. "I know. I think you are a good man. I cannot see anything in you that needs silencing." She placed a gentle hand on Gwyn's shoulder. "Do what must be done, but don't exclude me. I think we can make this work for you, too."

Gwyn took Nikos's hands in hers and closed her eyes. "Would you like me to take this pain from you, Nikos?"

"Yes, oh please!"

"Let it go."

At first, he wasn't sure what she wanted, but then he felt a tug inside, as if something was pulling towards her. He relaxed, letting the darkness flow. A cord of shadow swelled from him, linking him to the Fae. Her grip on his hands tightened, but no sound came from her as the dark ribbon corkscrewed into her chest. He suddenly became aware that the marii was singing, a deep sound, richer than mere music. He heard it as if hearing song for the first time, and its beauty made him cry.

"Listen, bard, and sing with me." She didn't seem to have stopped singing to speak, but the words were there inside his head. "Find your voice again."

He hesitated, but then Gwyn slumped against him with a small cry. He noticed that a second black streak stood out in her hair, livid against the white of her face. For her sake, he had to learn what the marii could show him.

He sang, tentatively at first, his voice rusty from lack of use, but gradually with more confidence, following the marii's lead.

"Deeper," she said or sang, he wasn't sure which. "Send the notes in as well as out. Feel them inside."

He tried, concentrating on each sound, letting the notes fill him. Letting go of his surroundings, he poured his heart into the music and noticed that the sound echoed. Notes were picked up from the earth and the trees, sung back to him from somewhere deep within each living thing. Many slid down the writhing shadow linking him to Gwyn, adding light and color briefly to the dark. He tried to follow the notes around him and realized they weren't all sung by the marii. Each living thing sang its own melody. Given time, he thought he would be able to pick out the individual tunes.

The marii pulled him to his feet, letting Gwyn slide to the floor. "Let her sleep. We have work to do." She took his hand and laid it upon the slim trunk of a tree. "Listen." He did, letting her song wash through him while searching for the notes of the tree. "Sing with it."

Lost in the music and slightly bewildered, Nikos sang, following the bass rhythm of the tree down through its roots and then soaring upwards. He was the tree, part of the World Song, lending strength to the forest and life to the land.

Fale's voice joined his, though her song was subtly different. She changed the song, adjusting and caressing the notes, questioning and cajoling. Nikos followed her lead, unsure of what he was doing but caught up in the music, unwilling to ever stop now that he'd gotten it back.

A long time later, or so it seemed, Fale drew him away from the tree. Exhaustion made his legs weak, and he sat suddenly.

"Very good, bard," Fale said. "Do you think you can find it again?"

Nikos listened. The notes were there, inside him, throbbing to the movement of the world around him. "Always."

"Use it wisely in your music; it is a powerful force. Once you are rested, see what further help you can give Gwyn."

"Of course, she saved my life." He looked to where the Fae had fallen, struck by how pale she seemed in the firelight. "And thank you, the music was—" He shook his head, lost for words.

"Look to the tree. You owe it thanks, also."

"What?" Nikos turned back to the tree he had been singing with. Propped against the trunk, bent of living wood, sat a harp.

"Your first gift from the World Song. String it and play it well."

He played it as the sun rose, picking out a new tune that came to him from the sleeping form of the Fae, from her notes in the World Song. So much sorrow made the tune mournful and sad, but he adapted it as the marii had shown him, lifting the grief in the notes, pulling them from minor to major, lightening as best he could. He couldn't cure it all, and he understood that—darkness was the heart of the Fae's gift—but he could alleviate a fair amount of it, and so he did. The color returned to her face, and some of the black in her hair paled to gray and even, in places, back to green and brown.

"I can see why the guild might fear your power," Fale said from where she watched.

"And yet I wouldn't have such power," Nikos said while his fingers continued the tune, "if they had not taken the music from me."

"Prophecies are often self-fulfilling," Fale said. "What will you do?"

"Nothing. Travel and play and be at peace." And stay away from the guild. He did not wish to lose his music a second time, and he had never had any desire to hurt them, whatever they chose to believe.

"Admirable aims," Fale said. "May you be blessed in them." She bent to pick up her pack. "Look after her."

"Aren't you travelling together?" Nikos stopped playing, surprised by her sudden move to depart.

"No, we merely met last night, travellers on the road. Lucky for you we did." Fale frowned. "Be at peace while you can, bard. I have a feeling fate has great things in store for you to have provided for you so well."

She hoisted her pack and left without a backward glance, leaving Nikos to play the sun up beside the sleeping Fae.

— AREST'S TALE —

Jeff Limke

The crackling fire lit the room and warmed the empty crib beside the hearth. Arest cuddled her sleeping son, Jotil, as she sat in the hut's sole chair. The babe nuzzled closer but never woke. She traced her slim finger along the child's forehead and down the bridge of his nose, and then kissed Jotil on the top of his head before she laid him down. She covered him with a wool blanket softer than the furs tucked around him. Once more she leaned in and kissed him.

A simple dream-watcher made of birch and bluebird feathers swung to and fro above the crib. The simple protection ward for the baby's sleep served its purpose, Arest thought as she gazed at it. With Jotil's father away fighting in the war, her simple magics were the best protection she could offer. A small sword leaning against the door was the best her husband had been able to offer her before he was called away. He had used it to protect them from marauding wolves that had thought the isolated family an easy target. The three skins she wore often showed how effective he had been.

She polished the sword weekly to maintain its edge. She smiled, remembering her man teaching her to fight before he left. The moves were basic, he'd said, but effective. If she could block and thrust, maybe slice, that would be enough.

Very pregnant at the time, her balance had been nonexistent for something such as sword fighting, but he had insisted. It had been disastrous. She couldn't move well with her swollen breasts and belly, but she knew that she needed practice, so she practiced every night. She continued to do so even now, after having placed Jotil down.

With Jotil now asleep, she stripped off her undertunic and laid it over her straw-stuffed mattress next to the crib. Stretch marks marred both her breasts and belly. Even though Jotil had been weaned over a year ago, Arest's breasts had remained enlarged while her body returned to its lithe form.

She picked up the wolf skins next to the mattress and criss-crossed one over her chest. Then she tied the leather cords of the other that served as a loincloth. Finally, she wrapped a third around her as a cloak. She felt her skin pock with goosebumps as she pressed the flat of the sword to her forehead. She brought the sword to midguard, exhaled, opened the door, and stepped outside into the pocket of pine woods within the outer borders of Harbrim's Forest beyond.

"Is she ever go head droopy?" a voice, like dried sticks underfoot, flitted across the air.

"Stupid, stupid, Bokey. Patience we've been told."

Bokey jutted out his lower lip. His canines glinted. "Patience not for Flickies. That for Doxies, Ofage."

Ofage wrapped her feathered wings around herself, her beak tucking underneath her plumage. "Shushed."

Silence ensued for two heartbeats of a mouse.

"I thinks we flap now. Changes now." Bokey's talons dug into the branch as he leaned forward. His translucence gave a waver to the atmosphere, the light passing through his body as though he was nothing more than a bubble of hot air.

Ofage tucked her beak deeper, picking at her underfeathers, scratching out a spark or two. "We do what we do when the chance dances."

Arest finished gathering pinecones. A smooth branch lay next to the hut. Taking it, she inscribed a triangle within a circle in the dirt at her feet. A hand's width apart, she placed pine cones until they encircled her. Finished with her routine, she returned to the hut's door and sat before it, pulling wolf skins around her to protect against the night. Her shoulders sagged as her breathing slowed and deepened.

Arest leaned back against the door. She let the wolf skin cloak fall away. Her skin reflected the moonlight. The air had warmed, or at least she thought so. She pulled her knees to her chest and gathered her arms around herself.

Looking to Lakshi, she counted the stars that framed the blue green moon. Each represented a dream to have, to lose, or to fulfill. She released herself, gripped the sword, and stood. The night air seemed to slip around her body as she stepped out into the clearing before the hut.

"Oh, so unsparkly." Bokey shook his head.

Ofage looked up with one eye. Below them, the naked human cut furrows in the ground. The energy of her magic glowed red with snaps of yellow where the point of her sword cut the earth.

She a nixy, Ofage thought. But the queen of the Flickernight had marked her long ago to have the child, and now they needed it.

Back amidst the forest, at the foot of the Mountain of Cats and Boggies, the queen had taken a turn for the worse, and, even more tragic, her lone offspring, Pej, had begun to make decisions for her. A cruel Flickernight with an unnatural beard, Pej had taken sixty Flickies for his ménage. The hue and cry had been loud and sustained, but Pej had boshed it, lounging amidst his pleasure slaves instead of leading and deciding. Amidst the Foresoldiers, a decision had been made: Pej's spirit would be swapped for a malleable one of light and goodness.

And the spawn of this ugly woman who twirled her folk magic was the one.

Ofage felt bad for this human, but the tribe needed a good leader, and the woman's spawn was true and valuable. Pej's spirit would be a trouble when it filled the spawn's form, perhaps even snuff its life light, but it would be better for all.

Arest shivered. The spells were cast.

The lilies around the cabin lifted their heads, singing their siren song of protection. Air twined between them. Pollen, dust, and petals moved about to show the silhouette of something almost bipedal.

"We ready the dawn, lady," sang a voice that seemed to come from within the shape, but with an ambience that surrounded Arest. You ready the dawn?"

Arest quivered, but she nodded. Her eyes closed as the shape flowed over her body, caressing it with quick slips of air. She gasped, her face flushed. Her mouth opening slightly, she moaned softly before sliding slowly toward the ground. Relaxed, yet energized, she let herself join with the form.

"No," Ofage whispered.

"Again?" said Bokey.

"Yes," Ofage said.

"Disgusting. Humans not dance like Floweren Fae. Makes things weirdy."

Ofage ignored Bokey. She opened her wings and glided to a branch hanging over the hut's thatched roof. Tilting her head to one side, she closed two of her four eyes. The remaining two perceived a faint bluish glow enveloping the hut. A humming pulsed as the Floweren coupled with the human. The nightly meeting satisfied the need of the Floweren, perhaps even sated it, but Ofage doubted that. Floweren were all about the coupling. In time, the humming ceased and the night sounds returned.

Every night, Arest now sat watch as her husband had once. Every night she heard animals. Growls, yips, and barks filled the nighttime after the forest Fae had left her. No man or beast would have been foolish enough to advance while the Fae was with her, but once it had left, only her cantrips remained. While effective, these gifts from the forest Fae were nothing more than alarms.

Now re-dressed in the wolf skins for warmth, she reclined against her home, sword resting beside her as she awaited the coming of day when the night's danger would pass.

The wolf stepped from the brush and had taken two steps before the buttercups sang, alerting Arest to its approach. Sunrise was not far away, but light in the forest didn't follow the laws of plains, fields, and open areas. The sun would not soon peak over the tips of the trees.

The wolf's growl seemed to make the earth tremble. Digging with her heels, never letting her eyes leave the wolf, she pushed herself backward.

The wolf stalked forward, teeth glistening as it advanced. Arest kept her gaze locked on it as she fumbled for the sword nearby. If the lilies did their part, she would finish the deal.

"Shap, not goodsy." Bokey tensed, his legs quavering as he balanced.

"Stupid Snarlteeth will ruin it all." Ofage began to slowly flap, building up speed as she moved to the tip of Bokey's branch.

"Stop." Bokey held out an arm, catching Ofage's wing with one of his three fingers. "Ugly choice timesy."

"Yes. I signal the others to come." Ofage opened her mouth wide. A shriek snipped away the quiet.

The flowers snaked out at the wolf's paws as it crossed their threshold. Caught off guard, the wolf snapped at the tentacle-like stems and tore at them with teeth meant for just that. The flowers cried out in death.

Arest rolled to her side, gathered up the sword, and continued into a defensive stance with her hands in front and the sword point up. "Those skins were not given to me," she spat. "I earned them."

The wolf stopped, cocked an ear, and growled.

"I don't bluff." She broke her grip and executed a neat figure-eight motion with the sword that sang with speed.

Two more flowers reached out. The wolf slapped them with its forepaws, clipping both, their petal screams audible only to Arest. The beast gave a measured growl as it padded toward her.

"Your decision," Arest said as she repositioned her feet, redistributing her weight. The tip of the sword never wavered. She kept its point just above the height of the wolf's head. "I can always use another skin."

Gold eyes flamed red as the beast ducked its head and gave a sharp bark.

Then the wolf sprang.

Bokey moved first. His leap took him right to the wolf's withers, his talons raking both sides. He tucked his head forward and exposed his canines, which grew far beyond any size that should have reasonably fit into his body, let alone his head.

"Off my back, air-sprite," the wolf growled. "She's my prey. I have right by murder to avenge her taking of my clan." It threw its head up as it bucked.

"Nokey, grrrowl. Flickernight made her whelp. That before she give herself your warmskins, after Nokey attacked her firstis."

Ofage swooped under the wolf, her beak forward, the claws of her wingtips exposed. She barrel-rolled, her claws ripping through the wolf's exposed belly. Blood spurted, but she missed disemboweling the animal.

Arest leaned back as the wolf bucked. Somehow, the skin of the wolf separated and bled, but she could not see what had created the damage.

She chopped downward with the blade, her eyes targeting the head and neck of the wolf, but she felt no resistance.

The wolf side-stepped out of the sword's arc and circled to her rear.

The blade smacked against the ground. The impact vibrated through the sword and stung her hands, but she held tightly. A copper taste filled her mouth; she had bitten her lip.

Automatically, she pirouetted left, keeping the sword extended but her elbow bent so as to protect herself from some attack as she momentarily exposed her backside. The wolf skins arced, obscuring any opening that may have presented itself.

By the end of the move, she once again faced the wolf, but the skins had loosened. The lion cloth was still intact and not in danger of falling free and fouling her movements. Not so the other. She had wrapped her chest to keep the movement of her breasts from making the swinging of the sword difficult. Her man had taught her well, but even though she had occasionally practiced without the support of the skin, her reactions were trained with it.

With her free hand, she tried to tuck the wolf skin over and around her breast, but unless she let go of the sword, there was no way to remedy the situation. She pulled the annoying garment free and flung it at the wolf. "Take it, then!"

The wolf collapsed on its side, snapping at the air and bleeding from the belly. Its eyes darted around as it growled and barked before forcing itself to its feet.

With a primal scream, she attacked. She swung the sword in short swipes and didn't intend to embed the sword in the wolf; that wouldn't stop its advance. It would be willing to drive the sword deeper into itself to get close enough to her.

Arest slashed across the beast's ribs, but the move threw her off balance. The wolf struck with a paw. Its claws tore across her forearm, knocking her off balance and to the ground.

Arest scrambled backward as she kept her sword at midguard, blood dripping from her arm. Behind her, she could hear the wailing of Jotil. In front of her, the underbrush rattled with growls, yips, and barks.

Leaves cartwheeled through the air as a harsh gale tore through the forest. Branches snapped and fell. Pinecones and acorns whipped through the air. One smacked against her side like a fist. She wrapped her arms around her torso for protection and retreated toward the cabin. Her eyes never left the wolf. It advanced, but it, too, was under assault from the trees.

Jotil's crying grew into screeching.

Tears formed in Arest's eyes. "Fae of the woods, I have given myself to you. Please don't let this beast have its way."

Golden eyes appeared between the trees, and growls rumbled from the shadows. The wolf pack assembled.

The birds' cackle erupted in random bursts, sounding like tin thunder over the low thumping of their wings. The sounds whirled around the hut's clearing, and the wolf paused.

"I will kill her," the wolf barked over the din.

Bokey reached back with a taloned hand and threw a pine cone. "Say you beforesy." The cone flew true and smacked the wolf on the snout. The wolf's eyes watered. "She ours."

Bokey turned away from the wolf and looked to Ofage, who hung perpendicular to the ground. "Beaks coming. Do they help us?"

Ofage grimaced. "They are with us now. They will start small with the sparrows first, follow with crows, then rooks. If more is needed, then the hawks, falcons and eagles will attack." Ofage turned her head in an impossible full circle. "We need for Jkavnd and Torxi to arrive with Pej's soul."

"Not good Flickies. Too uppsy."

"Don't pick a fight. Right now they are important. They have the crystal for the kidling and the prince." Ofage scanned the sky one more time. "They need to hurry."

From the undergrowth, a second wolf raced toward Arest. She had hoped the first defense and the coming of the sun would be enough to keep the rest of the pack at bay, but it was not to be. As the gap between them narrowed, Arest bent her knees and brought the sword up above her head. She coiled all her strength in her legs and shoulders.

The wolf leapt, mouth wide, teeth sparkling.

Arest leapt and swung. With gravity's aid, her sword carved the wolf's front flank.

But the beast's momentum carried it into her. Snarling, his mouth snapped shut on empty wolf skin as it rolled past.

Arest was pulled along. The garment tore free, but the force left her sprawled on the forest floor. Her left hand still clutched the sword, but she was in no position to use it

More wolves emerged from the trees, eyes aglow and teeth glistening.

The chirping sounded annoying and harmless. Ofage dove amongst the sparrows as they pelted the wolves. The wolves turned, snapping at the small birds, crunching some in their maws, but a few managed to damage the wolves' eyes and snouts with tiny, but sharp, beaks and talons.

The aerial attack spread the wolves apart, imbuing chaos into what had been a straight forward assault.

But three wolves persisted. They kept their attention on Arest.

"You can't get away," the lead wolf snarled. "I will treat you as you did my packmate."

Ofage sprinted along the ground, wings useless for lift as long as they were turned for weaponry. Alongside one wolf, she sliced out and severed the tendons on its back leg. The wolf tumbled snout-first into the ground and tumbled to a stop, where it let out a mournful howl. "Told you not to do this," Ofage said as it continued on to the next wolf.

The next wolf, having heard the howl, turned in time to see Ofage bearing down. The beast turned and lowered its head, hackles up.

"You are a pretty puppy when you do that." Ofage leapt into the air and barely glided above the ground.

Teeth glaring, the wolf leapt at Ofage.

Ofage stopped, pirouetted, and severed the wolf's carotid artery with her claw. The wolf's inertia toppled its body upon Ofage.

As she began to cut herself out of the wolf carcass, Ofage looked toward Arest and saw the other wolf attack.

"They finally skydown." Bokey cartwheeled along the ground toward Ofage, followed by the two other woodland Fae: Jkavnd and Torxi. Torxi clutched a golden amulet.

Arest was covered with a sickly mixture of sweat, dirt, pollen, and blood. Her chest heaved as she tried to gain a better grip on the sword. Her arms and hands burned with fatigue. The cut from the wolf trickled down her arm and into her hands. With her skin slick with blood and the skins gone, she couldn't clean her hands, but still she clenched the sword as well as she could.

The wolf slashed at her and leapt. Its growls echoed in her ears. The impact of the wolf onto the sword point wrenched her arms.

The wolf's head twisted to and fro. Its mouth snapped open and shut. Arest tilted her head away as its teeth gnashed desperately for her throat. Still she held the pommel before her. Her elbows buckled, but then the wolf's tongue lolled out of its mouth. Lifelessly, its head slapped against hers and drove both to the ground.

The world went black for Arest as the wolf's body came to rest beside her, its claws dragging across her belly, tearing the skin. She bled.

The remaining wolves regrouped and dashed toward the two bodies, ready to feast on Arest. Howls of anticipation along with yips of happiness rang throughout the air.

They never saw the wave of crows and rooks rain from the sky. The birds, while normally scavengers, were merciless attack beasts. With beak and claw they tore at the wolves, driving them away from Arest.

The wolves turned on them, teeth and claws inflicting fatal damage wherever they made contact, but their forces were thinned. By the time the first wave of falcons and hawks followed, they had retreated into the woods. Those left injured or dead became a buffet for scavengers. Above, vultures circled, awaiting their turn.

Bokey walked over to Ofage. "Not too badly."

"Thanks–I think," Ofage said before turning to the two accompanying Fae. "You have it?"

Torxi opened the amulet to reveal a small crystal vial in his lizard-like talon. "Perfectly ready. We have finish quickly."

Ofage's tongue extended around her head, lapping away the carnage. She took a deep breath and looked at Arest. "She is asleep?"

"More or less. She will not know that we have exchanged her whelp." Jakvnd glanced about.

Bokey smiled, his fangs wet and glistening. "So princey become baby and baby become princey!" With a paw he scraped the bloody hole that Ofage had created in the dead wolf and licked it. "Baby be better. You good teach."

Torxi and Ofage moved toward the hut. "Bokey, you and Jkavnd healtreat the lij. We need it to watch over Pej's new life. He may be bad, but he doesn't deserve to be dead."

Bokey arched two of three eyebrows as he moved next to the unconscious Arest.

"Trust us. This is a much worse punishment," said Jkavnd before both Torxi and Ofage entered the hut.

Arest awoke naked to the sound of Jotil crying. She lay inside the hut on a freshly skinned and tanned wolf skin. Her arm and belly were dressed with healing leaves. Her head throbbed, but she made her way to the crib. Jotil looked up at her with wide eyes, terrified as if he didn't recognize her.

"Shhhhh, it's alright. The forest protected us," she said as she brought the babe close. "We'll be fine."

The fire had been stoked and blazed nicely. Within the glowing embers, the remnants of the dream-watcher burned. Leaning against the side of hearth, her sword reflected the firelight.

She walked to the now barred door and looked through a crack between it and the frame. The clearing was torn up, but no bodies remained. She smiled as she noted the weave of viperweb that now fenced the woods around the hut, leaving a single exit only wide enough for one person.

She turned to the room where Jotil continued to cry. "My babe, we are safe. When you are older, I'll tell you of this battle and how the Fae saved us."

From above, Bokey looked down at mother and her transformed child. "Silly, silly, ugly lij," he said, his voice like the crackle of the burning wood.

— TIME AND TIDE —

Max Gladstone

"Heave!"

"I'm heaving! You heave!"

"Oi, Spindly, 'ware the net!"

Below, Aelfric, long and thin—"Spindly" to these northern people of rock and sea and iron—leapt back as a wet net full of flopping dying cod fell to the wood planks of the dock. The ruddy twilight lit their silver scales ruby and gold as they surged against the net, desperate.

One of the cod, a tiny specimen, poked its head through a hole in the net, straining against the mass of its brethren. Aelfric could taste its fear and little fishy dreams of open sea.

With a desperate wriggle the cod popped free and spurted through the air in a silvery arc.

Aelfric's long-fingered hand shot out from the dark wrappings of his cloak and snatched the fish from the air at the apex of its flight. It wriggled, wet and alive, in his grip.

"Hello," he told the cod in the language of fish.

Fish don't have many things to say to one another and as such their language is not particularly robust. They do, however, have a word for "Friend."

"Friend?" the fish asked.

"Sort of," Aelfric replied.

The docks stank of sweaty, salt-logged men and doomed fish. The men passed around him, seeing him and forgetting him soon after—even the fisherman who had warned Aelfric of the falling net was now wondering to whom he had shouted. This was all as Aelfric wished: here in Brailee's Steps newcomers were not unheard of but were looked on with suspicion, and Aelfric did not like suspicion. The fish saw him and remembered, but fish have short memories and most lij don't speak their tongue.

Aelfric cackled and danced down the docks, weaving a jangling jig between the day fishers coming in and the Diuntyne fishers going out. Some crates of wool or pork or rocks or whatever these dull mortals traded among themselves lay stacked at the foot of the pier. Aelfric climbed the stack in a trice and pirouetted there to the music of the wind.

He still held the fish in his left hand. He wanted to look the cod in the eye, but its eyes were on different sides of its head, so he settled for looking straight at it, which probably meant it couldn't see him at all. "Friend," the fish said.

"Of course," Aelfric replied. Then he stuck its head in his mouth and bit down, hard.

His fangs crushed through skin and flesh and bone.

In a moment his meal was done. He dropped the fish skeleton, sans head, in the water at the edge of the docks and walked away from the dusk and the stretching gray expanse of ocean. The sun fell beneath the horizon. Opposite it, eternal pursuer, the gray orb of Diun rose just above the waves.

Aelfric came from a place beyond these Dying Lands, where razor-sharp borders separated day and twilight and night. These prolonged dissolves as one orb rose and the other set were so intimate by comparison, so naive as to be almost erotic, like a prim young Yuinite woman lying nude on green grass in an apple glade beside the discarded husk of her best feastday dress.

Aelfric cackled and quickened his pace.

It was Diuntyne, and a need burned within him.

As Diun rose, Aelfric wandered over the rooftops of the little squalid fishing village, treading lightly on old straw and dirty flax, occasionally peering down into chimneys. The villagers didn't look up. They continued on their petty, pretty rounds amid their cluster of ramshackle stone huts: seeking joy and finding sorrow, or the other way around.

The day fishers all returned come Diundawn, as the twilight men went out with the receding tide. Those that could duck out on their wives and families for a few hours stopped home to change into something dry (or dry-ish) before escaping to the Sea Foam, the local tavern, to drink and jaw with the same men against whom they had cursed and fought on the water. Those that couldn't did not go home at all but drank wet.

In that tavern were singing and dancing, warm beer and warmer embraces. Aelfric crossed its roof without a second thought and leapt to land on the rocky soil behind, softly and soundly as a cat.

He had no business in the Sea Foam.

Paths led from the village down to the sharp cliffs of shale and granite, and still other paths led down those cliffs to the shore, where even now the tide receded. Aelfric didn't use the paths. He slithered over the cliff's edge and climbed down it face-first, hands seeking out invisible crannies in the rock face, his form but a shadow.

When the tide came in, it brought with it what the locals called sea hair—long strands of still-living seaweed that made good kindling when dried and when powdered leant a deep, meaty flavor to even the lightest soup. Prized in the Steps, sea hair properly collected, cleaned, and prepared could help take the edge off poverty.

The best time to collect sea hair was after the first tide receded, as Diun shone newborn down on the freshly uncovered sea floor, pitted by tidal pools and strewn with debris and scuttling sea-bugs. The sea hair lay in long black strands on the polished wet sand.

No fishermen had the time or energy to pick sea hair and their wives were too consumed by the endless war of householding to waste attention on such a painstaking endeavor. Boys not yet old enough to fish were stuck tying up their fathers' boats, or else spying and playing pirate. Girls had time, though—young maidens not yet married.

One, in particular, walked alone. She was short for her age and older than most of the other girls who picked sea hair. Her hair and skin were both dark, her eyes kind.

Every day her footsteps marred the perfection of the sand, little half-full puddles of destruction trailing her steps like they trailed the steps of so many others of her race. Every day the sand forgot her trespasses. It was more forgiving of the faults of the lij than was the rest of the world.

Aelfric crept up behind her, trying to still the fluttering desperation in his stomach and said, "Well met."

She didn't interrupt her stride. "Well met to you as well, my imaginary sir."

He danced out in front of her and threw back his cloak. What did she see? Her kind were always painting the world with those soft, gentle eyes of theirs. Aelfric wondered: to her, was he a study in black and white and luxurious green? Was he a courtier in her eyes? A cavalier? A pirate? Was he wearing a hat? "My lady," he said, "I'm hardly as imaginary as all that."

"Sir, you come to my side every evening as I wander, and you vanish before I can thank you for the pleasure of your company. I can hardly think what to call you, save imaginary."

"A fan, perhaps," he said.

"A fan?"

"A dancer. A music lover."

Her laughter came to his ears like bells as she bent to lift a long strand of sea hair. Her fingers flitted over its surface, brushing away the sand. "All the more proof you're imaginary. Nobody loves poor Lydia's songs. Look." She turned to the receding tide. "Even Mother Ocean runs away."

"Sing for me, Lydia."

For a moment, she hesitated as though she wouldn't, and his heart almost broke into two pieces. Then the first note escaped her lips.

Chills passed over Aelfric, through him, into him. His blood danced. The world expanded and contracted at the same time, squeezing his soul out through his pores. His left foot twitched. His hand began to move.

There were lyrics to the song, but he couldn't make them out, so thick was the dialect: "Mich moor dir'th'nacht..." But he was dancing.

His lips parted wide to show his jagged teeth, and he turned a back handspring. Lydia looked up from her work when she heard the light pats of his feet on the sand and smiled, but fortunately continued with the song. Had she stopped, he couldn't have born it. Fire coursed down his every nerve; her song flowed over him like soothing water.

By all the sleeping Gods, he thought, with that sliver of mind that still could think as he danced. By all the sleeping Gods, she doesn't know what she does to me. Beyond the sunset of this tiny mortal world rise towers of glittering gold and silver that these flawed little creatures with their so-brief lives will never touch, even with their highest, fiercest invention. I've walked the paths between those towers and romanced the women who live within them, down century after century. And yet she sings, and I…

And yet she sings.

They proceeded down the beach together. When Lydia reached the end of her song, Aelfric waited, sweating, starving for her to start again. He was in her hands. She could have asked anything of him—to dance on the surface of the ocean, to rise into the air, to set himself afire and light the night with his death—and he would have done it.

She did not ask anything of him, save that he dance.

As Diun rose, the tide receded and started to contemplate returning. Lydia walked out among the now-bare tidal pools, collecting sea hair in her canvas bag, and Aelfric followed her, a shadow on the sands.

Her songs reached a crescendo and faded, turned from slow to fast, from tragic to ecstatic, and his dance shifted to match. He wore thin, his legs trembled, and he faded, but still the song came on.

Until something broke it.

It felt as though his soul had been suddenly immersed in freezing water.

And then a voice beside him said, "Ey, Aelfric, give us a hand here, will you?"

The voice did not speak any tongue of these Dying Lands.

Next to him was a tidal pool, deep and brimming with black brine. A hand groped up out of it, slick and glistening with something that was certainly not seawater.

Aelfric shot a glance up at Lydia, but she had drawn away, unnoticing.

"Come on, help us up, Aelfric. We've been trying to make our way through for an hour now. This bastard's heavy."

He recognized the voice, though he hadn't heard it in months. Reluctantly, he gripped the hand and pulled. A thick forearm came into view first, then a squat, inverted-triangle head, then broad shoulders, over one of which was slung a remarkably full brown canvas sack.

"Hello, Schwarzalbe," Aelfric said as the woman finished making her way through the gate in the tidal pool and into this world. "I hadn't expected you."

"Who does?" Schwarzalbe gave him a grin that was all sharp teeth. "But you should have expected someone. You were due back weeks ago."

"Was it weeks?"

"Yeah." The canvas sack shifted, and within it Aelfric thought he heard a muffled complaint, like someone screaming through a thick gag. Schwarzalbe's features twisted in disgust, and she dropped the sack. It hit the wet sand hard, and the noises subsided. "We all thought ya'd be caught up in some mischief or other. I've been passing through the Steps last week or so, different little chips of rock every time." She cast a glance back towards shore. "You know, collecting bits here and there."

"Who's that?" He pointed to the sack.

"A new drummer for Master Nightmare."

"A drummer?"

"He's very good," Schwarzalbe said defensively. "Plays like nothing. Different rhythms on each hand, all that. He drums, and the earth shakes."

"I see."

"You look like shit."

He did, he knew. He had seen his reflection in a pool of still water last week, seen his features gaunt and lean, his hands trembling, bags under his eyes, wrinkles on his ageless forehead. He bore the marks of her music and of his abuse of it.

"I've been..."

"On the hunt, I see." She cast a meaningful glance up the beach to where Lydia wandered, humming to herself. "Only question is: have you caught her, or has she caught you?"

"I'm making it last." Aelfric drew close to her and whispered, "She's been getting better."

"You've been getting weaker, you mean." Schwarzalbe slapped him on the back, hard; he had to pinwheel his arms to avoid falling on her already well-abused drummer. "Weaker and more, whatsit, susceptible. You're going to end up like the Master, hooked up and drooling whenever anyone comes near who can play a scale." She distorted her body to make it long and thin and hunched forward, her features twisting into a clown-mask of Lord Nightmare's as she shambled towards him with mock-clawed hands. "Muuuuuuusic." With a leap and a spin, Schwarzalbe resumed her usual form. "Stick 'er in the bag and let's go on."

He turned from Schwarzalbe to Lydia, who had drawn away from them now to begin a dance of her own, turning dreamily amid the sea beneath the rising moon. Diun was well more than a quarter above the horizon, and the tide would be coming in soon.

"She's been getting better, Schwarzalbe. I swear. When I first came here she was just carrying tunes. I would have sacked her then and taken her with me if she hadn't..." he trailed off. "It was a pure note, you've got to understand. Purest I'd ever heard. I came back the next night, and that night she sang two."

"And then three, and then..." She nodded at the winding, spinning tracks he had left in the sand. His footsteps were lighter than Lydia's, but even he left a wake. "It looks like she's good enough for the master now."

His mouth went dry. If Lydia went into one of Schwarzalbe's brown canvas sacks and down through the tidal pool, she'd wake to find herself in a vast hall of black stone and thorn, branded and pledged. There was no moonlight within the halls of Nightmare, and no sea hair to collect. No smell of salt from the Diuntyne wind off the ocean. Little laughter there, and none pleasant.

Lydia chose that moment to look back over her shoulder and call out, "Sir, where have you gone?"

"Sir." Schwarzalbe laughed. "She's a fine one. Been teaching her courtly manners? You'd think you actually liked her, rather than just used her for her songs." She reached into a pocket in her heavy, dark jacket and produced a folded bundle: another brown sack, like the one in which she carried her drummer. "Come on, stick her in the bag and let's get back down the hole."

He looked from her, to the bag, to Lydia, to the moon. A tremulous song reached his ear.

"No," he said at last.

"No?" There was no anger in Schwarzalbe's voice, only confusion. Her head swayed like a cobra pondering whether to strike.

"The moon," he said. "The sea's coming in, and those gates are closed." He pointed to the tidal pool from which she had pulled herself.

"Really?"

"Didn't you ask anyone about these little pools before you decided to crawl up out of one? If the sea came in and the tidal gates were still open, then there'd be water all the time in the Dreaming Lands. The gates close before Diun reaches its height."

"So. There are other gates," Schwarzalbe said after some pondering. "I don't know this particular rock, but there'll be a gate off the edge of the boat dock when the moon makes its wee little road into the Dreaming." She mimed a person walking, with two of her long taloned fingers for legs.

"She'll go in of her own will in a moment." His voice sunk low. "We'll sack her then, once she's climbed the hill. No sense in carrying her."

"And in the meantime you get a final dance?" She cackled. "One last chance to play the courtly monster?"

His veins twitched and his blood burned, but he could deny nothing.

"Go to it, then."

"Sir?" Lydia called her question again.

"I'm coming," he shouted back.

He lost the world in that dance. Fire and ice ran through his throat, his stomach, and his legs, lightning crackling in his mind like the Finger of God. His arms spun in wheels, his legs flashed high, his feet circled above him encompassing the stars as he leapt and spun and tumbled.

When it was done, he landed before her and bowed.

"Thank you," he said, kneeling on the sand with his arms spread wide in a courtier's bow. "Lady." His voice, his body, felt as though it had been wrung out.

"Sir," she replied with an inclination of her head. "The sea is rising."

And it was, as Diun crested its peak and painted the land gray. Lakshi too now shone above, green and white, calling the waters back. The sea pooled silver around her feet and stained the bottoms of his trousers. Three shadows stretched out from her narrow form, one thick and two long and thin.

"We should go, then." The worship was easy to hear in his voice. He hoped it kept the sorrow hidden.

She gave him a knowing smile, turned, and led the way, skipping through the sand. Schwarzalbe stood some twenty feet away at the edge of the rising surf watching silently with her bag slung over her shoulder. She said nothing and drew into step behind Aelfric as he followed Lydia to the cliff's edge.

On the way, he knelt to pick up a long heavy piece of driftwood. He had brought no weapons with him. This would have to do. He whispered words of blessing and bargain to the wood, promising to return it to the sea in exchange for service now.

It took a long time for Lydia to climb the winding path up the cliff. Being fleshy, mortal, slow, she could not scale it as he had, and she did not race as the tide rushed in. Step by careful step, he drew close to her. Behind, he could hear Schwarzalbe's heavy, wet steps and wished she would walk more quietly.

They crested the cliff. Lydia stood silhouetted by the double moons. Aelfric raised his club. Scwarzalbe drew close behind him.

And, in a blur of blinding speed, he swung the club about and slammed it into the side of Schwarzalbe's skull.

What happened then was not what he had expected.

Schwarzalbe's skull caved in, yes, but it then reformed around his makeshift club. Tiny fractures appeared in the Fae woman's blunt face, extending down her jacket and her muscular body and even around the brown sack. Through those fractures, Aelfric saw something dark green and alive and writhing.

Seaweed. She had lent seaweed her shape.

Fool. Fool. Fool, thrice named and truly tamed.

The sky had two moons, but Lydia had three shadows. And he hadn't seen it. Too long in this stupid mortal world with its stupid mortal rules. Three shadows, two long and thin, and the other short and square.

Schwarzalbe had seen him coming. He was a damn junkie, and junkies were easy to predict.

He swung his head around just in time to see Lydia's shorter shadow bubble and distort, rising up and inflating with color: short, jagged hair, blunt features, a long dark coat, large, muscular arms. Schwarzalbe raised an empty canvas sack, gave a laugh of triumph, and brought it down over Lydia as the girl turned to look behind her. Lydia screamed briefly and kicked and fought in the bag, but Schwarzalbe tied it tight, slung it over her other shoulder, and took off running as if the sacks she carried contained bundles of cloth rather than imprisoned lij.

Aelfric tried to follow, but his arm was stuck and racked by thorns. The seaweed swarmed over him, a giant wet mass. He cried out in frustration and in pain, and then he had no time to cry out or to breathe. He pulled, ripped, tore in reflex, but the seaweed only tightened its grip.

Fool again, fighting as if this were a thing one could defeat by force of arms. Schwarzalbe had struck a simple bargain with the seaweed; she had no time to make a complex one. She had granted it form and strength in exchange for its holding Aelfric—but she did not know Aelfric's true name. She would have used a description for him: you will hold a Monarhig, so tall, with a dark cloak.

He needed to be something else. Some other shape. And he needed to change fast.

Breath left his lungs, and he dove within himself. Shapes. He surged against the seaweed net.

Ah. Yes.

Again, he surged, writhing, but now he was smaller, swifter, his skin a scaly silver as he spurted through the air in a glittering arc. The seaweed, deprived of its target, twitched and fell inanimate to the grass.

He shed the cod's flesh as quickly as he had assumed it and, recovering his footing, began to run. Above him Diun approached its apex, or perhaps had just fallen past it. Schwarzalbe might be gone already, into the depths of the Dreaming, the path closed behind her.

He passed the village on his left, a blur. Breath came unwillingly to his lungs. He descended the cliff that separated the town from the dock below in two great leaps, somersaulting through the air to land featherlight on the beach as Diun reached its zenith.

There, at the edge of the dock, stood Schwarzalbe, one sack over each shoulder. She faced round Diun, shining on the waves like a cold sun as the tide rushed in. The moon cast a shimmering silver-gray road on the surface of the water. She took a step off the pier and found her footing on the path of moonlight.

He sprinted past crates and nets and the detritus of the fishing day. Schwarzalbe took a step, and another, fading into light, and fading beyond the light into somewhere else, a place where Diuntyne shone like a polished jewel. Twenty feet from the end of the dock, ten, close now. He could see Lydia still thrashing in the sack, causing Schwarzalbe as little concern as would a flailing child.

He leapt for her as Diun passed the zenith. His hands closed around the canvas sack and clung for a moment, then it slipped through his grasp. They were gone.

Aelfric fell into the ocean with a dull splash. The water deadened his scream.

He floated there for a time he did not bother to measure, cursing and shaking. Need quickened within his breast. Music. Lydia.

Gone.

The rolling waves cast him up on the beach. His head lolled to the side.

Inches from his eyes lay the headless skeleton of a fish.

— ORCHESTRATION —

Max Gladstone

Before her imprisonment, Lydia had walked on the wet sand left by the retreating tide and seen the sky broken above, the four moons, Diun and Lakshi and Takata Shin and their angry little brother Nurom Misuer shining through the cloud-cracks onto the rolling silver sea. She sang to the sea and the sky and the shore, and to Aelfric, her gallant friend that no one else could see, who danced, transported by her music. Even in her innocence she had known he was not like her: not lij, not bound to the dusty, day-to-day world. He was different. Special. Her secret.

She had not seen him for a long time. Hard to judge how long, months maybe: he had cried a warning to her on a cliff above a Diuntyne sea, and she had tried to run, but a monster caught her in a canvas sack and carried her off to these tunnels of cool rock and earth, far from Brailee's Steps.

Here, too, she sang. Not for joy, but out of requirement, note after note ripped from her throat by the overwhelming need of the Nightmare Lord on his black throne.

Her first memory after the brown canvas sack was of waking in a dank cell with the monster crouched before her: a woman squat and strong like a great toad, with a toad's broad mouth and, row upon row of sharp, un-toadlike teeth that showed when she smiled.

"You're awake." The monster held out a hand, blunt-fingered and lizard-clawed.

Lydia screamed and scuttled back until her shoulders struck cold flat rock. Through glazed panic she saw the room about her: a pallet of straw, blank stone walls, a thick-banded wood door ajar.

"I'm called Schwarzalbe," the monster-woman said, "and I'm—"

Lydia surged to her bare feet, the stone cold beneath her soles, and sprang for the open door. In the darkness beyond, she could hide and escape this monster-woman—this Schwarzalbe, who cried "No!" and reached out to catch her, fast as sight but still not fast enough. Lydia leapt through the door.

There was no hallway beyond. No floor to support her weight.

She fell.

Fell for a brief eternity, the world a twisting blur. Far below she saw within the dark a deeper darkness yawning, opening many jaws, reaching with a hundred cold and hungry arms for her flailing warm limbs.

A calloused and hob-nailed hand grabbed her wrist from behind. Her shoulder jerked and bent wrong; she screamed and screamed but stopped falling. Through a haze of fear and pain she felt herself pulled up and in, onto the unfinished stone floor of her cell, where she lay on straw and saw Schwartzalbe's face contorted in unaccustomed concern.

Schwarzalbe placed her hand on Lydia's agonized shoulder, gripped her arm, and pulled hard enough to break bone. The right side of the world rolled and clicked back into place. Lydia's arm returned, through agony, to her own control.

"Don't," the monster-woman said when Lydia's deep-voiced scream faded to dull panting sobs, "try that again. Lord Nightmare's castle is not a place to wander unescorted. The halls can forget where they lead, unless you remind them."

"Why am I here?" Lydia asked when she recovered enough breath to form words.

Schwarzalbe rolled back off the balls of her feet to sit on her thick haunches. Broad, rippling with muscle, toothed and clawed, she looked nevertheless uncomfortable for once in her own skin. "Our Lord needs you to sing."

"Sing."

"Like you did for Aelfric." Schwarzalbe's attempt at a reassuring smile had the opposite effect. "You made him so happy that he forgot his duty was to bring you in for the Master. You'll make the Master happy, too, no fear. Your screams alone are..." She shivered. "Exhilarating."

"I won't sing."

"Won't you now?"

"Take me back to Aelfric. Take me back to Brailee's Steps." She tried to keep her voice from shaking. There was salt water in her eyes, like sea-spray.

"Listen, girl. There's only one door to this room, and it leads two ways: to Lord Nightmare's orchestra or to the black. You could stay here, too, I suppose. Not go anywhere. I starved a lij once, in a cell like this. It's a long death, and painful. And I like you." She held out her thick hands, palms up, open. "Your choice."

So Lydia sang.

But was she alone. There were other lij with her: some sang, and others played fife and fiddle and trumpet, harp and drum and horn, in the vast and bone-walled throne chamber. Their music made the femur buttresses and the scapula arches and the ribbed cupolas quake in rhythm. Before them all the Nightmare Lord sat, head lolling, eyes rolled back into his thin fragile skull, his wasted face framed by tangled, matted black hair. His limbs, marked and marred by music, twitched in the steps of a dance he lacked the strength to perform.

The other musicians she came to know—not personally, they were held apart—but through their subtle glances, through the twist of their fingers on strings or the particular hunch of their back as they drummed, through their chipmunk-cheeked facial contortions as they played tuba or horn.

The singers she knew best, though these she did not even see: they were separated from one another by walls of black silk as they sang, like small precious rocks in a collector's cabinet. Their voices grew as familiar to her as the waves: the deep bass who boomed behind her and to her right, the tenors in front, a cluster of soaring sopranos, a dotting of other altos.

Not many singers in total, perhaps fifteen in the whole choir. She knew the bass was large, perhaps fifteen stone, because when he inhaled she could hear his weight; it lay atop and beneath his voice like wet sand. She knew one of the sopranos as a light and willowy girl whose breath lay always a little too much atop the notes that slipped, pretty and fragile as fine porcelain, from her lips.

Lydia had never sung in a group before, other than the raucous chorus Steppers raised to setting Diun at midnight on festival days, but she had heard of the great port cities to the south and the choirs in the temples there, so she knew what was missing from Nightmare's hall: composers, written music, a director or conductor to unite their driving, variegated rhythm. So many musicians without a conductor should have produced mere cacophony, yet they sang and played and there was music, drawn from their souls by the Nightmare Lord's need.

Every night, after the swelling bittersweet finale, their captors drew the performers from the bone hall to their cells. The harpists' harps were ripped from them, and the fiddlers' fiddles boxed away. Brassy horns lay discarded on the cold throne room floor beneath the stretching bony fingers and sightless eyes of the enameled skulls.

But the singers' instruments could not be taken from them. Each musician was kept apart from every other, so there was no way for Lydia to know what the others did in their languishing hours in those bare cells. She sang.

The first song Lydia tried was one her mother had sang for her as she lay abed, sick with fever and chills at the age of five. Mother had rocked her then, as she rocked herself now back and forth on the pallet of straw. Late at night, free of the immortal hunger that pulled song from her throat, she found a quiet joy in old ballads and the privacy of her mind.

Her songs grew louder and more reckless over the weeks as she gloried in their needlessness. After the first month she noticed that when she sang, a weak and flickering light glowed about her in the dark cell. Joy leapt within her heart, and the rocks about her trembled with it.

One night as Lydia sang herself to sleep, she thought she saw eyes peering in at the small barred window of her cell door. Glistening, big wet eyes, like a frog's—but if Schwarzalbe had truly been there, watching, listening rapt, wouldn't she have said something the next morning when she came to drag Lydia to Nightmare's throne room?

When Lydia sang with the orchestra, their music confounded hours and minutes, and Nightmare's black eyes, his jerking addict's dance, devoured the endless beat. She feared him, first, for his rages and his madness and for his dark demonic melancholy. Then, she pitied him and his need, pitied the scars of music that showed through pale flesh when he ripped off his shirt in paroxysms of ecstasy. For a while after that she hated him, pouring her contempt into her song as he gyrated more wildly than before, lost in a dark world of desire.

She wondered at his addict's joy and at her contempt, because she was young and had not yet come to know even the simple, secret despairs of the lij of Brailee's Steps. This mixture of pain and need and contempt and desperation was a new, personal thing to Lydia, a private relationship with the Lord who never spoke a word to her, the Lord she would have murdered in an instant had the tools come to her hand.

After a time, the hatred too receded, but no love came to replace it. In the end, she only felt tired, her fear and sympathy and contempt all drained out like pus from a wound.

The day after the Dream-Lady strode haughtily into Nightmare's throne room and was caught in a web of song and made to dance, rigid and fragile and elegant as a china figurine atop a music box, face twisted with anger and ecstasy, Lydia tried to escape.

After returning to her cell, she waited for the light to die. When all was silent and dark, she began to sing, so soft she could hear the rats scuttle down their tunnels in the dank walls, so quiet her heartbeat could keep time. She sang moonlight reflected on the pool of her memory, and it shone about her. She sang to the rocks, which trembled like scared children, and the rats fled. Fixing in her mind an image of Brailee's Steps, of the sea road the fishermen plied, of star-speckled sky and wet beach, she sang herself a path.

This was a dark haunted dream. Music-shaped dreams. She seeded them and gave them force. She thought—hoped—she could follow her own song from dream to freedom.

Yet the dreamstuff pressed against her mind, resisting her with a flood's force: she felt like a child who, having lifted first a pebble, and then a larger rock, decides to lift the whole world. She pushed, strained, surged against the unyielding dream. About her it flexed. The four walls of her cell rippled. She could die here, she knew in that moment, trying to remake the world, and though the thought of death sparked terror in her, she sang louder.

The wall opened like a stone-petaled flower, and within that flower's center, simultaneously near and distant, she saw the ocean with Diun's sharp cold light falling on a familiar shore. She stretched out a hand to touch the water, but as she moved, the petals closed. She tried to draw back, but a powerful wind born of her own music forced her on. The wall closed like a mouth; it would crush her before she made it through.

A heavy weight struck her from behind, obliterating the world in white and yellow rainbowed pain. Power left her, and she fell limp to cold stone.

There she lay, rocking, moaning, the world a kaleidoscope, every shifting facet filled with Schwarzalbe's grim face.

"It was you," she said weakly, after a few failed attempts. The words came reluctantly to her lips. "Waiting outside."

"Try that again," Schwarzalbe said, "and I'll rip your tongue out."

"Nightmare wouldn't let you. He needs me to sing."

"Little girl." Squatting atop her, Schwarzalbe looked for a moment pensive and sad. "Just because I rip your tongue out doesn't mean I can't put it back in later."

"Then take it," Lydia screamed, beating at the fae woman's legs and stomach with her thin arms.

Schwarzalbe weathered her blows without comment and waited for Lydia to tire, for the strength of her arms to fade until they fell upon her like willow branches blown by a spare breeze. Lydia's breath came in ragged wet gasps.

"I would." The fae woman leaned in close, her large flat eyes inches from Lydia's own. "I would. But do you really want that? To lie here, twisting and mute until I drag you out to work? I'd do it." She feathered a clawed finger down the swell of Lydia's cheek. "But I like you, and I'd much rather you sing to yourself at night. I'm not cruel."

"What are you, then?"

Schwarzalbe rolled back onto the balls of her feet. With her great weight lifted, Lydia could breathe again. She could even sing—lay hold of Schwarzalbe's mind, make her dance. The fae woman had to know this, yet she waited still and patient, the cell door open behind her, the empty hall clearly visible beyond.

Lydia had grown accustomed to the need in the eyes of the strange, passionate, monstrous creatures that inhabited this Dreaming land. After months of captivity she could recognize it when their own kind could not: a tightness beneath the skin. She saw the need in Schwarzalbe—saw in her large eyes long nights spent outside Lydia's cell door, telling herself she only lingered to prevent Lydia from escaping, even as she tapped her foot in time with the music.

Lydia did not run. She closed her mouth and struggled with the floor and the nearby wall to prop herself up in a seated position. Disappointment flicked across Schwarzalbe's features; Lydia saw it, and at the roots of her mind, a contorted angry thing that had not existed before her confinement raised its hooked beak and crowed triumph.

Her hair had matted into elf-locks in the last months. She smoothed the thick locks behind her ears, behind her shoulders, and looked up. Schwarzalbe stood watching, waiting, the door behind her still slightly ajar.

"I'll be good," she said, as the sharp vengeful creature within her cackled.

Not long after that, the world ended.

Lydia was in the throne room when it happened. The thick wooden doors burst and a group of lij rushed in, bearing weapons of sharp steel, full of life and sunlight, clearly not servants of the dark lord. She wanted to cease her song and rush out to embrace them. No doubt the entire orchestra wished the same, but Nightmare's need bound them to their music. What did the newcome lij see as they stared about themselves in fear? Captives, certainly. Forlorn, skin slack over tired bones. Lydia imagined the deep pools her own eyes had become and shivered.

Nightmare hardly noticed the lij, so lost was he in the depths of the orchestra's music. But then something rose from the newcomers' midst: a great unsettling shadow, a half-forgotten memory of a demonic shape, eight feet tall and darker than night. It rolled forward, speaking words Lydia could not hear; when Nightmare heard its voice, he looked up, his whole being suddenly rapt.

Lydia had never liked Nightmare's palace, but at that moment she desperately wanted to be somewhere, anywhere else.

And, as the unfinished shadow advanced, Nightmare wanted the same thing, more even than he craved music from his orchestra. As the force of his need broke, Lydia's mouth snapped shut, and her breath quelled in her chest. She held fast to the lifeline of that silence.

She had lain often enough by calm ocean to know the swell before something great and hidden rose to the surface: a breaching whale or a vast collection of twisted lobster traps pulled from the deep. Nightmare's throne room, with lij running about waving their swords and Dream struggling to break free of her dance, was the ocean surface, and that shadow the swell.

Lydia tore her eyes from the scene, turned, and ran. The narrow door that led to her perch within the choir was open; Schwarzalbe had not bothered to close it, knowing Lydia could not free herself from the master's need. As she ran through that door, she heard behind her a scream. Many screams, cut short, and an abrupt splash that she knew, with sickening certainty, was spilled blood.

For months, Lydia's life had been a skein of thread wound tight between her cell and the choir. She knew intimately the turns that would lead her down the twisting taproot passages to her pallet of dry straw. But she could not hide from that shadow.

She had never thought the Nightmare Lord particularly nightmarish, in himself. His need was fierce and his power vast, but he relied upon wheels and pulleys, great machines and legions of servants to do his dread work. That advancing shadow needed no such assistance. Its very presence tinted the world.

Even now, was she imagining it, or was the hall about her growing darker?

Cold sweat slicked her brow. Behind her was the door to the throne room. To her right the hall ran down to the cells.

Steeling herself, she ran left.

As she ran, the shadows deepened, seeping like viscous fluid from cracks in the stone walls onto the floor, where they joined into spreading puddles. Ganglia of darkness dripped from the ceiling, and when they brushed her matted hair, mortal terror gripped her soul.

The narrow hall opened into a wide chamber carpeted in blood-red; the walls must have been decorated, and there had to be a door somewhere, but Lydia could see neither walls nor door nor ceiling beneath the slick thick coating of advancing shadow.

Her cell suddenly seemed a more attractive option, but as she turned back towards the narrow hall, viscous, oily shadow bled over the entrance and cut her off. She stood now in a room walled and ceilinged in advancing black; far away she heard muffled screams that had never come from human throats. Nightmare's servants, wailing in sudden terror.

The circle of red carpet around her diminished as ebon tendrils crept towards her, burrowing like insects through the echoes of remaining light. In a moment, they would have her.

At least she would die out of her cell and free of the orchestra. But she had never expected her end to come so far from Brailee's Steps, in a faerie castle beset by inhuman magic.

Magic.

Lydia's heartbeat quickened.

The darkness advanced, just like the tide back home. This blood-red carpet was her new shore. She opened her mouth and began to sing.

She sang a low note in her register. She didn't know that scholars in the bardic colleges would have called it an 'A.' To her, it was the first note of 'Mollie's Waterfall,' which her mother had sang for her on winter nights as a girl.

"Much more dark the night

Once Diun set behind the wall

Of father's house where Mollie left

To meet her love by the waterfall."

It was a slow song she'd chosen, death- and sorrow-ridden, a Brailee's Steps song where true love resolved in a moment of ruin. She'd always thought Mollie terribly brave, leaving her father's house for the rendezvous, traveling the dark sea at night without even Diun's light to sail by, to seek and find her love on a distant island in a cave behind a waterfall fed by a spring in the cleft stone. They lived together, joyful, until Mollie's father was seized by her love's enemy, a pirate who the young man had tricked. And then—

Three verses into the song, she noticed that she was still alive. The converging black had stopped five feet from her, thrown back by a halo of pale sea-green light emanating from her skin. Shocked by her own survival, she almost stopped singing, and as her notes faltered, so too did the light; spurred by terror she launched into the next verse. The green light hardened, the darkness rolled back, and she was safe once more.

As Lydia sang, she walked back towards the hall from which she had come, hoping to retrace her steps. The light moved with her, and the shadow rolled in to fill the space where she had stood. As long as she sang, they could not touch her.

It was hard to find the hallway, now that everything was covered over by oily shadow. Her first attempt dead-ended into a gold-ornamented wall, but she worked one step at a time counterclockwise along the wall's curve, singing softer now, until she came upon the edge of a door. She stepped into it, and the shadow receded.

Revealed beneath the lintel, blinking drops of slick black from her eyelids and nose and mouth, stood Schwarzalbe.

Lydia drew back as if from a serpent, even as Schwarzalbe leapt for her, desperate to remain within the light. Lydia would have hardened her song against her, but for the words she screamed as the shadow descended:

"Help me!"

The words, or the despair within them, arrested Lydia. Sticky black rolled in once more to cover Schwarzalbe, cover her straining, muscled arms, cover her rigid shoulders, cover her wide, flat hopeless eyes.

Lydia stepped forward and the black retreated. She wanted to speak, wanted to ask: why should I help you? What is this blackness and what was that thing that assaulted Nightmare on his throne? What elder terror has awakened in this castle and why do you fear it so? But she could say nothing while she sang. She moved so that her verdant halo enclosed Schwarzalbe's head.

Lydia fixed the monster-woman bent before her with an angry stare. Schwarzalbe quaked but did not draw back; back held more terror for her than did Lydia.

"Help me," Schwarzalbe repeated. "I don't know the words for what's happening now. The thing that came for Lord Nightmare owns this place more than he ever did. It's reclaiming the palace—and his servants."

Lydia took a step back.

"I never hurt you!" Schwarzalbe's cry almost deafened Lydia. Her face was a toothed mouth surrounded by wrinkled, angry flesh. "I didn't take your tongue. I cared for your wounds. I treated you like my own."

Lydia made to draw back another step.

"You don't know what he'll do to me." Schwarzalbe sagged, body and voice. "Once this dark stuff works me over, what's left won't be me anymore. It'll be older, angrier, stronger, and I'll be gone."

Lydia turned from her.

"And you'll never get out of this place alive."

Lydia stopped.

"You think the palace of Nightmare is some mud-and-grass hut, like the ones you lij crouch in when the rains come? Four walls, a hearth, a door, a dirt floor on which the dogs and children can roll together, and a cheap altar to your cheap gods? This building was made to trap the souls of waking lij. Take the wrong turn and you will meet horrors to stun your breath and take your song. And then the darkness will catch you."

Walk away, Lydia told herself. Don't listen—she lies, distorts the truth. You can do this without her. But singing took so much energy; if she gave less than her full heart to the song, the notes rang false and the black advanced. She was not strong enough to fight this elder darkness and riddle through a maze at the same time.

"I swear to serve you," Schwarzalbe said, stammering over her words. "I shall protect you, and I shall not harm you while I am in your service. I swear by bone and blood, by earth and by the hidden tree. There is no stronger oath. You know enough of my kind to know we do not break our oaths."

It was true. The Fae lacked lij music, the dancing tune that struck the heart and called the universe into order, but theirs was the magic of true names and true speech. Schwarzalbe would keep her word.

Lydia approached Schwarzalbe. The darkness rolled back from the monster-woman and she collapsed, gasping, to the plush red carpet. Then her collapse assumed a respectful rigidity, and Lydia realized the woman was kneeling before her.

With one hand, she motioned for her to rise, which Schwarzalbe did, carefully, recovering her breath before she shot Lydia a slanted grin and preceded her into the dark.

Lydia had expected them to stride across the red-carpeted hall to the other side, but Schwarzalbe scuttled clockwise along the gold-embossed wall instead, until they reached a small panel that looked no different from any other. This she pressed, and it swung back, revealing a small hole. Lydia sang her light within the hole, and Schwarzalbe crouched and crawled through first. Lydia followed.

The passage was short and narrow. At first Lydia had to paw through on all fours, but just as the walls closed in about her the passage shifted and she found herself crawling beneath a majestic gold-linteled gate, though darkness had covered most of the metal. The rest of the room, judging by its outlines in oil-black, was sumptuous, decadent: reclining beds, couches over which some Nefazo odalisque might drape herself. Around and atop those beds twined thorny vines of dark iron: loose enough that one might crawl inside their embrace, but once within (she knew, from the logic of Nightmare) they would tighten slowly: infinitely desirable flesh beneath the dreamer's touch, thorns bearing down on her naked back, piercing and drawing blood, but if you could last a moment more...

She concentrated on the story she sang: Mollie returned to bargain for her father's freedom, keeping her voyage secret from her lover, and was taken hostage there, while her love waited beneath the waterfall.

Schwarzalbe paid no mind to the decoration, to the hanging curtains and their velvet ropes, or to the iron maiden splayed open against one wall. Rather than making for the obvious exit, she chose a small door hidden behind a tapestry.

"The nightmare architects," she explained in a harsh hushed tone, "build to entice fear, enticing dreamers to flee from one terrible place into another. But they need to move about the nightmares, too, don't they, to build, tear down, modify. So they make small, hard-to-find doors that connect horrors to one another: a maze sideways inside the bigger maze. Easy to pick your way through if you know what you're doing."

And pick their way she did, leading Lydia through a shifting tangle of hells: trapped within a warm, jagged cave as it collapsed, they were ground to pulp and to ash to live forever on the wind, alive and aware and in pain; in one room they wound between immense, toothed statues that waited, watching for their slightest misstep. Through another door they entered a chamber of birds, big and little, long-beaked and short, stretch-necked or squat, elegant birds or birds of angry, torn feathers. There was nothing else in the room, save the ever-watchful birds.

The shadow-oil clung tight to their feathers, no longer opaque. Lydia could see hints of multicolored feathers beneath the slick. Yet the shadows were not fading—they were learning, she knew somehow, learning the world around them and taking on its appearance.

"Faster," Schwarzalbe said.

A hidden passage led from the bird room into an endless expanse with no walls or floor or ceiling, where she fell for an eternity. Past that, through a narrow crack between two stone walls, down a worm-ridden tunnel—the black had almost completely assumed the colors beneath it, here, the blue-black of earth and the jeweled hues of innumerable insect carapaces. And out onto a windswept stone ledge, where a beating wind and the sound of wings caused her to look up, even as the jaws of an immense dragon closed around her and Schwarzalbe both.

She screamed, the song broke, and that would have been the end of them—but it was not. She was rolling down a grassy hill under a twilit sky that had never shone above Baeg Tobar: she could somehow see all four moons and the sun in the sky simultaneously. Lydia rolled to a stop on the new earth and flopped out her arms; the grass was greener here than in Brailee's Steps and smelled fresh.

Above her stretched an immense stone tree that was not a tree, but in truth a building, its roots plunging below the earth and its great branches scraping the sky. The trunk seemed too narrow to support the immensity of the branches: like a bad dream, it seemed small at the entrance, but just got bigger the further in you went. This was the palace of Nightmare. Or of whoever, now.

Lydia couldn't have cared less. She was free.

Schwarzalbe lay whimpering on her side a few yards away, bent into a quivering, tight ball.

Lydia gripped the earth with her fingers and felt it damp, old, and alive. Pressing against the ground, she rose to an unsteady crouch, the crisscrossed grass abrading the calloused pads of her bare feet.

On her first free step, she almost fell; her second was steadier, and her third, stable. Under the stars, she began to run.

The gentle slope of the hill carried her down, stride accelerating, breath sweet. For the first time in months her heart beat with excitement, not with fear. Behind, distant, she heard Schwarzalbe call after her.

Then, though it seemed to continue unbroken forever, the sloping hill cracked beneath her like the crust on a winter snowbank, and she plunged through.

A startled cry escaped her lips; arms pinwheeling, she reached for the ledge. One grasping hand found a protruding rock, but the sudden pressure of her weight ripped it free, and it, too, fell. Far above, she saw Schwarzalbe peek over the edge of the cliff, shout something to her—she took aim and threw a ball of gray goo down into the abyss. Lydia was falling fast now, but Schwarzalbe threw faster, and as Lydia spun in midair, the gray ball struck her on the chest and stuck.

And as it stuck, it unfurled into endless lines of spider silk. Caught on the wind, the lines bloomed out like jellyfish tentacles; as she spun they spun, too, around her body and her arms, her legs and her mouth. A few strands struck and stuck to the canyon walls. Some snapped, but more held. Lydia's fall slowed abruptly, and she bounced to an uncomfortable stop, thin silk lines cutting her skin as the ball continued to unwind. She tried to call thanks to Schwarzalbe, who scuttled down the rocks towards her headfirst like a spider, but layers of sticky gray silk bound her mouth closed; desperate, she sucked air in through her nostrils until winding silk blocked them too.

She began to heave and struggle as Schwarzalbe approached, but the silk only bound tighter; her blood ached with panic.

Clinging to a ledge a few feet above Lydia's face, Schwarzalbe looked nonchalant, perhaps even smug.

"Stupid girl, stupid girl. Sees the free sky and runs, doesn't know to look out for sudden drops. Always sudden drops in the Dreaming. I told you I'd not hurt you," she observed. "And I haven't. I've saved you from certain death. But I never swore to keep you free."

Lydia stared at her with eyes suddenly full of rage.

Schwarzalbe pulled a slender knife from her pocket and cut the threads that bound Lydia to the near side of the chasm wall. Terrified, screaming through the silk, she fell and struck the rock on the far side. Sudden pain blinded her, and blood rushed to her head; when she opened her eyes again she was hanging upside down from the far canyon wall. Schwarzalbe gathered her limbs beneath her and leapt, landing on the rock above Lydia with colossal force, limbs splayed, hands and feet adhering to the rock.

"I promised to protect you, and protect I will. And I have." Turning about, Schwarzalbe gripped the silk lines that bound Lydia to this side of the narrow canyon, too, and slashed them off just above the rock. Lydia's full weight now dangled from her single arm. She began to climb, dragging Lydia back towards the night above.

Spots swam in front of Lydia's eyes. She tried to struggle, but her greatest efforts barely elicited a twitch from her air-starved muscles.

"But of course there's payment to be discussed. I can leave you here, bound, and walk away. Perhaps wolves will find you, perhaps they won't. And does your kind need air to breathe? I was never clear on the fine points of your biology."

The world faded to shades of gray. Lydia was vaguely aware of being hauled over the rough edge of a cliff and laid out, sprawled, on green grass. Her heart thudded loud in her ears.

"I've made my oath to you. I'll keep you safe and serve you. Now you swear your oath to me: swear to go where I tell you, and stay where I tell you, and sing when I tell you, and stop singing when I tell you, too. Swear it by bone and blood, by earth and the hidden tree."

Lydia tried to speak but had no breath.

"It's okay, love. Just nod your head."

Swear to go, and to stay, and to sing, and to stop as bid. So hard to think, without air, without breath. She wanted to kill this woman. Yet dark clouds were closing in about her, and she could not take vengeance if she were dead.

Slowly, hating herself, she nodded, and felt the oath settle in her bones.

Schwarzalbe smiled. "That'll do, I should think. You've done a good job on command performance, love. You're ready for the big time." She smiled. "So go ahead and faint. It's a long, long way to Maeda Criacao, and we'd best get started."

Lydia gave a final spasm, like a netted fish drowning carelessly on the shore, and slipped into unconsciousness.

— MARCH —

Max Gladstone

It took months for Aelfric to find his way back to the Dreaming Lands. The twilight paths and standing-stone gates were closed to him, rosebud doors and vine curtains alike shut tight. Even the secret passwords whispered to elephant-ear ferns did not yield him passage. Of course not: he was a traitor now.

Why had he tried to save Lydia? One human was near as good as another. They bloomed for an instant and vanished into time. When Schwarzalbe arrived to take Lydia to Lord Nightmare's court, Aelfric should have let her go, yet the girl's song had caught him like a fish hook in the mouth.

He had to rescue her, and hear her sing again.

So, though the traitor's mark was on him and all the gates he knew into the Dreaming barred, he wandered with grim purpose through the Dying Lands. He booked passage on a ferry from Brailee's Steps to the mainland where he forsook the dirty port cities for deep country, traveling alone down winding roads from town to town, asking a few questions at each hamlet before leaving at the next dawn.

After months he found the object of his search, a seventh son of a seventh son, a cobbler on his deathbed in a place called Farnham's Crossing. Children, grandchildren, nieces, nephews gathered round the old man's bed like rabbits in a warren. Aelfric watched through the window from his perch in a nearby tree, disguised by magic as a crow.

The old man died and was buried the next day, by local custom, in a plot of earth beside his predeceased kin. One of his children, a mason, chiseled a headstone. Words were said. In the crowd of mourners, Aelfric concealed himself and tried to feel sorrow. Lydia felt pain and joy as these creatures did, all the subtle range of their emotions, so he should feel them, too. It should have been no harder than learning their base tongue, but such mutable passions were harder to grasp even than their contorted grammar. One moment they mourned, the next rejoiced, retiring from the burial ground to wake the dead.

All this was to Aelfric's advantage. A seventh son of a seventh son was a powerful conjunction, made more powerful still as the villagers dwelt upon his passing. Such a man's death must have meaning and significance as a third son's second son did not, they said. As they drank they turned the dead man's life inside out and upside down and shook it for truths as though it were a garment with coins concealed within. Their collective attention pressed against the world they thought they knew, and made it fragile.

Setting sun and rising Diun cast a double shadow from the gravestone. The Aiemer resonated with drunken songs and stories. A rose lay upon the grave, the parting gift of a bereaved grandchild.

Aelfric could not return to the Dreaming by the regular gates and paths, but some doors opened only once, or never opened at all unless you knocked.

He knelt between the two shadows of the grave. The rose took fire in the mixed light as he picked it up and placed it inside his jacket. Bowing his head, he touched his left hand to the ruddy shadow cast by Diun, his right to the silver shadow cast by the setting sun.

By the gates of the cemetery, a drunken granddaughter come to pay her last respects saw a figure like a kneeling man before her grandsire's grave, and heard a click, as of a key turning in a great lock. She blinked, and when she opened her eyes the man was gone.

The gate deposited Aelfric in the deep talamhs, the vales and glens where order yielded to playful chaos. A desert hill at nightfall might be an island surrounded by shallow ocean come the dawn. In the Dreaming, Aelfric moved faster, free from the constraints of mortal realms where the distance between two points was generally a straight line. He left safe roads behind and commanded the shifting dreamscape to bear him forth. He flew, he bounded across plateaus at seven leagues a stride, he slithered through underbrush as a serpent. When all else failed, he walked.

Long before he reached Nightmare's realm he realized Lydia was no longer there. The land was closed, and wayfarers spoke in hushed tones of the assault on Nightmare's palace, of the dread lord's kidnapping and the death of his orchestra. Aelfric asked, when sharing campfires with a merchant too much in his cups or a local warden eager for gossip and riddles, if any of the orchestra had escaped. Someone must have, he reasoned, if only to spread the stories.

But how was he to tell truth from lie? The tales of Lord Nightmare's kidnapping he believed, or at least believed they were a version of the truth that suited the Nai'Oigher. None would spread such tales about a living god—he savored the quaint, human word—without the approval, tacit or otherwise, of others among their number. The rapacious claims made against the lij invaders, that they killed all who they encountered and bathed in the blood, were most likely false, rumormongers playing to the martial themes that spread like plague throughout the land. Country Fae practiced rank and formation. Even passing merchants with their multicolored wagons of tradestuff bore arms and wore soldiers' subdued colors. The land resounded with drums.

In millennia past he would have known what to think of such madness. A rebellion coming, an uprising against whoever was in power this decade. Some violence, some torture, a little dungeon time for those who needed it, and the system would right itself. But this time Fae names were not muttered in village squares, nor did the common folk rage against Fae crimes.

"I hear," he told the Ainghid Fas who shared his campfire one night, a winsome woman of scarcely a thousand springs, "that some escaped the slaughter at Nightmare's palace."

"A few," she replied. She bore the marks of her profession, wandering the Dreaming Lands and the Dying righting the balance between life and death (as she would put it) and feeding off passion, fear, rage. Shadows lingering upon her flesh made her cold; her pretty fingers ended in long claws. "So I have heard."

"I seek a sister of mine." He had given up asking after Lydia. To Fae, lij looked much the same. They were so mutable. Hair gold one year might be dark the next, or white; black skin paled and pale skin turned sallow. Height and girth shifted by the month, it seemed. Lydia he remembered frozen in time, dark-haired and beautiful, mouth open to sing, but how might she have changed? "Short and broad and blunt, sharp-toothed and sharp-eyed, strong of wit. Called Schwarzalbe."

The Ainghid Fas stiffened.

"You have heard of her."

"Seen her, I have." She did not want to say more.

"Where?"

She looked up at him through her bangs, strangely shy.

"She was the companion of my youth," he said, "a close servant to Nightmare. When we were young, we hunted together through the deep talamh." All true. Speak no lie in the Dreaming Lands, he had been warned as a child. "She was loyal."

"She- I-" The Ainghid Fas could not finish her sentence. She was a young Sin Eater, not without beauty in her shadowed way, but raw, like a branch with its bark stripped off. There was a thinness as of ice to her eyes. "There must be many Schwarzalbes in the Dreaming."

"People change," he said. It was not such a common name as that. "What have you seen?"

"Seen, and heard, and felt." She poked the burning twigs and brush of their fire with the copper-shod tip of her walking stick. "I am called Morgan," she said. It was not the way of travelers sharing a campfire at night to exchange names, even false ones. Any name given from one's own mouth was a handle. It could be used to grasp and to bind.

"You may call me Aelfspar," he replied. Like for like. She had not told him her true name, either. Even this sharing of aliases drew them closer. Their circle of firelight now enclosed two people who could address one another directly.

She bowed her head to accept his gift. "I am twenty Parades an Ainghid Fas." One Parade every 50 years, so his judgment had been true–she was just over a millennium old. "My travels take me through the land, one circuit roughly each Parade and ten years in Maeda Criacao. I'm not one of our great old champions, but I work with care. I resolved the Lean'Aghan Blight, and stopped, with my brothers, the Kamutu Flood. When the Attarin Healer rose in the Western Reach, I was there to receive him into the Death-house. I say this not to make you think I am great. I am not. But I am good at my job."

Shadows deepened around Morgan as she spoke, and the fire burned more brilliantly than before. Aelfric hugged his knees to his chest and listened.

"You have felt the changes in our land. The masses prepare for war. The shepherds speak of it, and the merchants plan for procurements and profits to come. I thought I should be in the capital. That is where we will need the most balance soon. As we lumber towards war, some must protest for peace.

"In Maeda Criacao I met friends I had not seen since before I became a Sin Eater. We rejoiced. Five comrades from five different paths, united again. We toasted one another and decided to see what we could of these Dying Lands with which war seemed inevitable.

"So we went to the Mist Market."

She flinched a little as she said it, as if expecting a blow or a cry. Aelfric listened and watched the fire.

"It made sense, to me, though I was drunk at the time. To resist the war, I had to understand the men and women of the Dying Lands. What is their greatest distinction from us? Death, but that I could not taste. Behind that, music.

"My friend, a lord of the city, led us through the Delledier Market until we found the Mist. Once there, we paid no heed to the lesser pleasures on offer. According to him, there was a new joy in town greater than all the rest: a lij singer, caged for our amusement. Every night she sings, and the city comes to hear her.

"I had never seen such a dense-packed crowd, cheek pressed to cheek, reeking of sweat and rotten flowers. The room grew dark but for a spotlight on the stage, and a woman stepped into the light. A lij woman.

"I knew she was lij, not an illusion or a glamour. There was something brief about her, unreal, as of a soap bubble or a cloud. The audience screamed. They hated her. She was pinned in that light, poor lost thing.

"The lady of the place bid her perform, and she opened her mouth and-" Morgan could not finish her sentence. Words clogged her throat. She breathed in slow, measured gasps. Aelfric shifted around the fire until he could lay his hand on her shoulder. Her skin beneath the fabric of her chemise was hard and smooth as old stone.

"What happened then?" he asked.

"She sang. What do you think happened?" Morgan shot back. "She sang, and the room erupted. The dance was stronger than I've ever seen it in Fae, mad and wriggling. I've never..." she said, tasting the memory. "I have felt passion. I have felt death and birth and brought balance between them. And I have heard music before, so don't think this was a...a neophyte's first brush with the stuff."

"I know," he said.

"She sang joy and sadness. It mixed with the rage in her audience like different oils mix when shaken, piercing one another. I tasted that passion, felt it build. I tried to feed upon it before violence erupted, but it was too strong. I went mad with the rest, screaming and dancing, and when the time came we rushed the stage to grab the little lij singer and tear her flesh to rags. The madam of the place expected this. She called her guards, big burly terrors whose ears were stopped with wool and wax, and they fended off the crowd, laying about them with thick staves until blood stained the floorboards. All the while, the woman sang.

"I ran. I've been running since. And I do not know today whether I deserve the name of Ainghid Fas." Noticing for the first time his hand on her shoulder, she made to brush it away. He did not let go. "I cannot guide myself. How can I guide the flock?" For those of her calling saw the world as a flock of wandering sheep, and they the sheepdogs.

"You were surprised. You did not go there to bring balance; you went to learn. And so you learned."

"There is no excuse for failure."

"There is no room in the world for stories without it. Great lords and ladies make the best fools, and country farmers may be wise.

Secret-keepers miss the secrets that lurk within their own mirrors. Servants fail their masters, and friends their friends. If it's a good story, though…" He had thought on this often in the weeks past, about the look on Lydia's moonlit face as Schwarzalbe seized her from behind. "If it's a good story, our failures do not destroy us."

"You believe that?" she said without looking at him.

"I have to. That is why I seek her." He found, to his surprise, that he trusted the Ainghid Fas. "The girl, the lij. She suffers from my weakness. Tell me the name of her captor. The madam of the Market of Mist."

"Schwarzalbe," Morgan said.

They sat longer by the dying fire and spoke of other things.

The next morning he left her sleeping by the embers of their fire, laced his boots, and walked on, ceaselessly, to Maeda Criacao.

— CAESURA —

Max Gladstone

All roads lead to Maeda Criacao, but once they pass beneath its gates they spawn a tangle of bramble-paths and thorned alleyways. Bumpkin Fae from the deep talamhs stare around themselves in awe; one might think they'd never seen water falling upwards before, or ten-story palaces made of tightly woven, still-growing grass.

Aelfric did not gawk. Long had he skulked in the fishing villages of Brailee's Steps and yearned for these golden streets, but he did not return today a conqueror or even a supplicant. Maeda Criacao's immensity weighed upon him from all sides, compressing him into a single idea.

A single mission.

His hands shook. He stuffed them in his pockets and kept his eyes on the faerie-dust flagstones.

He knew what he sought here, amid the military drumming and the young recruits who marched in rank and file down gold-paved streets, bearing truncheon and spear and sword. He avoided the marchers and skirted the edge of huddled, angry conversations:

the lij celebrate the death of parents and friends with food and drink, they build temples to glory in the horror of death, their rulers oppress the peasants and the peasants slay the rulers at the slightest opportunity. Animals, all.

The Delledier Market was easy to find. Wander Maeda Cricao without a firm destination and let enchantment guide your feet; soon you heard the hawkers' cries, smelled spices and cooked meat, and came upon the caravanserai in cloth of saffron, red, silver, and green. Spice-sellers and water-sellers, tailors and tinkers and toy-makers and merchants of liquor. One row of stalls sold childhood memories, kisses, love, first sorrows three to a bundle. Another bought and traded body parts, your fingers for a thief's, your eyes for a hawk's.

Aelfric sought amid the tangled alleys the Street of Smiths, smelling of oil and salt sweat and molten steel. A hugely fat woman screamed "Knives, Knives" at the top of her voice; next to her stood a half-naked merchant with the word "Knife" written in red paint on his pot belly. As his partner screamed he demonstrated the sharpness of her blades, slicing paper and feathers and raw meat and stones. Aelfric walked on, past the burly master smiths who sold swords by the dozen to soberly dressed recruits; walked on, past the propaganda posters and the crowded cutlery shops. Near the end of the row he found a dusty stall stacked high with broken pots and pans. A wiry woman sat within, bare feet propped up on the counter beside a wooden flask of some foul fire-water. Her eyes were closed, and she was snoring.

He rang the bell on the counter. She did not move, but the snoring stopped.

"You are Aiobheann the Smith?"

"Ev," she said, shortening it. "Who wants to know?"

"I want a blade."

"Nah." She waved dismissively, eyes still closed. "You don't."

"I do."

"You want some little pricker to go stab lij with. You don't want a blade, you want a piece of pot iron to make you feel all maley-like."

"And yet here I am, to buy a blade."

She opened her eyes then. "Buy, you say."

He ran his fingertips over the counter, making tracks in the dust near her bottle and her feet. "It seems to me that some centuries back, if one wanted a blade in the City, one sought out Aiobheann the Smith."

"Such things were said," she acknowledged with a slow nod, as though her head were too heavy and her neck too fragile for swift movement. "It was also said one should not seek her out lest one was willing to pay her price. So." She moved first one foot from the counter to the floor, then the other, then leaned forward. "What have you brought?"

From within his ragged jacket he produced the rose. In two hours lying on the old man's grave its petals had begun to wilt, but in weeks or more of travel through the Dreaming, the flower had suffered no further decay.

Ev cradled her chin in her hand and squinted as if the rose were a bright flame.

"A flower from the Dying Lands," he said. "Placed on the grave of a seventh son of a seventh son, by one of his own blood." She reached for the blossom, but he pulled it away from her clutching fingers. "Sorrow, and memory. Joy, decay. A child's first taste of death. Don't see that much here, I think. Not lately."

Again she grasped for it, and again he pulled it back. In her heavy-lidded gaze he saw a quickening hint of desire.

"I want," he repeated, "to buy a sword."

Petulant, she pursed her lips and narrowed her eyes, as if about to leap across the counter for the flower. "A sword, you say." She raised one finger, then disappeared beneath the counter. He heard the heavy clunk of pottery and the light ting of tin, the scuttering of little feet and an unearthly scream, followed by a hammering noise and a crunch. She rose again, hair mussed, bearing two swords in rough and inexpert scabbards, hilts and pommels made from braided leather thongs. "A deal. Choose your sword. If you choose the good one, I'll sell it to you for that flower. Choose the bad one, and I'll sell it to you for the flower, and take your hand as a tip." She waved inconclusively at his arms. "I don't care left or right. I can find uses for both."

"Done." He examined each sword first sheathed, then naked. Both were straight, both sure, both blades dark in color save their cutting edges, which were chalk-white. Both balanced well in the hand, fair and strong, flexible. A cut in quarte shifted to a parry in prime easily as the opening of an unlocked door. There was no choice between the two. He almost touched their edges, but thought better of it, and instead pointed to the bottle resting on the counter. "May I?"

She nodded.

He tipped the bottle on its side and worked the stopper out until a small, steady stream of clear liquid flowed from the neck. The first sword he touched to the fire-water, blade pointing up to cut the flow. A thin stream of red issued from the blade's rear edge, tainting the liquid; Aelfric wet his finger in the red, touched it to his lips, and tasted blood. With the second sword he repeated the experiment, but this time when he cut the fire-water the stream bifurcated a half-inch above the blade, only rejoining an inch below the sword's trailing edge.

"I'll take this one." He righted the bottle.

"Well chosen," Ev said. "I'll take that flower."

He gave it to her gladly; the thing had caught at his soul as he walked. Like a child she received it from him, two hands cupped. As he left the stall, sword slung over his shoulder, she peeled a petal from the rose and placed it between her full lips, humming as she chewed.

To find the Mist Market required desire, not for the Market itself but for something within that could be found in no other place. Those who wanted the Market for itself were likely as not law-keepers or righteous lords and ladies, looking to win renown by destroying an acknowledged evil. Over centuries, the denizens of the Market pulled the mists around themselves for protection. Without such defenses they would have been destroyed a hundred times over, hounded into deep nightmare.

As Aelfric left the Street of Smiths, he chose a direction at random and began to walk. When that direction bored him, he took the next avenue that diverged, a grungy side street lined with hawkers of barbecued scorpion. Turn, onto a lane of multicolored silks. Turn, onto a booksellers' alley, every book here that had ever been written and many that had yet to be written, the rarest the books that could never be written. Then turn, onto a street that sold every form of nail and spike and tine and barrel-hoop.

He realized as he proceeded down the Street of Nails that he was walking through a faint fog like finely pulled cotton. This was the hardest part. He ignored the mist entirely and thought of Lydia, of her smile and her long black hair and her light footsteps on the sand. Step, and the mist was thicker now. He could no longer see the stones beneath his feet. Her dress swayed as she spun, arms spread. Step, and the Street of Nails was gone. Her song. Her beautiful, damning song.

Though he did not remember willing himself to turn, he felt a turn nevertheless, in him or around him or maybe only in his mind. He heard voices ahead in the gray.

"Give us it again." The high-pitched whine of a man with a child's unyielding needs.

"Not 'less you pay." Quiet that one, almost whispered.

"Come on. I tell you, I'll pay. But give us it again."

"Will not. Unless."

"Unless what, Shae?"

"That's an awful nice finger you have there. The third one."

A shocked silence. He was almost upon them, two shapes in the fog, one taller and rich in clothing but bent forward, shaking, and the other short, stout, resolute. The shorter form stood nearer Aelfric, so Aelfric saw him first as he passed: bald pate and fringe of tangled hair, leather vest and bare sagging flesh beneath. A boxy contraption hung around his neck, and a pair of earmuffs; each of his hands had eight fingers, and they did not match. From a belt around his waist, more fingers dangled, impaled on hooks. Some still sparkled with rings.

As Aelfric passed closer he saw the taller figure, dusty and elegant, three fingers on his left hand, four on his right. A Monarhig, a lord of the city, face wan and eyes desperate.

"A taste," the shorter figure said. He placed the earmuffs over his ears, and pressed with one of his fingers (this one slender and long—it had once belonged to an elegant lady, and its nail was still lacquered) a button on the side of the box. The box's lid opened and a small china dancer appeared within, spinning. From within, also, came a tinny, harsh, repetitive sound.

Music.

The Monarhig's eyes glazed over and he shook, this time with pleasure; Shae removed his finger from the button and the music stopped, and the Monarhig began to weep.

Aelfric hastened deeper into the Mist Market. He did not pause as he passed more streetside music-sellers. There were no craftsmen or salesmen here. Their stolen music boxes did the work for them, and they stood by, collecting. First taste free. After that, it starts easy. Memory of an unimportant lesson or an afternoon wasted on unpleasant tasks. Later, after the need set in, maybe the memory of a lover's quarrel or the whole emotion of jealousy. When the hooks were deep enough, love itself could be traded. How vast the Mist Market was, Aelfric did not know. He had never plumbed its depths, though his steps had wound here more than once, drawn by curiosity and by fashion. These delights went in and out of vogue, and if this was not a peak of the trend, neither was it an ebb. The deeper into the market he walked, the more real it became around him. The mist split down the middle until it obscured sky and cobblestones but left the intervening space clear, peddlers and customers and buildings.

Others walked with him in the Mist Market. They did not talk to one another, did not laugh or skip or dance, though they trembled when they heard a trill from a nearby music box or from within one of the music dens they passed. They were men, mostly, but he saw a Riddari woman glancing about her as if afraid she might be attacked and a few prim ladies with trembling hands.

These were his people. That thought tasted sour. The sword belt chafed his shoulder.

Following the current he came to a tall, broad, thatch-roofed building with a door of thick wood and barred windows. No decoration here, no enticement beyond a single sign, tall and broad above the door: Schwarzalbe's. The building, like its lady, did not pretend to elegance or subtlety. Aelfric's companions of the road, these silent salmon swimming ceaselessly upstream, entered Scwarzalbe's darkness. He followed them.

Even before his eyes adjusted to the dim light he could see the inn was near-full, though it was only midday. Most of the building was one large chamber with a raised stage at the far end. Before the stage, scattered tables interrupted a sawdust floor. All the tables were occupied, though none by friends. Each individual had come here apart from every other. A bar near the door sold drinks, but few drank. All waited.

Before the stage stood a row of thick-chested men in green and silver, Schwarzalbe's colors. They were armed with cudgel and truncheon, and their ears stuffed with wax.

Aelfric remained near the door, his back to a wall so as to camouflage his sword.

The lights dimmed. A hush fell over the hall. As one, the guards near the stage beat upon the ground with their truncheons, a measured rhythm growing faster and faster still until their blows fell, never-ending and harsh, a summer rainstorm. The audience seemed transmuted into stone. Not a head rose or fell, not a breath stirred the air. Aelfric felt his heart flicker.

Schwarzalbe stepped onto the stage.

She was broad and squat and potent as ever, moving with a shipmaster's assurance, dressed more richly than he remembered, in leather breeches and a fine green tunic belted incongruously with what looked like black rope. "Ladies," she said, raising her hand. "Gentlemen." She strode to the stage's edge, hands on her hips and elbows flared. "Are you ready?"

The stunned silence shattered in a roar like a collapsing building, a roar that could not have come from the thin mouths and threadbare throats of the addicts arrayed in audience. Schwarzalbe's smile was jagged and joyful.

"I don't think they're ready, Mil," she said, kicking a guard in the shoulder. "Do you?" Mil shook his head.

The roar of protest was even louder than the roar of affirmation–loud and rote. The onlookers knew their role in this drama. Like a crowd at a Duinite service, they made their proper answer, and leaned forward to receive the blessing of their spiritual shepherd. Schwarzalbe reveled in the ritual and in her control.

"Come out, pet!" she yelled over her shoulder. A door swung open behind her, hesitantly, revealing shadow beyond.

Lydia stepped onto the stage. Herself, unmistakably, but changed.

Her hair was short now, barely half an inch long and ragged as if cut with a sword. She was slender and taller, the Dreaming working into her blood and body. Before, she had always worn a peasant girl's dress of coarse blue and brown cloth, suitable for work and not much else. Today she wore a white blouse and a flared green skirt with silver trim, no lower than the knee, and high stockings. A doll's clothes. A green and silver ribbon bound her jaw shut, and was tied atop her head in a bow. Her eyes were open and older.

He could not look away. What had he expected to do here? Rush forward, sword in hand as he forced his way through the crowd. Need made the air thick and his body heavy. Lydia strode to the front of the stage. Schwarzalbe reached into her belt pouch and removed two pieces of soft wax, which she inserted into her ears. Then she gripped between thumb and forefinger a loose end of the bow atop Lydia's head, and pulled. The bow untied itself and the silver-green ribbon came away in her hand. The world shrank to Lydia's eyes, brown, deep, round, and hard.

Aelfric tried to speak. Call out her name. But he did not know the person who looked out from behind those eyes. Had he ever known her? Really known her, not known her as a toy, to use and discard as needed?

The brown eyes that were his world revolved and pierced him. They widened, seeing him, knowing him. Reflected in them he saw himself turning a somersault beneath vaulted, starlit skies. Her mouth drifted open, and it was black within, a hole into which he could crawl and hide and die.

She was about to sing. Sing, as Schwarzalbe had some way of forcing her to do; sing, as she had back in Brailee's Steps before he let her slip away. And he would stand here against the wall and watch her, transfixed like all these others by her goddess-song. Just another trembling shade.

A small beast woke in his chest, and its name was Rage. It stirred like the expectant audience, and as it felt the outline of his past and the shapes of his betrayals, it swelled in size and majesty, spreading wings and baring claws. The air around him was still composed of mud and rock, but he was stronger now; as expectant groans rose from the assembled crowd and Lydia inhaled, his hand rose to the hilt of his sword.

Another hand settled about his wrist like an iron cuff. Without thinking, without even looking, so strong was his rampant anger, he pulled against this rude grip, but it did not resist him. Rather, it following the trajectory of his wrist down and brought it back up behind him, pressing and twisting. Pain erupted in his shoulder, the world twisted, and he fell. His back struck the floor with a painful crack and galaxies unfolded before his vision, then resolved into Schwarzalbe's face. She knelt over him, smiling with jagged teeth. Her left hand held his arm and wrist. He tried to pull free, but only pain rewarded his efforts. The flat of his sword in its scabbard pressed hard against his spine.

"Welcome back," Schwarzalbe said.

"I-"

He never finished the sentence. She looked to someone Aelfric could not see, and he heard a whisper of wind before a cudgel struck the side of his head. He swore, loudly. Schwarzalbe did not hear. Of course not. Her ears were stopped.

She reached down to his throat, found the points to either side of his windpipe where his blood flowed, and squeezed there. He flopped against her, desperate for freedom.

"Shhhh," she said. "I do not mean to kill you. What kind of welcome would that be for an old friend?"

He pulled harder and felt a muscle within his arm give. Brown rolled in from the edges of his vision, and he fell into a hole dark and deep and warm as the inside of Lydia's mouth.

Aelfric heard a voice, as if from a faraway country, singing. He went limp.

"Well," Schwarzalbe said. "Let's get him into the back, boys. No sense disturbing our customers."

— CRESCENDO AND FINALE —

Max Gladstone

Eyes open or closed, Aelfric saw only darkness. He was moving. No dream could have produced so varied a spectrum of pain. Awake, then, and blindfolded.

Carrying hands set him down. He tried to move, weak as he was, and felt ropes around him, wood at his back and beneath his haunches. He was tied to a chair. Someone ripped the darkness from his eyes.

He sat in a dirty, candlelit room between two tattered cots. No windows in the clapboard walls. How long had he been out? This was not a good place to torture someone: people lived here, to judge from the ratty blankets on the beds and the shaving kits and the dirty pictures on the walls. There were abandoned warehouses aplenty in the Mist Market, and dungeons for rent if needed, and this was none of those. They must've been within Schwarzalbe's inn, probably in the quarters of a pair of guards who boarded on the premises. Which meant Lydia was nearby.

He heard the lady of the house before he saw her. "Outside, boys." Heavy boots tromped on thin floorboards. A door closed. Bootsteps, again, a single pair advancing.

Blunt fingers ran through his hair. He pulled away.

Schwarzalbe walked into view and sat on a cot well out of Aelfric's reach. She wore still her green and silver tunic and carried his sword.

"Let me go," he said.

"Hardly any way to greet me after months of absence, Aelfric, to come into my place of business with hard steel and hard words." She patted the sword's sheath. "I should think you might ask how I've been and what path I took to get here-queen of the undercity. Who'd have thought, decades back? They'd have laughed if you'd told them, 'Schwarzalbe, give her time and she'll be a woman of substance.'"

"What did you do to Lydia?"

"So it's Lydia now? Decided to think of her as a person? Or is that just what you're telling yourself, because you think an addict doesn't travel halfway across the Dying Lands and Dreaming for a fix?"

"What did you do to her?" he repeated, tone flat and sharp.

"I made her promise to do what I say: sing when I bid her, and stop when I say stop. That done, I asked myself, how can I profit by this poor girl?" She patted the cot beside her. "Not a bad place, this. Not bad work either, for her. In the Dying Lands the streets are full of girls who hope for this kind of gig. Two shows a day, no errands to run or water to fetch."

"She doesn't want to be here. She wants to go home."

"Maybe she does, now. But once she got back there she'd find it's grown smaller. Will she fit there any more, after men and women have torn themselves to pieces over her?"

"I hear they try to kill her as she sings."

Schwarzalbe shrugged.

"You claim she likes this life? Let her go. See how long she stays."

"Just because a dog runs away when you leave the door open doesn't mean it isn't happy where it is," Schwarzalbe said. "You don't want her free any more than I do. If you did, you'd have left her on Brailee's Steps and found another singer for the master. You wanted her all to yourself, your singer-girl on your private island. I'm doing the same thing as you, only I share my toys. You're just here now because you have the shakes for her."

"Not true."

Schwarzalbe stood in a creaking of wood and fabric and towered over him, arms crossed. "You're pissed I stole your toy. Get over yourself and see the big picture. We need a night manager here. You've been unemployed since His Dreary Nibs got nicked. You could hear her sing as often as you like. I'd even arrange a private show."

He spit at her. She laughed, wiped his saliva from her cheek, and punched him hard in the jaw.

Rubbing her knuckles, she walked past him, giving him wide berth. "Don't believe me? Still think you're a hero? See how long you can sit face-to-face with your princess without begging."

He heard a rustle of cloth, and darkness settled over his eyes again.

Light returned, bright and warm. Dazzled, Aelfric heard a door close behind him. One blink, two, and the shining haze resolved into a well-appointed room. The lace on the soft green curtains of the four-poster bed matched the warm off-white of the walls, matched the doily draped over the maple writing desk and the coat of arms on the armoire. Gas lamps lit the room. Night sky hung close beyond the single, massive, barred window.

Lydia stood by that window, her back to him. She still wore her stage outfit: white blouse, green flared short skirt (she must, he thought, feel so exposed, used to the layered furs of cold winters on Brailee's Steps), stockings, sandals.

She turned around. He realized that he had said her name; its syllables hung on the still air. Trying to read her expression, he found his judgment slipping. There was too much there for him to read, too much even for her to know, sparking from one mood to the next like blooms of lightning in high clouds.

Her clothes were more a part of the room than of her body, leaving her face and hands to hover disconnected from their surroundings like the features of a ghost. Her expression grew tense with the effort of memory. She knelt before his chair, drawing her face level with his. He wondered how he looked, to her eyes. Terrible, probably. Sick and wan after months of rough living, a purple bruise spreading across his face.

"Hello again, imaginary sir," she said.

"If I were imaginary," he replied, "I wouldn't hurt so much."

She reached for him, for the bruise on his jaw, her touch light as the fall of an autumn leaf. Her fingers explored the contours of his chin and lips and cheeks as if his were the first face she had felt in the world. Her skin was paler than he remembered. She must have been locked in Nightmare's palace for months. That pallor was a wound he had dealt her.

If she wanted vengeance, she would have it. No great effort would be needed, not even a weapon. Just sing, and he would dance and thrash and break himself on these ropes.

She withdrew her touch and stood. "Who are you?"

He had never given her his name. One did not give names to lij, especially not to lij one intended to betray.

"You see a humble man, once hight Aelfric of the Nightmare Court." He met her eyes as he said it. "My dread Lord sent me into your world to quest musicians for his orchestra."

"Your Lord was..." Her language did not have the right word. "Like the people who come to watch me. He needed the music."

"Yes. He sent me, and others like me, and Schwarzalbe, to find musicians. I think he was not a well man," Aelfric said tentatively. "Nor a happy one. He had been ill for thousands of years, tens of thousands. He needed song to prop him up."

She circled around behind him, trailing one finger down his cheek, over his chest, onto his shoulder and back. "So you came to steal me away. But you did not."

"Yes."

She pressed against the ropes that held him. "Why?"

"Because you were..." he trailed off. "Your music was honest and rich. More powerful than I had ever heard. That was part of the reason. But…you seemed so happy. Dancing. Gathering sea hair."

She revolved around to his front again and paced toward the window, standing in profile against the bars. "You collected musicians before this."

"I did. I tricked the others, mostly, into signing contracts to enter Nightmare's service. Sometimes, if their talent was great, I stole them away without their consent. I was never so rough as Schwarzalbe, but I did serve my lord."

"Until you met me."

"Until I met you."

"And decided to keep me for yourself."

"Not for myself," he said. "For yourself. But you did not mind singing to me, and that was all I would ask in return."

"Had you betrayed your master before?"

These were deeper questions than the Lydia of Brailee's Steps could have asked. She had been a girl of light step and dreamy eyes. A kind of slime had congealed about her into a hard, slick shell, and that was his fault. "Never."

"But you did, for my music."

"For you," he said. "So you might sing for yourself, and I might hear you."

"For me." She turned back to him. "Would you like me to sing for you now? I can, when Schwarzalbe's not in the room — so long as I don't try to escape." Her words ran together, so fast did she speak. Eager, as if afraid he might disbelieve her. She clutched her hands together above her stomach. "I can sing."

He felt sick. His body was slick with sweat. *You're only here now because you have the shakes*, Schwarzalbe said, and she had not been mistaken. He had passed untouched through the Mist Market, because Lydia still sang in his head. Because he needed her.

Before his mind's eye he fixed the girl he had known, the dancer on the Diuntyne beach whose life he had destroyed. He cursed himself and said: "No."

The oval of her head inclined to one side. She had not heard him, so weak was his voice. Or perhaps she heard him but wanted him to repeat himself.

"No," he repeated, taking strength in his decision and making it seem inevitable. "Don't sing. I couldn't bear it."

No sound. The room smelled of dust, of long-dead things and still air. Floorboards creaked under Lydia's sandaled feet as she shifted her weight, considering him. Behind her brown eyes he was weighed on a pair of scales vast as the cosmos.

"It's a pleasure to meet you, imaginary sir," she said at last. "I wondered how long it would take you to find me. I had almost lost hope."

"I'm sorry," he replied, with a courtly bow of his head. "If you were awaiting a gallant rescue, I fear I've disappointed." He strained against the ropes but they were no less tight than before. "We're both in need of succor now."

"My sweet Aelfric, what made you think I needed you to rescue me? I stayed here because I knew that here you could find me, and here I would be some manner of safe. It is dangerous, after all, for lij to travel your land alone." The shell was broken, and what emerged, incongruous in those doll's clothes, was a girl no longer. Her richness startled.

"I'm trussed," he observed. "Your music is useless when Schwarzalbe is around. The two of us would be hard-pressed to overpower her alone and without her guards."

"Leave the guards to me."

"What are you planning?"

"Better you not know. Your disbelief might spoil the whole thing. Just be ready to move when the moment comes. Even if everything works out as I hope, we'll be in terrible danger." Footsteps in the hall outside. She smiled. "I intend to be original."

A heavy hand knocked upon the door, and Lydia's mouth snapped shut. Schwarzalbe entered, and the floor shook beneath her heavy stride.

Without a glance towards Aelfric, she moved to Lydia, produced the green ribbon from her pocket, and tied the other woman's jaw shut. Lydia did not flinch, long since accustomed to this process. "You've more fire in the eyes than usual, pet," Schwarzalbe said, patting her on the cheek. She turned back to Aelfric. "Guess she realizes who got her in this mess, eh? And wouldn't sing for you, it seems, no matter how you begged for it. I'll fix that." She bared teeth that were longer, sharper than Aelfric remembered. "We've saved you a front row seat."

The house was packed when the guards carried him onto the stage, still bound to the chair. With the spotlight in his eyes, Aelfric saw the audience as a persistent, writhing darkness beyond the world's edge, united into one organism by need. Though he could not see them, he heard their roar of disappointment and rage. He was not their idol, not the source of their release. Morgan had described the smell of sweat and rotten flowers. There was a harsh edge under that, like chemical smoke.

The roar grew, stretched, twisted into a living thing apart from the frail Fae whose throats birthed it. Violence crouched there, waiting for its cue.

The door behind him opened and Schwarzalbe emerged to cries of rapture. She raised her arms as she advanced, commanding her petitioners to their feet. They rose together with their voices. "Good evening!" Schwarzalbe shouted. She was dressed more richly than before, in a green and silver tunic with more frills and a wider cut in the sleeve, belted with the same dark rope. Aelfric realized in revulsion that the belt was not rope but human hair, Lydia's hair, cut from her head and worn as a trophy. His stomach turned, and he yearned to hold the sword now belted across Schwarzalbe's back, the good blade purchased from Aiobheann the Smith but never used.

He was about to die. Lydia's plan, her hope, was foolish, the delusion of a woman too long held captive. Promises bound her to Schwarzalbe, and promises ran deep in the Dreaming Lands. Schwarzalbe would bid her sing, and sing she would, and he would dance. The thought turned his stomach, and a rotten kernel of his soul rejoiced.

Schwarzalbe was talking again. He ignored her. Whatever she said caused the floor to shake as the addicts in the audience leapt and screamed. She stepped aside, gestured back to the upstage door. It swung open readily and Lydia emerged from shadow, chin up, shoulders back, defiance radiating from her skin through the bright-colored, tawdry doll's outfit.

That defiance touched flame to the audience, who erupted in outraged chorus. They cared nothing for Aelfric or for Schwarzalbe, but Lydia they wanted to destroy, to break her fingers and rend her flesh and spray her blood over their bodies like rain. She was lij, she had power over them, and they would end her for it, throwing themselves against Schwarzalbe's guards like the tide, bashing their own heads against the stage in ecstasy. People would die here tonight.

He tested his bonds. Weaker, he thought, than they had been before. The guards who had brought him in were distracted, as was Schwarzalbe, by the roiling crowd. Nobody would notice a little extra movement on the stage. He worked his bound wrists against one another, trying to loosen the knots.

Schwarzalbe ended her oration and undid the bow atop Lydia's head. The green ribbon floated to the stage floor as she stepped back. The seconds of its fall were Aelfric's last chance: three, and he felt the ropes give a little; two, and he pulled, but his hand was too big to fit through; one. He tried, frantically, to loosen the knots. Zero. Contact.

"Sing!" Schwarzalbe shouted, stepping back.

Silence. Every crazed member of the crazed audience crept forward, united in a grim silence more terrifying than their furor. Lydia's red lips parted. She drew in a deep breath, steeling herself for some great undertaking. What was her plan? To overwhelm them all in a burst of song-magic? Could she manage it, untrained as a spellsinger and barely trained as a musician?

"Sing!" Schwarzalbe commanded again.

Lydia replied, in a perfectly normal tone of voice, "I am singing."

The crowd was too startled to respond.

Schwarzalbe's ears were plugged with wax, but she could read faces and lips well enough. "Sing, girl! I command it!"

"I am singing, right now," Lydia said.

Unruly murmurs from the assembled crowd. Schwarzalbe shot them a worried look. "You," she said, taking a menacing step forward, "are not singing."

"I am, indeed." Lydia looked cool at first glance, collected in the face of Schwarzalbe's wrath, but Aelfric could see her hands shake.

"You're not making music!"

"Am I not? Words are music. They have pitch." By demonstration she shifted that pitch as she spoke, now high, now low: "All we like sheep have gone astray." She smiled. "Rhythm. Pitch. Rhyme if you have the time."

"Sing what you sang this afternoon! Or last night!" The angry rumbles from the crowd were getting louder now.

"You're prejudiced. You think every song has to sound like this-" She sang a tripping, trifling trill of descending notes. The audience spasmed in pleasure and cried out in pain and fury when she stopped, but Aelfric paid no heed to either: those few notes she sang had an effect neither audience nor his few guards could see. The ropes that bound him to his chair lost their strength. He twitched his wrists, and the hemp cords melted to ash. He was free. "But they don't," Lydia shouted over the crowd. "A song is what the singer cares to make it."

Schwarzalbe's hand rose to the sword. "Girl, if you don't sing-"

"You pledged to do me no harm."

"If you don't sing right now, you'll see how far I can stretch that promise."

"I promised you I would sing, and I am. But I never promised to let you call the tune, nor to abide by your definition of music."

The audience had become a mob, and they were hungry. This paltry lij defied her mistress, and her mistress had not brought her to heel. They surged against the stage. There would be vengeance. Blood for music withheld. Great Mother, but Aelfric hungered for it, too, in his stomach's pit, the music, and failing that... He thought back to Lydia's face in that doll's room. The mob pressed towards the stage. Schwarzalbe's guards formed an uneasy battle line, truncheons out.

"You I can't kill," Schwarzalbe said. "Or harm. But your friend here?" She ran across the stage, sword flashing free of the scabbard. Fast as a viper, she took position behind him, between his flanking guards, and placed the blade against his neck. He felt its edge dimple his throat, felt her breath hot in his hair.

Lydia looked from her, to him, to the crowd, and back again. She licked her lips.

Aelfric stood.

Not for nothing had he brought a flower across the Dreaming Lands to trade with Aiobheann the Smith. Some said any blade would do, if it was sharp and bloodthirsty, but a true artist crafted blades that knew when to cut, and whom. Schwarzalbe had always been the stronger of the two of them, the better with the swift and cunning stroke. Why bring a blade to her lair that could be used against him?

The diamond-sharp sword brushed like a cobweb against his throat. He grabbed the blade and pulled. The hilt slid free of Schwarzalbe's grip easily as if dipped in oil, leaving a vicious red welt on her palm. Schwarzalbe roared in pain.

As Aelfric spun on her, the riot began. It was no great event: an angry woman pushed an angry man, who stumbled into one of Schwarzalbe's angry guards. The guard did what guards do and struck with his truncheon. The crack of a skull was inaudible in the bedlam, but the man fell, and others saw him fall, and, screaming, they leapt for the offending guard. His comrades moved to aid him. The maelstrom spread.

Schwarzalbe stared from her wounded hand, to the riot, to the tip of Aelfric's sword. One of her attendant guards leapt forward, swinging his club; Aelfric's sword flashed to parry in quarte and cleaved the club neatly in mid-swing. The guard's momentum bore him crashing to the floor. He scrambled to rise, but Aelfric touched him with the sword-tip and he kept still, trembling with sudden fear.

The riot blossomed. The audience tore through the guards and struggled toward the stage, toward Lydia. Schwarzalbe cradled her wounded hand and looked to Lydia with desperation, desperate as

Aelfric had been for a fix back on Brailee's Steps, desperate as these mad Fae for their music.

"What will you do now?" Schwarzalbe screamed. "I can't keep you safe any more! You think they'll listen to me?"

The first rioters crawled onto the stage, slick with sweat and blood, clothes torn and bodies bruised. They staggered forward. White teeth flashed between thin dry lips.

"They'll listen," Lydia said, "to me."

She sang.

She believed, of course, that she had been singing all along, but this was music Aelfric recognized. The first long, pure note stilled the rioters and bowed Aelfric to the ground. Swiftly he knelt beside the fallen guard, pulled the wax plugs from the man's ears, and with shaking hands placed them into his own. Schwarzalbe took a step forward, but Aelfric stood and re-trained the sword upon her before she could try anything.

As Lydia advanced, the mob gave way before her, bowing like night creatures before the sun. Aelfric followed, keeping his sword en garde and pointed at Schwarzalbe. The song continued, though he could not hear its words, if there were any. He glanced about, alert to any threat, but none among the audience dared stand against him.

Schwarzalbe stared after them, growing smaller, a sailor overboard, swept back by powerful waves.

Behind him, a creak of hinges: Lydia opened the door. He stepped through it without looking and closed the door behind them on the dark and bloody room. The song stopped. He turned to her, stunned.

"They won't move for a few minutes more," she said. "We don't have long."

"We can hide. I know places." Already they were farther away than he could have guessed: neither of them required the Mist Market any more. One step from Schwarzalbe's door and the fog clinging to the cobblestones began to dissipate. They took the first turn they came upon, and had they looked back down the way they had walked, they would not have seen Schwarzalbe's theater.

Lydia stopped. The Alley of Silks surrounded them with rainbow colors. Merchants and customers and stock boys scuttled by, painted figures on the backdrop of a play.

She held her head up, breathed slowly, blinked rapidly.

Something wet shone in her eyes.

Aelfric stood in front of her, and a thousand miles stretched behind. She had seen more than a lij from Brailee's Steps expected ever to see, had been stretched beyond all comprehension, had grown. It hurt. She felt it now.

"We're okay," he said.

"We're okay," she replied.

She was about to say more, or he was, but a scream interrupted them both. Multicolored silk covered the ground to Aelfric's left, stained by mud, and a woman stood above the silk, pointing with a shaking finger at Lydia's round lij skull and her short lij hands and all about her that was not Fae.

Aelfric and Lydia exchanged a quick glance. They were a picture frame falling from a great height, frozen in one another's eyes.

"Let's run," he said, as the frame hit the ground and shattered.

She laughed, and together they ran.

— TRADITIONS —

Andrew Schnider

The gong sounded low and deep, its thrumming well beyond the hearing of most creatures. But most creatures were not shuen, gifted by Wian Liung, He of Storms and Leviathans, to hear as easily below the lapping waters of the ocean as in the too-thin air above.

With the thought of Wian Liung, Asa once more touched his head to the variegated coral of the altar and gave thanks. Spiraling up and around him on all sides, the living tower of coral breathed its pleasure, releasing a spray of phosphorescent particles and filling the tower interior with a soft green mist.

Asa held his arms wide and inhaled deep of the tower's munificence. This was his time, his moment. For seven years he had tended to his tower and the focus at its peak, singing it the songs sorely earned from the leviathans of the deep. For five years following he had walked the path of the shark, hunting the bounty of the oceans so his people might live in comfort. And for three years he had nurtured the living coral of the city, guiding its growth into houses, halls, bridges, gates, and this tower. His tower. It was a perfect copy of the First Tower, save one annoying problem: the seabird that dared soil its roof, resulting in Asa's focus that sprouted forth from it like a needle toward the heavens. Poisons, traps, wards—that damn gull foiled them all, stalling Asa's ascension in the process.

The gong sounded again, high and bright and full of harmonics, and the coral pulled into itself. Slowly, the tender mist floated to the floor and Asa was left alone, his glowing body the only light in the tower. As mandated by tradition, Asa closed his eyes one membrane at a time. Then, too, he closed his ears, as if he were diving deeper than the orca, the grey, the blue. Deeper even than the great kul whale and his kraken prey.

Without sight or sound, the pungent scent of coral filled his nostrils, and Asa was meant to reflect in isolation upon the wealth of his people, the rightness of their path, and their promise to this world and its oceans. Yet Asa could not contain the thrill of excitement and triumph swelling within his breast. After fifteen years of service and learning, of memorizing the long songs of history and the short chants of hunting, building, and caring, Asa had been chosen. Chosen!

With the coming of the third gong—that which sounds neither through the core of the body nor through the fragile bone at the base of his skull, but rather through the middle space of air where it would be audible to all that walks and flies and swims —then would Asa emerge from his tower, his place within the community, as an adult assured.

Not any adult, oh no. Asa suppressed a chuckle as he opened his senses once more to the world. He would be a wavesinger, one of the priests of his people, that bird be damned. By evening he would have his choice of wife. Perhaps the fair Shu Ta, who had sat so often by his side, mending nets or gutting fish in proper anticipatory silence.

Asa blinked, the membranes of his nostrils convulsing shut in consternation. Surely the appointed hour had passed? The long chant running through the back of his mind like the deep ocean currents had come to an end. Asa counted back through the stanzas, wondering if his premature exultation had caused him to miss a verse or two. No, no, he was quite sure he was in the right. And there, the light of dawn filtered through the tower porthole.

Suddenly another shuen, far smaller than Asa's muscled frame, burst into the tower bearing the great whale-bone trident, the symbol of his office.

"What is the meaning of this, shark bait?" Asa bellowed. Such an interruption was unheard of in the annals of his people.

"The high priest Choubatsu begs your indulgence." The smaller shuen, the patterns on his back marking him as a bird-singer, prostrated himself before Asa, trident held high. "By virtue of your long training and diligence, you are immediately raised to the rank of tidewalker. Your presence is beseeched immediately at the sacred tree."

Asa took the trident, let its weight become an extension of his arm as his emotions churned like a blood foam frenzy. Not even out of the tower and already he was a tidewalker, a position he might not have held for a decade or more? And yet, what of the banquet, the grand celebration, the songs sung in his honor? The deep violation of tradition tightened his grip on the trident, and by mere degrees he refrained from taking the messenger's head.

"Why is the ceremony not complete?" Asa demanded. "Why was the third bell not rung?"

"Oh, great one!" The messenger looked to Asa, his voice quavering. "Unbelievers. From the sky, out of the morning sun. Even now they slaughter the living coral with their iron-shod feet and shred the life-pulse of the city with their blasphemous touch. And with every step they—they approach the First Tower!"

Asa's gaze darkened as the membrane of blood and battle descended over his eyes. Messenger forgotten, he strode out of the tower.

Asa stepped out and looked towards the sun. A shadow blocked the light of life, long and narrow, swelling at one end and tapered at the other. It was the shape of a great kul whale, made of metal and pulsing with orange blood. Sitting in the air as easily as one might float in the waters of the Jie Meng, it was a mockery of the great leviathans, of the living coral, of all the shuen hold sacred. Asa nearly fell into the battle trance then and there, but the blasphemy was well beyond his reach, and other prey beckoned.

A wavesinger's duties were many—care, build, hunt, and song—but foremost among those there was the sanctity of the city, the shuen, and the Oaths of Wiang Lung. Against all comers, there was battle.

— THISTLE —

Scott Colby

I'm not one to do things halfway. I'm a man with standards. When there's a job to be done, you'd better believe I'm going to do it better than anyone else. When I want something, I always make sure I get the best, price be damned. If something's worth doing, it's worth doing right. So when I decided I wanted to become a Riddari, one of the guardians of knowledge in the Dreaming Lands, I sought out the most famous of all the Secret Keepers: Old Bramble.

Finding the man was no easy task. A rarely-seen recluse, Bramble is none the less a bona fide celebrity (or a notorious villain who steals children, depending on who you ask), and everyone who thinks he's anyone has some crazy story of having met the man and gleaned a bit of wisdom from him.

I visited each of the eight talamhs at least three times, using Maeda Cricao as my base of rumor-chasing operations, until I finally came across a lead I could feel in my bones would get me to Bramble's doorstep. I bought the tip from a Delledeir merchant who'd acquired the information from a Feirnann in exchange for a few rocks, who'd heard it from some family who'd been visiting from Admi's talamh, who'd learned it while sharing a camp along the way with a Riddari from the wind talamh. Even if my feeling of certainty turned out to be no more than the result of a Delledeir bargaining trick or just some ill-timed gas, I knew it was worth checking out. I'm immortal; I have all the time in the world. Besides, this one was far too complicated to be just another simple lie made up to impress gullible strangers.

The wind talamh was one of my least favorite places to visit. It's so…windy. Much of it is little more than open space where the air is allowed to flow freely. I hired a ferryman with a little winged boat to move me between the scarce islands of floating rock that were the talamh's only solid ground. He didn't like the direction I asked him to go, claiming that he'd heard stories and that a little Lean'Aghan like me couldn't possibly find anything of interest that far out in the wilds, but a few extra beams of sunshine in his pocket greased the wheels.

The trip was not fun. For three days nothing separated me from the never-ending sky but the paper-thin walls of my guide's tiny boat. I couldn't tell what the little brown dinghy was made out of, and I didn't ask because I truly didn't want to know.

Every time the wind would whip up and send us spiraling in a new direction, my stomach would leap up into my throat, my palms would sweat, and visions of falling forever would dance before my eyes. But my guide, despite his dour unfriendliness, was quite the skilled navigator. He kept us upright and moving in the proper direction with naught but his tiller and an occasional curse.

I could've kissed him when I spotted our destination far off in the distance. I would've sprung up and danced a happy jig if I hadn't been afraid of capsizing our vessel. As we drew closer, I discovered it was exactly as the Delledeir had described: a tiny, unassuming slab of ragged brown rock with a monolithic chunk of granite sticking straight out of its top. The perfect place for an antisocial recluse to make his hideout.

My guide scowled at me when I insisted that the only way to land on Bramble's island was to sail around it three times before trying. "Rutting hogwash!" he snarled. "Current's bringing us right in!"

We were about to make landfall (and I was seriously beginning to doubt the accuracy of the information I'd purchased—after all, if this bit was incorrect, then maybe Bramble didn't live there at all) when an impossibly strong gust lifted us up and hurled the little boat over the island. When my guide regained control of the vessel and I regained control of my bladder, I realized that this must be how a stone feels when a child sends it skimming across the surface of a pond.

"Just a random burst," my guide growled as he brought us around for another try from a different angle. "Happens all the time out here."

After four more progressively angrier attempts produced the same result, he finally capitulated and tried it my way. Three quick turns around the island later we landed without incident. I stood up arrogantly, proud that I was right and my rude guide was wrong, and then promptly fell on my face while climbing over the gunwale.

The rock was as hard as it looked. My guide laughed and busied himself about the boat.

I dusted myself off (there wasn't much land in the wind talamh, but there's more than enough dust constantly blowing around) and approached the granite monolith like a supplicant approaching a totem. Bramble was here; I could feel it. There was an energy about the place, an atmosphere so different from the surrounding talamh that it was almost palpable. He was here. He had to be.

Just as I'd been told, I placed my palm on the surprisingly warm granite and made one slow clockwise circle across its face. Then I knocked five times.

Nothing happened.

Behind me, my guide laughed again. I was really beginning to dislike that guy.

I was about to try it again when suddenly a voice rang out from the rock. "Who the rut is that? Hold on, hold on, I'm coming! I'm coming!"

My heart leapt into my throat when a small slab of granite slid aside and a pair of piercing blue eyes locked onto me from the darkness within. "Who the rut are you?" Bramble asked.

My response came from instinct. I'd been practicing my introduction for years. "I am but a humble Lean'Aghan who'd like to become a Riddari. I've come to learn from the greatest of all the secret keepers, sir."

His eyes narrowed. "Secret keeper, am I? Pffffffffffffffffft. I wouldn't be caught dead with those stuck up bookworms. You've got the wrong guy, kid."

The slit closed with a heavy thunk, echoing the fall of my spirits. I'd come all this way, worked so hard, just to be rebuffed in a few seconds. I couldn't believe it. I stared at the monolith blankly for what seemed an eternity, wondering what I'd done wrong. How could I have screwed up my first impression badly enough to effectively make Bramble slam the door in my face? Had I come on too strong? Was I too reverential?

I turned dejectedly toward the boat. It was gone. My guide had already taken it several hundred yards off into the sky. I was stranded. No doubt he was having a hearty laugh at my misfortune.

I don't think he realized he was doing me a favor. With nowhere to run, I had to face my failure head on. I whirled back toward the monolith and pounded angrily on the stone. A few moments later, the narrow slit whooshed open again. "Eh? Still here?"

"I've been tracking you for years, sir," I said as firmly as I could. There was a slight whimper in my voice, but I fought to keep it under control. "I spent a small fortune. I crawled through the armpit of every talamh hunting for clues. I chased a few dozen false leads. I will not be turned away without a proper audience."

He rolled his eyes. "Typical. There's one every millennium or so. When are you young bucks going to learn that there's a damn good reason people like me make ourselves so hard to find? It ain't because we want to lead you on a merry chase that tests your mettle and builds your character. In your case, I couldn't give a lij's ass about either of those things. Did it ever dawn on you that I didn't actually want to be found?"

"It did, sir. But I thought it worth trying, anyway."

"Hmmph. Well, then you're smarter than most of the other fools and maybe also a bit dumber to boot."

The slit slammed shut again. Before I could protest, I heard another click, rather like that of a lock, and the entire face of the monolith faded away. In its place was a short unassuming man with leathery skin and deep, knowledgeable eyes. His white linen tunic and loose pants fluttered in the breeze, and he leaned heavily on a thick walking stick.

"But as it stands I happen to have a task perfect for someone that stubborn. Come on in, kid."

I nearly tripped over myself to obey. The rock reappeared behind me with a rather ominous click, leaving us in the dark. Bramble lit a lamp on the wall, casting an eerie glow over the inside. Surprisingly we were in a long hallway, built of wood rather than stone, with a long red carpet running down the middle. Doors lined the walls as far as my eye could see.

"Come on, stop staring!" Bramble beckoned. He was already several yards away and moving quickly. "What did you say your name was again?"

I hurried to catch up with him. I noticed that each door had a slightly different knob, many shaped like the faces of what I could only assume were various types of Feirnann. They were wild, animal-looking things, and I could've sworn their eyes followed me as I passed. "I didn't. I don't have one yet."

"Ah, right. Lean'Aghan. Rutting annoying custom. Pick something I can call you."

I spat out the first thing that came to mind. "Call me Thistle!"

Bramble sighed heavily. "Kill me and take my rutting job, why dontcha? Shove the hero worship, or I'm dumping you in the middle of Nightmare's palace. In the scary end, where he keeps his collection of really sharp things."

Bramble wasn't at all what I'd expected. Where was the sage, compassionate trainer of the world's greatest warriors? The most learned scholar of all things Duine? The crotchety old man I'd found was downright crude. It had to be an act, a test of some sort, a trick to try to rile me up. I wasn't going to fall for it. I kept my mouth shut and walked a step behind him and to his left, my eyes locked on the floor.

"I am too old for this shit," he continued. "Tassel, when you get to be my age, you'll understand the value of staying the rut away from everybody. Helps keep you focused on the things that are really important."

We stopped in front of a door with a rather ugly knob shaped like a goat with six rolling, curling horns and three eyes above a nasty set of fangs. "Here we are, Tussle! Ready for your first assignment?"

I was speechless. I figured there'd be some training involved, or at least a bit of conversation. We'd barely known each other for five minutes, and already he was sending me away on some errand?

"Eh? You look like you ate someone what didn't agree with you. Speak up, Thimble!"

I barely choked back the urge to correct him. He was supposed to call me Thistle, damn it! But I knew it was another cheap trick trying to make me angry. "Sorry. I—are you sure I'm ready for something like this?"

He closed his left eye and sized me up with his right. "Can you walk straight? Talk straight? See straight?

I nodded.

"Then you're perfect! I need eyes in a certain area—eyes that aren't going to be watched in turn, least not by anyone that matters, and since nobody gives a rut about you Lean'Aghan..."

I was used to that. All of the other Fae, the ones with names and castes, treated we Lean'Aghan like dirt. But it was different hearing it from the lips of someone I idolized.

The doorknob bleated angrily when Bramble took hold of it. "Quiet, beasty!" he warned it, adding a quick whack to its jaw with his walking stick. It quickly stopped protesting. Bramble turned the knob and shoved the door open, revealing rolling hills, a pristine river...and an obviously mortal city, a ramshackle collection of brick, mortar, and wood that was a real stain on the surrounding landscape.

"That's Terre Haute. You're to wait there for something very interesting to happen. When it happens, you follow it. But you keep your distance, see? That's the important part, Tattle-my-boy: you follow it but you do not, under any circumstances, reveal yourself to anyone involved. You follow it until you can't follow it anymore, and then you contact me."

I was suddenly very afraid. The mortal realm was a place of legend, an untamed frontier of strange creatures with even stranger customs. They aged. They died. It all lead to a lot of selfishness and short-sighted decision making. I didn't want to go.

"But how will I know when this very interesting thing happens? And how will I contact you?"

Bramble sighed again and took firm hold of my arm. His grip was surprisingly strong. "You'll know. And now that you're working for me, just ask a raven. Little monsters will smell me on you and act accordingly."

Before I could protest further he shoved me headlong through the door and into the Dying Lands. I landed in a heap on the grass, looking back just in time to watch the door close between the trunks of two trees knotted together in a sort of heart shape. The door had disappeared before I could so much as stand.

I stood, brushed myself off, and eyed Terre Haute nervously. If waiting and watching was what Bramble wanted, then that was what he'd get.

WELCOME TO
— THE DYING LANDS, THISTLE —
Scott Colby

The closer I came to the mortal city, the more I realized I was completely out of my element. Perhaps it was the gradual fading of the Aiemer as I walked further and further from the faery gate my mentor had closed behind me. Perhaps it was the brick and mortar monstrosities looming bigger and bigger on the horizon. Or perhaps it was the traveling merchant who'd sicced his ferocious hound upon me when I'd surprised him by stepping soundlessly from the woods. The terrible beast chased me deep into the swamp outside the city before finally giving up and turning back.

In that swamp I stayed for several weeks, taking shelter beneath the collapsed branches of some sort of cypress. My new little home was cramped and muddy and wouldn't have been much good for entertaining company, but it kept me out of the rain (mostly) and the harsh sun (mostly). In the Dreaming Lands, I simply would've willed the land into providing me with shelter. Having to actually find a roof over my head was an odd experience, but one that I felt proved I could make it in this strange realm.

I spent my days wandering as close to the road as I dared, careful to keep myself hidden in the dense foliage, watching the endless stream of merchants and adventurers moving up and down the road and listening closely for any mention of events that might fit my mission. I may not have been in the city, but I was sure I was close enough that I'd know if anything interesting were to happen. Truth be told, the snippets of conversation I heard almost bored me to tears. I didn't think Bramble was interested in Besnia's three-legged cow or how the fishing had turned sour in Hanter's Creek. If he was, he'd sent the wrong person. Some of the wilder stories about the nearby mah'saiid ruins were entertaining, but they were obviously fantasy and rumor.

I slept little, so at night I took in the stars. The night sky in the Dreaming was often transient and fleeting, quickly replaced by Diuntyne or daylight or some strange combination thereof, but there in the swamp the world actually gave me time to admire the heavens, the way the stars slowly danced around each other and the moons. I don't know if I'd go so far as to say that the Dying Lands did this one better than the Dreaming, but it certainly was fantastic to watch.

One Diuntyne, after a long day of skulking and eavesdropping and various other clandestine activities, I found a group of trappers had taken up residence in my lean-to. Three men, two older and one younger. They'd lit a small fire beside my shelter and set a piece of unidentifiable meat above it on some sort of metal contraption they turned every few minutes. The lifeless corpses of several small furry creatures hung limply from a line strung between two nearby trees, staining the mud below red with dripping blood. I gagged and looked away from the macabre scene, shutting my eyes tight. I'd read about the brutality of the Duine, but I'd always assumed such commentary to be the result of the author's To'Sidhe'Lien bent, repressed or otherwise. No combination of ink and parchment could've prepared me for the gruesome reality.

Something hard and sharp pressed into my back between my shoulder blades. I knew I'd been caught. I kept my eyes closed and stayed stock still, hoping in vain that whoever it was would go away.

"Stand up," a rough voice commanded. I did as instructed, slowly so as not to startle the fellow and his blade. "What business 'ave ye here?"

"Th-this is my home," I stuttered. "I l-live here."

"Yer home, eh?" I'd studied the Duine languages and spoke many fluently, including the local Nefazo tongue, but the speaker's harsh inflection and obvious lack of proper speech education made him difficult to understand. "Ye weren't here last we come through two moons ago. Or two moons 'afore that. Been trappin' these swamps fer years and ain't never seen ye before."

"I-I'm new to the neighborhood," I replied, trying hard to keep my bladder from overreacting.

"Oh, new to the neighborhood?" he said mockingly. "Well, let me be the first to extend a warm welcome, ye rutting pile of habback sh-"

"Rody!" an even deeper and rougher voice interrupted. The old man at the camp was on his feet now, the firelight flickering across the impressive girth of his bare chest and bulging stomach. "What's 'at ye got over there? Ain't a lawman, is it? If'n it is, ye let him go!"

"Naw, Pap!" Rody responded. "Jes' some smart ass thinks he owns our camp!"

"I was just borrowing it," I sputtered meekly. The blade pressed closer, ending my attempts to reason with Rody.

"Well, bring him here," Pap replied. "Let's 'ave a look at him."

Rody shoved me forward so hard I almost fell. "If I see ye so much as thinkin' 'bout runnin' I'll gut ye where ye stand."

The thought of myself strung up on the line with the rest of the creatures unlucky enough to have crossed these hooligans was almost enough to make me throw up. I stumbled down the bank and across the water as quickly as I dared, desperately seeking to reach the seemingly more reasonable Pap as soon as I could without making Rody suspect I was *thinkin' 'bout runnin'*.

"Close enough," Pap muttered when I reached the fire. The man was truly huge, about my height, his skin like leather and his linen pants fit to burst. One of his eyes had been replaced with a milky ball of glass I couldn't help staring at.

The third trapper, who was even younger than he looked from afar, stayed seated and picked at his fingernails disinterestedly. Rody stayed behind me, out of sight but constantly reminding me of his presence by dragging his blade across my back like some sort of demented painter would a brush. These were rough, hard men, men who lived short lives in an unforgiving wilderness. For the first time, I legitimately wished I'd never set out to find Bramble.

"What's ye name, sonny?" Pap asked, his thumbs hitched inside his belt.

I didn't understand why he was comparing me to daylight, but I answered nonetheless. "Thistle."

The boy beside me laughed. "Stupid name," he squeaked.

"Ye be a strange one, Thistle," Pap replied thoughtfully, appraising me up and down. "Ye look like us, mostly, but ye move differently, like a slow summer breeze. Ye face is different. Taller. Long toes, even longer fingers."

I knew all this, of course. The differences between we Lean'aghan and the Duine, specifically these lij, were subtle and easy to miss if one wasn't paying attention. Some Riddari wondered if we were related somehow...and then those whimsical theories were laughed away by their fellow Secret Keepers, and they focused again on hard facts and figures.

"I know what ye are, Thistle," Pap droned on. My heart leapt into my throat, beating against my flesh as if trying to escape. Many Duine thought poorly of my race. "Ye're one o' them mah'saiid!"

I took a deep breath and rolled my eyes, thoroughly insulted. "I am not mah'saiid. They are a disgrace upon my kind—"

Rody silenced me with a quick cuff to the back of my head. "Just what a mah'saiid would say if'n he didn't want to admit he was mah'saiid."

Pap and the boy nodded wisely. "Bind his hands, Rody. We know what's to do with ye mah'saiid. None of us is fool enough to go trouncin' through yer ruins like a bunch of nervous nallions, but we knows a man who is. An' he pays good copper for anythin' mah'saiid."

I spent the night lying in the mud beside the dying fire, my hands tied behind my back and my feet lashed together. The cold, Mother-forsaken rain came down in sheets starting around midnight and then trailed off before dawn, soaking me to the bone while my three loutish captors snored loudly from beneath the shelter of collapsed branches. I rolled onto my side so the rain wouldn't hit me square in the face and propped my head up onto a nearby rock so I wouldn't swallow any of the mud creeping up my cheek. I cursed Bramble and the names of every Riddari I knew. Nothing was worth this.

Rody was the first to awaken a few hours after sunrise. He stumbled out of the shelter, scratching his ass as he stepped beside me and unbuttoned his trousers to urinate not far from my head. He looked down at me groggily, as if he'd forgotten I was there. "How'd ye get so wet?" he asked, feigning innocence. I tried to spit at his ankle, but I missed miserably. He roused his companions and they relit the fire to prepare breakfast. Thankfully they ate in silence. I wasn't offered a single morsel, but I wouldn't have eaten their slop anyway.

After the camp was broken down and distributed amongst their three packs, Rody ran a rough length of rope around my neck and cut my feet free. "Act out, and it gets tighter," he growled when he saw me straining my neck against the scratchy fiber, trying to find a comfortable spot. I nodded and gave up. If I cooperated, maybe I could lull them into a false sense of security. Then maybe they'd stop paying close attention to me. Maybe they'd leave a knot a little too loose or stand me up near a rock or tree with a rough edge I could use to saw my way free.

And maybe, if I closed my eyes and wished hard enough, I could've grown wings and flown out of there. Fantasies of escape kept my mind occupied and my spirits from collapsing completely, but I knew deep down I was going to be sold to some mah'saiid collector and there was nothing I could do about it. My only real hope was that the buyer would recognize me for what I was and inform my captors of the truth. Surely then they'd see reason, apologize, and send me on my way.

The trappers set a brisk pace through the jungle and back to the road. Pap lead the way, swatting vegetation aside with a bent old machete. The boy followed close behind, bent nearly double beneath a heavy pack loaded with their equipment and the fruits of their hunt. Rody and I brought up the rear.

"Stay in front of me, where I can sees ye."

I tried my best to match the stride of the boy up ahead, but Rody was never satisfied with my attempts. When I went too fast, the rough rope bit into my throat like fire. When I went too slow, he'd shove me in the back and send me tumbling forward into a patch of mud or a nest of ants or a bunch of prickly foliage. The bites and scratches healed almost immediately, but my pride was not so easily repaired. Never in my life have I wished death upon another living being, but Rody so infuriated me that I prayed to the Mother asking that he be horribly maimed.

We turned toward the city when we reached the road. Traffic was sparse, more people were heading for the settlement than were leaving it, and nearly all traveled slower than us, burdened with heavy wagons loaded with what could only be described as absolute crap: chunks of broken buildings, twisted pieces of useless metal, piles of ruined clothing, bones and hair and even a tree uprooted from the earth and dropped across a cart. "Idiots," Rody spat. "Ain't none o' that shit mah'saiid. We gots the only thing on this whole road worth a damn."

Few of those we passed even bothered to look my way, though I tried hard to look as pathetically desperate as I could, limping and coughing and staring at them with pleading eyes. Nefazo, it seemed, was short on idealistic heroes and good samaritans. At least Rody had grown bored with torturing me, though I suspect this was because he was too busy leering at the very friendly, very scantily clad ladies following close behind us. I suppose a roll in the sheets with a couple of flea-bitten, toothless, malnourished, illiterate, diseased strumpets was the best a despicable, dirty, abusive, sociopathic kidnapper could aspire to.

The road turned into a steep slope as we approached the city. Rody's two lady friends took one look at the imposing incline and turned back the way they came. The city above was nestled in the bosom of an impressive mountain range. It could've been beautiful, I suppose, had I the slightest appreciation for construction, but I wondered why the lij had marred the natural beauty of the mountains, why they bothered building in such a difficult location. Such folly could only be the product of a people painfully aware of their own transient existence.

The outskirts of the city were like a scab on a painted face. Random bits and pieces of wood, stone, and fabric climbed all over each other as if expelled from the ground and left where they'd fallen. People lived in the spaces in between, filthy and vile. Hungry eyes watched us pass from innumerable dark corners, held back, I believed, only by the blessed sunlight.

The boy fell back to walk by my side. "Welcome to Terre Haute," he said. "The real Terre Haute, not the whitewashed little paradise further up. All these people thought it was a good idea to go digging through your ruins. Thought they'd make their fortunes. We ain't ending up like them. Leave the treasure hunting to the fools."

Shut the hell up!" Rody commanded, giving the rope a firm tug that almost put me on my back. The boy rolled his eyes and hurried back ahead of me. "Boy reads too damn much," Rody growled.

The shantytown gradually faded into small squat buildings made of a single material, usually stone or raw chunks of the local trees. I couldn't imagine living in such a dark, dank space, but apparently these mortals cared little for the breeze or the sunshine or the haunting beauty of the moons and the stars. The next neighborhood was even less inviting, the walls and roofs thick and square and intimidating. The people became cleaner, their hair tamed and their skin polished, their clothing layered and intricate and crisp. It was as if money and status gave one the power to keep the real world at bay.

We stopped before the massive iron doors of a building twice as tall as its neighbors. Tendrils of steam wafted skyward from three stout chimneys atop the roof. Pap banged the pommel of his machete against the door, sending a metallic hum rattling through my teeth. A small slit squealed open to reveal a pair of beady, suspicious eyes.

"Ugh, not you again," the man on the other side of the door squeaked. "Master Lancois is not in the market for squirrels or their hides or their bones or whatever part you want to sell this time."

"Tradiciol, my friend, I come bearing a singular opportunity!" Pap declared, speaking slowly and carefully in a terrible parody of intellectual speech. "Why should your master set and wait for a bunch of dirty jungle humpers to bring him mah'saiid treasures when he can go right to the source with a mah'saiid of his own?"

I couldn't help rolling my eyes. Rody slapped the back of my head.

The ferret-like eyes swiveled to examine me, but only briefly. "You have a point," Tradiciol replied. There came a series of clicks and whirs as the locking mechanism disengaged, and then one of the doors eased open far enough to admit Pap's ridiculous girth. The rest of us followed him inside.

The anteroom was a massive, cavernous space lit by the ethereal, flickering flames of a pair of torches mounted in heavy iron sconces in the far wall. Tradiciol stood beside Pap, half as tall and half as wide as the big trapper, his silver hair and powdered face shimmering in the half light. He pulled a lever on the wall once we were all inside, slamming the heavy door shut behind us. My fate, I felt, was sealed.

Tradiciol looked me up and down. "Quite the specimen you have there. Master Lancois will be pleased. Follow me."

The attendant lead us down one of the many hallways branching off the main anteroom like spokes on a wheel. Master Lancois had quite the collection of mah'saiid relics. We passed a jade fresco of Guil Ghemmal stripped away from its original home and reinstalled on the wall of the hallway. I stopped to admire a table set with blue and gold clay pottery obviously from the Third Insistine Era before Rody shoved me forward. The arches in the ceiling were sandstone laced with veins of gold, obviously lifted from a mah'saiid structure. This Lancois knew his mah'saiid—surely, he'd recognize that I wasn't what Pap thought.

The hall ended at a heavy set of double doors hung from ancient golden hinges. The air here was humid and warm, as if we'd stepped into a swamp. A vast cloud of steam wafted out from the next room as Tradiciol opened the door and beckoned us inside.

"Visitors!" a deep voice bellowed gregariously from somewhere in the fog. "Tradiciol, where are your manners! Lower the steam so my guests and I can do business face to face!"

"Yes, master."

I heard the heavy clank of another lever, and then a series of clicks as the wooden slats in the walls flipped upwards to allow the steam to escape. The room cleared slowly, finally revealing a great pool of white and black marble set in the floor, the crystal clear water bubbling with heat. Seated against the pool's far wall was the largest man I'd ever seen, a great hairless whale of a lij with a bulbous body glistening with sweat. His face reminded me of a canine I'd seen once, an ugly beast with big jowls and a droopy brow that looked rather dumb but also rather content. A long, narrow strip of what appeared to be platinum studded with enough jewels to buy half of Terre Haute dangled from his left ear. Six naked women flanked him, three on either side, beauties in every sense of the word save for their shaved heads.

Lancois locked eyes with Pap and frowned. "Oh, not you again. That last batch of pelts gave my ladies an awful rash, and that liver paste did nothing for my ingrown toenail. Get out."

Pap was unabashed. "If ye insist, my dear Master Lancois," he said, feigning defeat. "But then I'd have to sell this here mah'saiid to Fenssaint the Spade, and I knows he won't give me as good a price."

The large man's gaze swung in my direction. A wide, shimmering grin spread across his chubby face. He'd replaced all of his real teeth with gold replicas. "My apologies, Pap. You were right to come to me. Will five hundred copper suffice?"

"Six hundred."

Lancois rubbed his chin with one meaty finger. "A fair price for a mah'saiid. Tradiciol, escort Pap out and see that he's paid. Throw in a few pounds of salted beef while you're at it."

Pap bowed deeply to Lancois, then he and the other trappers followed Tradiciol out.

"S-s-sir," I stammered once the others had gone. "I do believe you've been swindled."

"Swindled? How so? Six hundred copper is more than a fair price for a mah'saiid," he said mischievously. "But six hundred copper is a bargain price when one is purchasing Fae."

ALL HAIL LORD — THISTELONIOUS! —

Scott Colby

I heard Lancois' effusive voice clear as day from just beyond the other side of the thick black curtain. "Ladies and gentlemen… and Fenssaint the Spade…"

The lords and ladies gathered in the ballroom chuckled politely at this. I was later told that the drunken guffaw echoing over them all belonged to Fenssaint himself.

"It is at great personal expense that I've brought to you this evening's guest of honor. He hails from a faraway land, a mystical place where dragons soar across the sky and beautiful mermaids roam the seas!"

His audience oohed and aahed. I rolled my eyes and shook my head. Did none of these pretentious mortals have any clue as to the nature of the Dreaming Lands?

"I give to you Lord Thistelonius, Prefect of Maeda Cricao!"

The crowd burst into applause as the curtain fell away, exposing me to the piercing judgment of the crowd. I'd been dreading this moment since Lancois first told me of his plans two weeks ago.

"It'll be the grandest party Terre Haute has ever seen!" he crowed from atop the over-stuffed couch in his parlor. Somehow, despite the couch's sturdy frame and thick cushions, Lancois' girth managed to make the thing look like a piece of children's furniture. His eyes glittered as he spoke, either with pride or from the three bottles of wine he'd inhaled since breakfast. "Anyone who's anyone will be there!"

"But I'm not royalty!" I protested from the little chair across the room to which I was shackled. "I'm but a humble lean'aghan, a nameless soul wandering the world in search of— "

"Pish-posh!" Lancois snapped with a wave of his fingers. The motion sent a little quake through his flabby form. "These suckers will believe whatever we tell them, and they'll love us for it!"

"But if the Courts of Twilight were to find out that I'm impersonating—"

"Enough! You'll do as I say, or you'll end up like them!"

He pointed angrily to the mounted heads of a family of thul bears—father, mother, and three cubs—attached to the wall to my right. I swallowed, my throat tight and rough. "P-P-Prefect Thistle, at your service, sir..."

I took a few hesitant steps further onto the stage. I'd never worn so much clothing before and it made my movements slow and deliberate, as if I were trapped in a pit of thick mud. The tailors had dressed me in black leather pants that were two sizes too tight ("All the rage in Priyati!"), a heavy fur tunic studded diagonally across the chest with gold and gems ("Emperor Pileaus wore one just like it at the last fête!") and an extremely heavy cloak streaked black and white with smelly dyes ("The tailor in Ouillaine simply can't make them fast enough!"). A platinum crown sat cockeyed on my head; the smith spent a day reshaping it to fit around my skull, and he'd twisted it a bit too far.

I didn't ask why the Prefect of Maeda Cricao would wear mortal clothing.

But by far the worst of it all were the shoes. Why anyone would wish to stick his feet in those things on a regular basis was beyond me. They were like the mouths of some vicious beasts trying to crush my delicate toes in their jaws. The cobbler had never seen feet as long as mine, and it had taken him a few tries to produce a set of slippers that he could declare "right." It took me three days to learn to walk in the Mother-forsaken monstrosities.

Lancois beckoned me forward from his raised platform near the front, decked out in a silly purple robe covered in gold moons and stars and an impossibly tall, impossibly pointy hat tipped with a black feather. I shuffled to his side, taking small delicate steps so as not to lose my balance or my crown.

The crowd on the floor below was a motley collection of the rich and the learned and those who were just good at faking one or both. These were the cream of Terre Haute's crop—and they were the silliest looking group I'd ever seen. Their outfits made mine look positively normal. All the colors of the rainbow were well represented, occasionally on a single tunic or gown. A stringy old woman in the very front wore a duck on her head that was still alive and quacking. A man beside her wore a glittering gold robe with his face reproduced on the breast in sparkling rubies. I spotted a pair of twins in the back who'd shoved themselves side-by-side into a single giant gown, each wearing a thin strap over her outside shoulder. It was all I could do to keep myself from bursting into hysterics.

I stopped beside Lancois and offered what I hoped was a benevolent, kingly wave. The heavy rings covering most of my fingers made the motion awkward. My master's guests applauded politely and generally seemed glad to see me in an I'm-impressed-but-I'm-too-important-to-show-it-and-anyway-you-should-be-more-impressed-with-me sort of way. I was just glad I hadn't tripped.

"And now, if you'll all adjourn to your assigned seats," Lancois said dramatically. "Dinner is served!"

The guests dispersed to their tables, using their invitations to find their way. Young men in crimson shifts and black masks stood behind each chair, pulling it out for its owner with a smile and a flourish of the right hand. They then hurried off through the servants' entrance to their duties in the kitchen. Lancois and I sat at together on one side of a round table, joined by four others who I'd been trained to recognize on sight.

The duck lady to my right was Madame Hoost, widow of Terre Haute's former authority on textiles. To her right in the gold robe sat her latest companion, Hoctor Hanhuis, a man of some repute in Priyati. They were joined by the Almais brothers, Lantel and Remly, who came in matching black tunics and silversilk cloaks. We barely finished introductions before the serving men returned, each bearing a plate piled high with meats and vegetables and cheeses I didn't recognize.

Lancois attempted to engage me in conversation with Madame Hoost, but it was the discussion across the table that caught my attention.

"I swear to you, Lantel, I saw the arrows go right through her!" Remly said as he bit off a big hunk of cheese and washed it down with a gulp of wine. He was the younger of the two brothers, the one who spent most of his time in the jungles hunting for mah'saiid relics. According to Lancois he was damn good at it. His curly blond hair bounced as he spoke, making his babyface look even younger. "Check the gouges in the door of Simonez's shop. Clean through her, and not a drop of blood came out with 'em."

"Boruin's woman is a strange one indeed," Lantel replied thoughtfully. He took care of finding buyers for the priceless antiquities Remly brought in from the jungles. Supposedly, he was also damn good at his job, and Lancois was hoping to butter him up a bit that evening to get a better price on some such-and-such he wanted for his steam room. "But it's that slave that worries me. The man looks right through you, like he'd cut you in half just so you'll be out of his way."

"And that short one—what's his name, something like Heap?—he'll pick your pocket just as soon as shake your hand. Got to watch your coins around that one," Remly replied. "Strange crew."

Lantel nodded. "Strange men keep strange company. Any man dumb enough to cross their boss, though, will more 'an get what he deserves. Boruin walks around with this bearing like the whole world is out to get him. And like he's daring the whole world to try."

Hoctor turned to the two of them. "Friend of mine had some dealings with Boruin's crew recently. Said they were to ride to Priyati, but then the whole lot of them just disappeared somewhere along the road. One moment they're talking business, about how they're going to split the whole deal fifty-fifty, and the next Belok's on the road all by his lonesome, swindled out of the delivery. Couldn't find them anywhere."

Now, that really caught my attention. That was interesting. Very interesting.

Madame Hoost reached across the table to put her hand on my arm. The duck on her head flapped its wings and tried to snap at me with its bill. "You're not going to eat, dear?"

"Mortal food does not sit well with me," I said quickly, getting rid of her so I could address the men. "Hoctor, where is this Belok now?"

He shifted in his seat and looked down at his plate, seemingly uncomfortable at speaking with me. "Priyati. He rode on. A letter came from him the other day. He writes a lot of letters."

"Such a charming hobby!" Madame Hoost crowed. The duck on her head quacked angrily; it didn't agree. "And such a charming man! That Belok would surely be the life of this very party if he were not busy elsewhere!"

I ignored her and looked to Lancois, hoping he'd get the message. "I'd rather like to see this spot where Boruin disappeared. It could be most…enlightening."

He was confused for a moment, but then realization slowly crept into his eyes. He smelled a potential profit, just as I'd hoped. "Why, yes, Hoctor will be good enough to take us, won't you, Hoctor?"

The man across the table nodded stiffly. "Of course, Master Lancois. Anything for the Prefect."

Conversation picked back up around the table. Lancois leaned in close to my ear a few moments later. "Excellent work, Thistle. You keep this up, and the chains will stay off for a very long time."

Dinner was a flurry of uninteresting conversation interspersed with stupid questions and asinine declarations about my person and my lands.

"Those long fingers must make you an expert piano player!"

"Are you concerned at all that Pileaus might push to incorporate your nation into his Empire?"

"Surely there's a Lady Thistelonious! Is her head as big as yours?" I answered politely to keep Lancois happy, silently cursing them all.

After dinner, the party relocated to an adjourning room where a twelve-piece band awaited us under a canopy of sparkling streamers. My heart fluttered at the sight of the musicians. I'd heard others tell of my kind's affinity for music, but I'd never experienced it for myself. This is more common than it might sound: we Fae make no music of our own, and so we are dependent on mortals for song, but Duine living in the Dreaming Lands are all but unheard of.

The first haunting strains of a low horn lifted my spirits like a warm sunny day, literally pulling me up onto my tiptoes. My heartbeat shifted to match the slow thump-thump-tha-thump of the bass drum that joined in next. The rest of the instruments came to life in a joyous crash that washed over and through me, setting every nerve in my body on fire. I couldn't fight it; I gave in to the music, letting it pull me forward with a force as irresistible as gravity, drawing me rudely through the crowd. Lancois stood at the front, bowing low to gallantly invite a pretty young woman to dance. I grabbed her around the waist and pulled her along with me, finally whipping her into a tight twirl that I pulled back into a deep dip. She looked up at me with wide brown eyes, exhilarated and surprised and a little bit frightened, and then I whirled us back into time with the omnipotent rhythm.

Lancois—I was told by one of the servants the next morning—laughed heartily, grabbed the two nearest women, and hurried out to join me.

I didn't stop until the music ended. I couldn't have even if I'd wanted to. My body, mind, and soul existed at the whim of the cellist, at the pleasure of the harpsichord. Sometimes I danced alone, a dervish storming through the crowd. Sometimes I was joined by a partner, a momentary soul mate to whom I felt myself joined completely. I felt like I could live forever. I felt like I could die without regret.

The last few notes felt like organs slowly being dragged from my body. I would've collapsed if the twins hadn't caught me. Words can't really frame the loss I felt, the emptiness that cried out to be filled in every cell of my body. I wanted to shout at the band, to demand that they continue even if Lancois and the rest wished to retire, but I hadn't the strength.

Lancois threw my limp arm around his broad shoulders and helped me to the entrance so we could bid his guests a good evening. The best I could offer was a weak wave or a subtle nod to each departing group or individual.

"Excellent work tonight," Lancois slurred drunkenly after everyone had gone. "If Pap could see you now, he'd shit himself!"

Two servants had to help me up the stairs to my chamber, one at my head and the other at my feet. They dropped me angrily on the hard pallet and locked the door behind them. Normally I would've fought sleep for a few hours, staring longingly at the hard stone ceiling and pondering what I'd done to deserve my fate, but sleep came for me quickly that night. My dreams of the music were sweet; sweeter still were my dreams of a particular spot on the road from where Boruin had disappeared and where I might hope to do the same.

I woke the next morning to a throbbing headache and a body on the verge of mutiny. Climbing out of the bed took a concerted force of will I didn't know I could muster. I swayed back and forth as the servants straightened my Lord Thistelonious outfit and replaced the jewelry I'd shrugged off during the night. They helped me down the stairs, one of them taking each arm.

Lancois was waiting for me at the head of the long table in the dining room. One of his concubines held a poultice to the back of his head as he cut greedily into the hunk of pork on the plate before him.

"You really think there's something to Hoctor's story?" he asked slowly, as if every syllable were a mountain to climb.

"I do," I replied just as slowly. Every word sent waves of pain echoing through my skull. "I'd stake my prefecture on it."

We departed at noon, when we both felt somewhat better, borne in a metal and wood contraption pulled by a pair of habback. A man with a whip kept the burly beasts moving in the right direction. I still don't understand why Lancois insisted we travel inside a portable room when we could've been out in the open, enjoying the sunshine and the breeze. It seems to me that the Duine are deathly afraid of that which is beyond their control, of forces of good and evil alike. Perhaps that's why so many insist on surrounding themselves with barriers of stone and wood that nature can't penetrate.

Lancois drew the shades as we entered the slums. "Some day," he said wistfully, "I will turn all this filth into a great series of parks like those in the mah'saiid cities of old, where people can come from far and wide to see the ancient wonders I've rescued from the wilderness."

"I don't understand this fascination with the mah'saiid," I replied. "In my lands, the name of their fallen empire is anathema."

"Then the thinkers of the Dreaming Lands are surely small-minded and foolish," he snapped. "The empire of the ancients was the greatest civilization to ever grace our land! Its secrets are all around us, hidden in these very jungles, just waiting for us to find them!"

"Have you ever considered why their empire is gone in the first place?"

"Who cares? What they can't use, we will!"

I let the matter rest. There's no use arguing with someone who can't see past the tip of his own nose. One day Lancois would purchase something he'd regret. Perhaps, I thought proudly, he already has.

Hoctor met us outside the city, where the slums abruptly became lush jungles. He rode a white charger with red tassels braided into its long mane.

"Good morrow, my lords," he said after Lancois snapped the shades back open. I'd forgotten that I was still supposed to be Thistelonious, Prefect of Maeda Cricao. I returned his greeting with a regal nod.

"Hoctor, my friend!" Lancois boomed. "Lead on to riches and glory!"

I stifled a snort. If my suspicious were correct, Hoctor was guiding us to a wild place of untamed power, a crossroads that cared nothing for the profits of man. It had always been there and it always would be, a rare confluence in space and time where the Dying and the Dreaming were as close as lovers under the sheets.

We rode on. I didn't need anyone to tell me we were getting close to our destination; I could feel it, as one can feel hot or cold on one's skin. The Aiemer thickened as we traveled, a miasma clinging to the land and the air and the very carriage in which we rode. There wasn't a lot of it, not like there is in the Dreaming Lands, but that small touch affirmed my suspicions. Truth be told, it made me a bit homesick.

Hoctor called for a stop and Lancois and I clambered out of the carriage. We'd stopped on a rather non-descript piece of road, flanked to the left by a dense swamp and to the right by a thick jungle. To the naked eye, there was absolutely nothing special about it, but to someone with my senses, it was very interesting indeed.

Hoctor dismounted. "Through that stand of trees there's a small hollow. Boruin disappeared somewhere in there."

I lead the way, pushing through the thick brush abutting the road. It was as Hoctor had described: a small bowl dipping down into the earth, surrounded by vegetation. I strolled down into its center, letting the Aiemer guide my steps.

"This is useless," Lancois growled. "All we're going to get out here is a damn rash from the flies. I'll be taking a piss if you need me." He trundled off to the side of the bowl and began to untie the front of his breeches.

I closed my eyes and focused on the Aiemer. There wasn't a gate here like I'd expected; rather, the two lands were close enough to have built a miniature realm between them, a sort of intermediary that was more Dreaming than Dying. The Aiemer flowed into the hollow from between two trees to my right, swirled around a bit, and then exited through another pair of trees to my left.

And Lancois was practically pissing on the exit.

A plan began to take shape in my mind. The one problem was Hoctor; the man was watching me like a hawk. If I made a move on Lancois, he'd surely stop me. Unless…

I took the crown from my head and offered it to Hoctor. His eyes lit up. "Go silently back the way you came and don't come back."

His eyes bulged out of his head, and then he nodded and accepted my offer. He was gone without a word.

I ran, not away from Lancois but right for him, throwing all of my weight into his broad back. The man stumbled forward and through the two trees in front of him, shouting something that was immediately cut off as he disappeared into the paths between realms.

I turned and ran the other way, a smile creeping onto my face as I leapt between the two oaks. The transition was shockingly cold and painful, and then I was through. I was in a different jungle, one awash with reds and purples and pinks rather than greens and browns. The air was heavy and humid and it reeked of Aiemer. I looked up and saw the Dreaming Lands in the far distance, the wild talamhs strung out around the glittering city of Maeda Cricao in the center.

I laughed heartily. Never in my life had I been so happy. I was free. And I was going to Ouillaine, to track down this Boruin and his companions and to find something of value to report to Old Bramble.

— END OF THE LINE —

Scott Colby

The trail of blood was maybe a day old. It began in front of a trade house. Undurlund, the sign read. Why here? Did Boruin have business with Underlund? The trade house was serene, untouched, so I decided to follow the trail. I could come back to Undurlund later if it was necessary. I doubted it would be.

Priyati was eerily quiet despite the weather. The bright, sunny day had failed to draw people into the empty, cavernous streets. It was a shame, really, that my visit came under such circumstances. Here was a city where I could've felt somewhat at home, where the construction was a part of the landscape rather than a barrier built to keep it out. Buildings were nestled under rocky outcroppings or among the lower boughs of tremendous old trees. Windows were wide and open to the elements. The roof was just another floor, a place to observe and enjoy nature. These Easlinders got it right.

But for all the city's beauty, the lack of people on the streets left Priyati feeling downright eerie. Something bad had happened here, something that seriously spooked the locals. The few I encountered on the outskirts of the city went about their business furtively, suspicious of everybody and everything, as if they would've preferred to be anywhere but out in the open. These people, the Easlinders, were very different from the Nefazo I'd met in Terre Haute. They were darker and earthier, their hair wilder and their skin shining with sweat. Their bright, homemade clothing would've been considered downright garbage in Terre Haute's elite social circles. Bare arms and legs were hard with taut muscle. Breasts swung freely under loose, airy dresses. Some carried bags or boxes of belongings or dragged young children or elderly parents behind them.

I passed an old woman seated on the road, her back against a nearby building, beseeching some unnamed god for assistance with blood-soaked hands. Something terrible had happened in Priyati, and these people wanted no part of it. The boy to whom I'd traded Lord Thistelonious's shoes for directions to the city warned me to stay away, but he refused to say more.

I followed the trail of blood in a general southerly direction, winding through alleys and side streets. Time and weather and foot traffic had diluted the trail, leaving it spotty in sections. More than once I lost it and had to carefully examine the area to pick it up again. Did the blood belong to Boruin or one of his companions, or to one of their victims? Did it lead to a trap or was it a call for help? I had so many questions and so few answers. Such would be the life of a Riddari: a neverending search for truth through a dangerous sea of mystery. I was looking forward to it.

The homes and shops soon gave way to a district of thick, blocky warehouses. I noticed people working inside through the occasional broken window, hauling crates and barrels of uncertain contents. Food, I guessed, maybe fish given the area's proximity to the water. Here was a novelty I wished I had time to examine further. We had no need for such things in the Dreaming Lands. Each of us knew how to gather his or her own particular brand of sustenance from the land itself. I shook my head and focused back on the trail.

I noticed something strange. Sections of the cobblestones seemed a bit depressed at regular intervals. Footprints, I realized. What in the name of the Great Mother could leave footprints in a stone street? Something big. Something dangerous. Something I hoped was long gone.

My heart sank when the trail split into three directions. This was obviously some sort of a trap, but was it still primed and loaded? I didn't want to find out. I paced around the area where the trail split, trying to find some way to differentiate the three lines of blood. One had to be safe to follow, I reasoned. Why bother dividing the trail if all three led into danger? But which two were the diversions? They seemed identical. There were no markers to identify them. I bent down and sniffed each line, but they all smelled the same. Tasted the same too.

Suddenly I knew exactly which line to follow. I leapt to my feet as if I'd been shocked, then took off at a run along the line flanked by the footprints. I laughed at my previous indecision; this was why I was going to be a Riddari, a secret keeper, and not a Feirnann, a land shepherd. I was so thoroughly useless in the field that my only hope for success was to lose myself in the world of books and maps. Exactly where I'd always wanted to be.

The trail brought me alongside the Oriune. Its rushing waters were a constant stream of sound and a mixed blessing; the background noise of the river would surely mask my approach, but it left me similarly deaf to the movements of anyone lying in wait. The buildings ahead were broken and crooked, long ago abandoned to the elements and left to rot. This was the perfect place for an ambush; dozens of men could hide in the nooks and crannies created by the collapsed walls and dilapidated foundations. I slowed my pace, taking care to examine every shadow.

I didn't see the tripwire. Suddenly something was pulling my feet out from under me, and then my face and hands struck the cobblestones hard. I rolled quickly onto my back, gasping to regain the breath that had been forcibly expelled from my lungs. The first thing I saw was the tip of a sword, sharp and glittering in the sunlight. I traced the lines of the blade upward to the hilt, to the strong set of fingers holding it in place, to the burly man in a blue and gold uniform who looked none to happy to see me.

"Whatcha doin' here, boy?" he asked.

Possible answers whirled quickly through my mind. Surely, I couldn't tell him I was lost; he'd obviously seen me following the blood trail before my fall. He didn't look like the type that would tolerate any sort of half-truth or incomplete response.

So I told him the truth. "I'm here on Fae business, tracking a man named Boruin. I have reason to believe he was involved in whatever happened further up the street."

The man relaxed visibly, sheathing his weapon. These Easlinders were obviously more familiar with my kind than the ignorant Nefazo. "That's a crime scene up ahead. I'm not supposed to allow anyone past this point without a judge's permission."

"Can you tell me what happened?"

He shrugged. "No harm in that; most of Priyati knows. The man you're after got into a bit of a tussle with the local Makua'Moi. He and his crew wiped the floor with those rutters. A lot of us are grateful he did it, but where there's one Makua'Moi, there's always more. We'd like to bring Boruin in for questioning, to find out if he can help us track down the rest."

"He left no further trail?"

The officer shook his head. "If he did, it ain't as obvious as these bloody rilk tracks. He and his crew are long gone and no one knows where. We think the rilk might have some idea, but they ain't talking."

The rilk. I should've known. A rilk was certainly heavy enough to leave the kind of trail I'd been following, especially if it had been moving quickly.

He wiped his chin, considering something. "And...there's something strange in the back. Something none of the brains can figure out. Brought in a Ha'ha'welo, but even she had no idea what she was looking at. And now you're here. It makes a man think... it might be Fae."

Here was my chance. It was refreshing to meet an honest, intelligent lij who was trying to do his job to the best of his abilities. He was worth ten of every single one of the bastards I'd met in Terre Haute. "Let me through, and I'll share anything I learn."

He answered by offering me his hand. I took it, and he pulled me to my feet. "It's not pretty in there."

"I've been following a trail of blood. I didn't expect to find a rainbow at the end of it." We shared an awkward laugh. Despite my attempt at humor, I was petrified of what I was going to find—especially considering that my companion, a rather hard looking man, still seemed haunted by the things he'd seen up ahead. We parted with a handshake, and I soldiered on.

THE TRICK
— TO TRICKING A TRICKSTER —

Alana Joli Abbott

The first clue that she wasn't a marii was the fact that she had extra tails. I like to think I'd have figured it out regardless, but the poor creature made it a little extra obvious. And while it's true that marii from the forests that border the Shoro take particular pride in their tails, I've never seen one of my kin with more than one.

I've certainly never seen a marii with six.

"Come sit by my fire, traveler," she purred, shifting ever so, maximizing the fluff of her tails and the toss of her mane. She'd managed the canine tilt of our mouths quite well—I have to give her that—but the rest was so far over the top, I think it flew right over the Aiemer sharks and hit an airship on the way by.

Still, I'd be no proper storyteller if I didn't sense a story when one was so clearly in front of me. I know you're thinking, "Kath, if you knew it was a trap, and you thought she was Fae, why in the Emperor's name—rest his soul—would you sit by her fire?"

First, I didn't think she was Fae, I knew it.

Second, the Emperor's soul can rot. I said it. Don't care who hears it.

And third, didn't I just tell you I sensed a story?

So I wandered right over to the log she'd set up near the fire—if she'd actually set it up and hadn't magicked it into existence—and settled myself a good distance away, just watching her. She twisted a claw in her mane nervously, like that lij tic they have when they wrap a curling hair around their fingers, just for something to keep them busy. Another clue there, if I hadn't figured it out already.

"Please, good traveler," she simpered. "I have so much food to share. If you'd just take one bite..."

I couldn't help it then. I'm ashamed to admit that I laughed. Not a little titter either. No, my laugh was a full bellied guffaw that startled a flock of Uju's thrushes right out of the tree they'd been nesting in. Those birds might have been as annoyed as the Fae trying unsuccessfully to hide her scowl, but I doubt it.

"I'm sorry," I apologized, and I was. She was trying awfully hard. "It's just, I'm not going to eat Faerie food."

She blinked long and slow. "I'm sure I don't know what you—"

"You have six tails," I interrupted.

She smiled again, thinking she'd gotten the conversation back on track. She reached back and dragged one over onto her lap, petting it like a lij would pet a lap dog. "Aren't they beautiful?" she asked, admiring her own work.

I allowed that they were. "But there are six of them," I said, trying to let her figure it out.

I wasn't dressed in near the finery she was (another clue; you can do the tally), given that I'd been traveling the borders of the Shoro between villages for most of a week. Still, I slung off my pack and twisted so she could see my own tail, not so prettily brushed, but still a fine enough specimen if I do say so myself.

"One," I said.

She blinked again. "One?" she repeated.

"Just the one." I sat down again. "I heard about a litter of kits born with their tails twisted together once. Took a skilled healer to separate them. But I've never heard a story about a marii with more than one." I thought for a second, then had to reconsider. "Two at the very most, and I only heard that story the once, so I think it was made up on the spot."

She slumped so dejectedly I almost felt bad for her. I figured that might be part of her ploy, too, but no, it seemed genuine enough. "I knew T'anai couldn't be trusted! He's after a promotion, and wouldn't it just be the thing to make him look better if I failed?"

Do you hear that, my friends? That's the moment where my instinct was proven correct. There was indeed a story.

"Never trust an ambitious colleague," I agreed. "Want to tell Ol' Kath all about it?"

I have a nibling—I have several, but there's just the one of them who has this way of giving off a sound that's not quite a snort or a huff, but it expresses, all in one release of breath, both dejection in the self and a complete denial that anyone could possibly understand her suffering. Imagine my surprise when the Fae made the exact same sound!

"No," she moped. She adjusted her legs so they weren't tucked with such attempted allure, leaned her elbows on her knees, and cupped her chin. "That would hardly look good, would it? 'There's Hanagisa, talking up the mortal she's supposed to be practicing on.' I'll never be anything but Assistant Chaffer."

My fingers itched to take out a scroll and quill from my sack, but I made a mental note instead. "Oh, I'm sure it's not all that bad," I said, channeling my inner Elder, the way I'd encourage my nibling to open her soul to her dear Ommer Kath. "If this was just practice, it's not as though you've failed a test."

I swear on the World Song, my friends, she hid her face behind two of her six tails.

"Oh, it is that bad," I said sympathetically. Don't think for a moment I felt an actual twinge of sympathy for one of the Fae—you give them an inch and they'll take ten leagues—but you'll recall I have quite a reputation for my early performances on stage in… well, that's neither here nor there, and I can see from your expressions that this is not a moment to sidetrack.

It's been said that the Fae can't weep, that they simply don't have the heart for it. I don't think that's true at all—no one who loves music as much as the Fae do could possibly be lacking the heart needed to appreciate it, after all. If it is true, though, this particular specimen did a fine job of performing the equivalent.

Foolish as it was (and I'd already been plenty foolish), I sidled up closer to her and offered her a handkerchief. In the firelight, her fur fairly gleamed, as though she had little dewdrops or stars glistening all over her body. "You know, I could…" I gave myself the one chance to reconsider this before I pressed ahead. "I could give you some feedback."

She lifted her eyes above the tail fur and sniffed. "Why would you do that? You're a mortal. You don't like us."

Yet another snippet of information for my notes! Why did the Fae think we mortal folk didn't like them? They knew we didn't trust them, obviously. But I'd known plenty of mortals, young and old, who believed in every tale of Faerie sung on pleasing notes and dismissed the scarier ones as mere propaganda. "You remind me of my nibling," I admitted.

She shoved down her tails. "Your who?"

"My niece," I said, using the term she probably knew better. "She's an apprentice herself. Not much of a musician, not like her Ommer Kath, but she's a fair hand at carving instruments for others to play. Could make a name for herself someday if she gets the right advice from the right person at the right time."

I lost her there for a moment, based on the way her eyes glazed a bit above the fur of her tails. "What I'm saying is, I could be the right person at the right time for you," I tried. When she still didn't seem to understand, I sighed. "If you're supposed to be practicing, practice on me."

At that she brightened and stood up from her own log. "I could use the practice," she said, then splayed her six tails out behind her. "Obviously," she giggled.

I rubbed my hands together. "Well, then, we'd best get started."

She tensed, still as a board, and I looked behind me, wondering what had her spooked. "Nothing is free," she said, almost like it was a religious tenet. "What's in this for you? What will it cost me?"

I made a show of considering this question. "A story," I said finally.

She scowled. "You know we can't make our own stories," she said, an edge to her voice for the first time that reminded me who—what—I was dealing with. "We can't make our own music or write our own tales."

"Ah, I see where we went wrong," I said, rising slowly as well, in case I needed to run. "I didn't mean for you to make up a story. I'm curious about some of the details of how you came here, to the Dying Lands, and for what reason." I gestured to the lute strapped to my pack. "I'm a performer, you see. A storyteller, and a fair musician myself. You only need to give me facts and details, and I'll turn it into a story."

Still, she hesitated. I knew I had to sweeten the pot.

"And I'll make absolutely certain that T'anai's the villain of the piece," I offered. "He'll get what's coming to him at the end—in my version, at least."

"Done," she said instantly. She spat on her hand and offered it to me, the way I've heard stories that some lij urchins do in Deos.

World Song help me, I spat in my hand, and we shook on it like a pair of street rats.

Hanagisa was right; she was a truly awful storyteller. Her details came out of order, and the events were misplaced—although that could be the nature of the Dreaming rather than any fault of her own. This is the story I finally put together, once she'd finished.

In the Dreaming, in the talamh of Polorun, Hanagisa worked as an apprentice to Conasuari Renn, a notable merchant with aspirations to become a primary supplier of ephemera to Polorun's rulers. Hanagisa couldn't describe exactly what Renn sold—her answers and descriptions were nonsensical, like "the smell of the breeze on a crisp day" and "the particular color of purple that you see on the backs of your eyelids after a flash of lightning." Apparently, Hanagisa and the other Delledir, her particular caste among the Fae, were trained from birth to work as the deal makers in the Dreaming.

But even being born to a job didn't guarantee success. "It's a good position," Hanagisa told me, shedding her six-tailed marii form for a more comfortable, but no less strange, shape: long fingers, ovaloid head, a pair of short antlers surrounded by a brush of riotous hair of leaves and feathers, and a slender body covered in short, blue fur. Her clothing had been, it appeared, genuine: the deep red of her dress still sparkled when the firelight flickered just so. The extravagant spread of food before us faded as well, revealing a more modest fare. "I don't mean to sound ungrateful."

"You don't," I promised her. "Wanting to succeed at what you were born to do is only natural. Mortals only wish they had their destinies so clearly transcribed."

She smiled faintly at that, showing tiny, sharp teeth against almost purple lips. "Another way I'm lucky," she said, but there wasn't much hope behind it. "When T'anai told us he'd traded a small bead for a full head of a mortal's hair—left the lij shaved utterly bald and bewildered, especially when the bead got eaten by a squirrel the next day—it was clear he'd mastered Iomlai."

"Iomlai?" I repeated, taking notes openly now so I wouldn't forget the details.

"The Art of Bartering," she said wistfully. "It's our code, the dream to which we all aspire. It's also our law. I can't reveal much to you—you're not initiated—but I can explain a little. We mustn't cheat, you understand, or go back on our word. A deal is a deal."

I looked at the spread of food in front of us—roots and berries from the Shoro that she'd clearly gathered to enchant into something more extravagant. "You offered me food without asking anything in return," I pointed out.

The look she gave me was utterly scandalized. "Of course I did!" she said. "What kind of merchant do you take me for? Any Chaffer worth their weight draws the customer with food first. Hospitality is a vital part of bartering."

I rolled a berry with my claw, careful not to touch it too thoroughly. "So it wouldn't have made me more amenable to whatever you offered next?"

Again, she appeared baffled. "Yes, it would have. That's the point." Her hair rustled as she shook her head. "Do your mortal merchants really know so little?"

I had to grant her that yes, of course quality merchants offered at least tea in order to begin a discussion, and she was somewhat mollified.

"If I'm not promoted, I could come here and teach a course," she muttered. "Imolai for the Dying Lands, learn while you're still alive."

T'anai's success had brought great praise from Conasuari Renn, and subsequently drew the master merchant's attentions away from her other apprentices. In order for any of them to earn their Liam's Weight—a rite of passage that would have elevated them to full-fledged merchants on their own—they had to win back the approval of their master.

I considered that. "How many of you are here, now, in the Dying Lands?" I asked cautiously.

Hanagisa shrugged. "Just the three of us. And possibly T'anai, if he came to gloat."

A chuckle formed in my belly, and I let it rumble out, the joy of its natural music fusing, just momentarily, with the World Song—a quirk I've never quite been able to eliminate from my own practice—and sending lights into the air above us, dancing in the campfire's smoke.

"I don't know why that's funny," Hanagisa sniffed.

"That," I told her, "is because you don't know how to tell stories."

We needed to pull off several tricks in a row—fooling the other Fae over several details—to achieve the ending to the story that I wanted for young Hanagisa. I know, I know, I said you should never develop a fondness for one of the Fae, but so help me, I found I liked her. And through her retelling, I didn't like T'anai a bit. He'd get what was coming to him.

But in order to get the best of a Fae, I needed to understand what they valued. "Song, of course," she instructed as we walked through the Shoro the next morning, toward the nearest Imorin village. "We bottle them up on occasion, but they never last more than one opening."

"But what would T'anai value? That he already had?" I asked. "In order to show you've mastered Imolai, you need to get something of greater value for a lesser offering, is that right?"

She considered this for a moment, as though admitting it might be revealing too much of her people's secret code. She gave a shallow nod, and I took that for a yes.

"So we need to offer something that seems better than it is—"

"Without lying," she interjected.

"Without lying," I promised, though my friends, such a thing pains me, as what is a good story without a bit of embellishment. "We'll be sure to describe it very carefully and accurately. But that's where your glamour comes in."

"Ah!" she said, waving her hand as she stepped under a branch. The branch lifted upward so she didn't have to dip her head, then descended after she'd passed through. "We have a word for that."

"Oh?"

She grinned, tiny shark teeth gleaming. "Marketing."

The village was most of the day's travel, and we stopped for lunch, each eating our own stores, presumably because sharing food was not a part of our current deal, and neither one of us fully trusted the other not to gain advantage. As she sucked on a strand of honey wheat, she watched me eat.

"What?" I asked finally, wondering if I had something stuck to my whiskers.

"I'm just curious why you didn't respond at all to my form. Six tails not withstanding, I thought I did a good job on her."

I laughed. "You did well enough. Your gestures didn't quite fit the form—your body language was more lij than marii, although your snout was particularly well done."

"Thank you," she said, willing to take pride in a good detail. "So the gestures were off. But the body itself was unappealing?"

I saw where this was headed. "I know we mortals have a reputation for thinking with our desires rather than our brains, but you can't count on that. I admit, for many it's not a bad place to start. Pretty people do tend to make good marketing."

"But not you?"

Was she actually curious, or trying to find an angle in our strange relationship? To be fair, I was genuinely curious about her—how often did a mortal get to spend a day or two plotting with a Fae?—so I decided to answer accurately. "Not me. I have to know a person a bit before I lose my head over a pretty face. And then, they don't even have to be that pretty—not if I care about them."

She grimaced. "My poor luck to have you as a target then. Some other fool would have traded me their whiskers on a lark if I'd smiled well enough."

I shrugged. "Perhaps. But then you wouldn't have a partner in crime, helping you pull one over on your arch-nemesis."

She tucked the last of her food back into a small pack that seemed far too little to fit all the things she'd withdrawn from its pocket. "I suppose that's so," she agreed. "But it's not crime or pulling one over."

"Of course not!" I said amiably, putting away my own food. "It's simply getting the better deal."

You may be wondering why I brought a Fae with me to a village, but that was also part of the plan. I wanted Hanagisa to have practice walking among other marii, getting her gestures just so, counting her tails correctly, before we found T'anai.

In fact, finding her nemesis would be the hardest part. The thing he wanted was easy enough: I'd bottle up a song—something she knew how to do—and we'd admit how valuable it was, given that it contained part of the World Song itself. This, as I'm sure you know, is true of all music. There's not a note sung that doesn't harmonize with that greater melody, not the slightest hum that goes unnoticed in the orchestra of the ground and water and sky. I'd add a bit of glow and glimmer to it, of course, with the smallest bit of my own skill. Hardly any effort at all.

Getting T'anai to trade the hair of the lij—which he'd made into a wig—would be trickier. What on earth could a pair of marii possibly want with a wig? But that came easily, too: I was a traveling entertainer, so there would be no lie, and I did frequently use costuming in my tellings. Not lij wigs, per se, but we didn't need to mention that.

No, the hardest part would be finding the Fae in the first place. And for that, I needed the help of a Singer with greater skill than mine. Fortunately, Singer Bastona owed me a favor I was more than happy to trade for the sake of the story we were penning.

Hanagisa's new marii form was far more subdued: one tail, thankfully; less dramatic clothing to be more in tune with my own; and the same perfect snout.

"Don't twist your claw in your mane," I reminded her as I strung a few of my old beads into her glamoured fur—she gave me a small stone in exchange, because I told her the beads had very little value, so she found something equally dull in her own pack to offer.

"Don't keep counting to make sure I only have one tail," she countered.

And together, we walked into the village. I introduced her as Hana, a temporary apprentice. When I promised I'd be singing that evening, she scowled at me. "You'd give away your songs for free?" she hissed, in a way the crowd didn't hear.

"No, of course not," I promised. "My songs are paid for in food and a roof over my head, every village I visit."

"But you didn't barter," she insisted.

I laughed. "That price is already established on my regular route. But you could barter."

She harumphed, again looking so much like my nibling I felt a wave of fondness I had to tamp down. "I can't sing."

I cocked my head, ear twitching in amusement. "I understand you can dance..."

So it was that Hanagisa traded dances for trinkets all evening long, bringing more joy to a host of marii youth in one evening than my songs would do in ten; if she got the better of any of those deals, I'd be surprised, but based on her smile, I suspect that even a Fae can realize a fair deal, where both parties win, is one to be celebrated.

Singer Bastona, though none too pleased when she realized Hanagisa's true identity, was able to locate not only T'anai but the three other apprentices roaming the Shoro.

"They're together," the old marii said, displaying what she saw in an illusion she cast in the water, humming all the while. "Your foe, it seems, has gathered them, promising to show them how a real Chaffer does the job."

Hanagisa sniffed, sounding every inch a disgruntled marii, and I laughed. We didn't stay the night; instead, we set off, looking like weary travelers, easy marks for tricksters and traders in the night.

The Shoro can be tricky to navigate for newcomers, but I knew the region well, and Hanagisa was Fae enough to simply change the world around her as it suited her. She'd have had more trouble in Deos, I imagined, but in the Shoro, the Aiemer flow is strong enough she hardly noticed she was using it.

"Be wary of that," I told her. "You'll give yourself away."

She hesitated. "But you sing it to do what you want," she said.

"But you don't sing," I reminded her. She huffed, but there was no more adjustment to our path. Instead, she put a hand on my shoulder, and we traveled on together.

T'anai had set up a campfire so similar to Hanagisa's the previous night, I almost did a doubletake. But instead of an attractive, over-tailed marii sitting at a log on the other side, there was a far-too-pretty lij man, with eyes just a bit too large for his face and perfectly symmetrical features. He looked like a drawing advertising a new opera or one of those books with the tales of dashing pirates on the inside pages.

I stilled on the edge of the firelight, holding an arm in front of Hanagisa protectively.

"Hello there!" he greeted cheerfully. "You needn't be afraid. I'm just a simple traveler."

And I was a Mana'Olai diplomat. Was that the type of lie he'd get caught for? "Late for a fire," I called back to him, stepping a bit forward into the light. "We didn't expect to run into any fellow travelers tonight."

Because he wasn't a fellow traveler, this was not a lie. Hanagisa didn't even stiffen behind me, so I figured I'd done well enough so far.

"I think we should stop to rest," she said from behind my shoulder, shyly. "The fire looks cheerful, and he's been very friendly."

All true, all true. "If you think we should," I said with a nod. We stepped more fully into the light, and I let Hanagisa take the lead. If she was to earn back her master's approval, this had to be her show.

And what a show it was. As she sat, her bag, now a humble thing like my pack, slipped open just so, and out of it tumbled the swirling, sparkling song we'd bottled. It was a thing of beauty, I don't mind telling you. I'd chosen my favorite lullaby, filled with images of stars; you may know it—one of the lines describes a shower of wishes cascading from the heavens, alighting around the crib of the young listener. Like the song itself, what filled the bottle was darkness brightened by twinkling lights, some of which would cascade together from top to bottom.

Hanagisa gathered it to her and let out a deep breath. "Wouldn't want this to break," she said to me before tucking it back in her pack.

I eyed T'anai, who was trying very hard not to look interested. "That looked very precious," he said casually. "I'm glad it didn't break."

"Me too," Hanagisa said, a bit effusive for my taste, but T'anai didn't seem to notice. She worried her top teeth along her bottom before withdrawing the vial again. "It's beautiful, isn't it? I probably shouldn't say this, but it's Fae magic."

T'anai laughed. "Fae don't give magic to mortals freely."

"Oh, no," Hanagisa agreed. "We traded for it."

"A song," I supplied, sticking to our script.

"And now it's in the bottle, too," Hanagisa said. "Part of the World Song, held just so."

She held the bottle up to the firelight, and if I hummed just under my breath to make sure the flickers within the vial glimmered even more brightly, well, I can't say that I regret it.

"That must be incredibly valuable," he said, trying to look nonchalant, but I could see he'd been hooked. He leaned back against his log, letting the fire play over his features. "I don't imagine much could make you want to part with it."

She clutched it to her chest for just long enough. We'd practiced that move as we walked, and I was far too proud of how she'd mastered it. "I'll likely have to eventually," she said. "A marii has to eat, after all."

From there, it was just the haggling. T'anai did his best to subtly feel out what it would take to procure such a thing, and while Hanagisa had promised we wouldn't lie, T'anai's way of stretching the truth—he was, of course, a merchant interested in oddities, but not nearly in the way he described it—pushed the boundaries of what I thought reasonable. Still, she made a hefty profit for a thing we'd created just that day: a ream of Aiemer sharkskin from T'anai's wagon, bits and baubles and coin, and finally—

"It's too bad you don't have any costuming," she said. "We really had been looking for a wig for that one story—the one with the lij who gets tricked by the Fae."

That, I thought, was quite risky, but just the right amount of daring. "It's hard to find a lij wig that would fit me," I admitted. "We don't often get lij merchants in this part of the Shoro."

That was a bit risky on my part, I thought, but still, it sold the detail.

"I happen to have just such a thing!" T'anai said triumphantly. "But it's quite precious—I use it to cover my bald spot. I'd have to renegotiate on some of the other items."

Hanagisa pondered it, looking at the song in the bottle longingly again. But at the end, she accepted the wig and a number of other pieces T'anai had offered, though he kept the sharkskin for himself.

After the deal was struck, we made camp on our side of the fire, and T'anai settled down on his. We were both still awake when he stood, did a little jig at the fireside, and vanished into the Shoro, presumably making his way back to the Dreaming.

After making absolutely sure he was gone, Hanagisa and I sat upright and laughed, drawing the other apprentices out of the treeline before they, too, followed him back to their master. Hanagisa placed the wig on her head and transformed, her leaves and feathers miraculously fitting under the blonde lij mane.

"Hanagisa?" one of the other Fae asked incredulously.

"What in the world—?" began another.

"It's quite a story," Hanagisa said, "but I'm rubbish at telling it."

Which is how I told this story first to an audience of Fae. Soon after they all left for the Dreaming, and I continued on my merry way, one story richer. While I doubt I'll ever find out if Hanagisa earned her Liam's Weight, I'm positive that T'anai got his comeuppance in the end, outsmarted by one of the lower apprentices for a single, hastily made song in a bottle, not nearly as rare as we'd made it seem—and good only for a single opening.

I see from your faces that you don't believe me, but these things really happened! And even better, the stone Hanagisa gave me in trade for my beads only needed a bit of polish before I realized what it was: a pebble from the Dreaming itself, worthless to a Fae, but shaped by the Aiemer itself. Here, look and you'll see: the way the colors shift, the way, if you hold it just so, you can hear the rustle of leaves and see the twinkle of stars.

— THE SOUND OF BETRAYAL —

Emma Melville

The throwing knife thudded softly into the guard's heart. He slid slowly down the door frame with a gentle sigh and keeled over to sprawl across the top step.

His partner on the opposite side of the imposing entrance barely had time to glance at the flicker of movement before his own death winged its way in. He fell, half-across his compatriot, their arms reaching out to each other, their surprised faces reflections in blood.

The assassin strolled out of the shadows across the street to climb the stairs in swift silence. He retrieved his blades and wiped them carefully on his victims' clothing before replacing them in their sheaths.

Then he left, leaving two more bodies for Arthus to find in the morning: another stab into the young man's confidence.

Marcos Darkanian stretched lazily and stared at the ceiling. The distant sound of morning drills and sparring rose from the colosseum in the valley west of Lowridge. The early light slipping through the boughs of the fire oak outside threw shadows and leaf patterns on the ceiling overhead. He followed the dancing light with his eyes while his fingers stroked the back of the young lady lying next to him. Her beauty was a bonus because Darkanian—Dark to those he left alive long enough to know him—was working.

Katya stirred beneath his touch and rolled over to stare up at him. "Oh," she whispered, her face flushing. "You must think me dreadful, I—"

He placed a long, slim finger against her lips. "Hush."

"But I don't usually—I—it's not that—"

"I do not, my lady, believe you would stoop so low as to sleep with someone in order to obtain their services. Not even to help your brother." She let out a small gasp, but he continued. "So, I can only imagine my lady must find me pleasing in some way." He kept his tone light, a smile pulling up the corners of his full lips and straightening the scar line across his cheek. She'd slept with him for precisely the reason he'd first given, and it was that memory which brought the color to her cheeks.

Dark wondered if her cherished brother would approve; he doubted it. But then, Arthus Movanian had stubbornly avoided asking for help. Dark could hardly make any conscious efforts to protect someone who didn't want to be protected.

"How is Arthus?" He slid his fingers along her thigh to distract her from the seriousness of the question.

"Two more dead yesterday morning."

He knew that; the frequently found corpses of Arthus' guards had been the talk of the town for days. "Still no attempt on your brother's life?"

"The house is well protected. The two at the door are only for show."

Dark rolled his eyes at the ceiling; he knew that, too. He wasn't sure he would risk dying for a master who openly used such simple defenses as decoys. This wonderful "protection" his guards were dying needlessly for was the main reason Arthus wasn't clamoring for Dark's help.

"But Arthus' enemy is effectively keeping him in the house after nightfall."

"I've told him he needs to do something." The desperation in her voice indicated she'd told anyone who might listen, including the emperor himself, hence Dark's ostensible presence.

"I know, I know." He leaned down and kissed her cheek. "Will he see me? You did tell him about me?"

"Yes, he'll see you. He's meeting some friends here today. He'll talk to you first."

Dark nodded, intrigued to see if his charm would work on her big brother as well as it did on the lady beside him.

Arthus was a pale youth of barely twenty whose arrogance greatly outweighed his good sense.

"My sister believes you can help." Nothing in the young man's tone suggested he agreed with such a claim. Dark raised one eyebrow, but he chose not to confront the implied insult in the man's tone.

"I know I can help," Dark said.

"Because you did some work for the emperor?"

Dark smiled slightly at the irony of the comment. "I have helped in a couple of small matters."

"My guards are being killed by an invisible assassin. I'd hardly call that small."

"No man is invisible, and I've never met an assassin who only kills bodyguards."

"You're telling me I'm in danger? Do you think I don't know that?"

"In fact," Dark said, leaning forward in his high-backed chair, "I was suggesting there might not be an assassin, since the murderer is making no move to kill you."

"Oh." Arthus was momentarily speechless. He leapt to his feet and turned to stare into the garden beyond the window. "I think," he said, "that you underestimate the deterrent effects of my home's security on any potential assassin."

"No protection is foolproof," Dark said, throwing the bait casually into the conversation.

"So you say. Well, Mr. Darkanian, here are my terms: I will have a contract for your services prepared and left in my study tonight. If you can reach it to sign it, you're hired."

Dark kept his amusement hidden; some people were so predictable.

"Arthus, that's unfair," Katya protested sharply.

"Is your tame guard not up to it?"

"I believe," Dark said smoothly, "that your sister is disappointed because we had arranged an outing tonight. Perhaps, if you would be so kind as to invite her to spend the evening at your home, I might visit with her once I've signed our agreement."

"A double disappointment, but by all means."

Dark grinned, showing all his teeth.

It shook the youth's certainty but not by much. A slight widening of his eyes and the briefest of hesitations before he spoke might have been missed by someone less skilled in reading people than Dark. "Goodbye, sir. I don't expect to see you again." Arthus left the room, his back straight.

"You can't do it," Katya said, clutching at Dark's hands. "I should never have asked you."

"I'll see you in your brother's study tonight."

"You can't be that good!"

"There's only one way to find out." He disentangled himself from her embrace and followed her brother from the room, whistling cheerfully.

Once Dark had noisily let himself out of Katya's front door, he silently let himself back in. He snuck through the house and out into the expanse of beautifully appointed garden behind the luxurious townhouse. Moving as if he belonged there, he made his way around to the marble plinth just outside the open drawing room window and sat down to listen.

Dark wanted to know what made the pompous young noble a target—and he suspected the man's friends would be the best people from whom to learn that information.

Three young men had joined Arthus. Dark recognized them all as the supposed cream of Pilean society—youths with hot blood who had grown up in the refined cities of the northern empire and had no understanding of their fathers' battle to leave the islands. Not long ago, Dark may have counted himself among them, though he thought his own arrogance had been less misplaced.

"He's just a pirate," one of the men said. Dark recognized the son of a general who had died in the last campaign. "He needs to be retired."

Dark smiled to himself. Pileaus—who he assumed they referred to—was proud of his heritage and had never been "just" anything.

"Forcibly, if necessary," Arthus agreed.

Dark almost laughed. The fools discussed treason without first ensuring the secrecy of their conversation. How did they think they would manage such a plot?

"Are we safe?" asked the general's son, making a belated effort at discretion.

"Of course. Pileaus has no idea. He has sent some bodyguard chap to keep me from being attacked by this assassin." Dark could imagine the smirk on Arthus' features. "This idiot is going to prove how good our security is tonight."

The four of them laughed.

"I hope Pileaus hasn't sent his best," Arthus continued. "It'd be too easy if he left himself unprotected."

"We'll finalize details tonight, then," the general's son said. "You have all the papers."

"Safely stored," Arthus assured them.

"Really?" Dark muttered, squinting up at the rising sun. "I think I can see why you need a bodyguard, my lord. A good thing Pileaus did send his best. It's about time I did a little research."

Sauntering leisurely, he made his way to the back wall. He silently jogged the rest of the way and arrived on top of the wall in a cat-like crouch.

Having checked that the street below was empty, he dropped to the cobblestones and strode off.

Reconnaissance took place in the main bar of the Sailor's Arms, a seedy establishment at the base of the Steep. The pub occupied a highly trafficked corner at the edge of the docks, the slums, the city market, and the soldier's district of Saltedge. If there were secrets to be bought, Dark knew this conflux of societies would be the place for their purchase. As expected, the Sailor's Arms had for patrons an architect, a locksmith, and a bard—three very useful individuals.

Dark knew just about anyone who was anyone in Pilean society, though it could not be said that this was reciprocated. Since he was fifteen, any who had claimed to know Marcos Darkanian in any depth had rapidly discovered just how little they knew. Quite often in the last two dozen years, such knowledge had been fatal.

Armed with the right knowledge—always the most useful weapon in his arsenal—and a length of rope tied to one ankle and wound tightly round his leg, Dark set off as Diun set and the silver twilight faded to black.

Arthus' manor was a daunting building situated on east side of Lowridge, further from the bustle of the entertainment district than his sister's beautifully appointed townhouse. There, the semi-rich could look over the valley and its governmental buildings, or even up to Eastbreak to envy the luxurious mansion of the phenomenally rich.

Two guards stood nervously on either side of the grand entrance. Dark briefly considered approaching them—sometimes the easiest way in was through the front door—but decided against it tonight.

Leaving them to stare out into the street, he slipped into the shadows of the alley alongside the east wall. Once out of sight of the main thoroughfare, he climbed the wall and let himself down into the garden.

Ignoring all the paths toward the house, Dark crept along the wall to the corner where he hid amongst a copse of fire oaks. From there, he could see the two guards positioned at the back door.

Dark crouched and gathered several small stones which he then threw out onto the path alongside the house.

The guards jumped.

He didn't blame them: guarding Arthus had not been a long-lived occupation this week.

After a whispered discussion following a couple more thrown stones, the pair decided to investigate together. Dark silently applauded their predictability whilst gliding unseen across the lawn. Using a small twisted hook retrieved from his boot, Dark let himself into the house and locked the door behind him.

That was the easy part. Reaching the study wouldn't be nearly as simple.

According to the secretary of the Khaiamus who had charged handsomely for the knowledge, he was safe until he made it to the hall. He hoped the musician was right as he took a deep breath and stepped out across the luxurious carpet of what was plainly a dining room.

Nothing happened.

Dark reached the doorway and peered into the huge expanse of the hall, taking care not to cross the threshold into the next chamber.

Arthus' manor was a square built around this massive central hall. Rooms sprouted off on all four sides and a central stairway led up to a landing, which was also a square and ran around the perimeter of the hall with more rooms along each side. The study that Dark was attempting to reach was built into the space under the grand central staircase. He could see the door fifteen paces away.

Fifteen paces he couldn't take.

"The hall and landing are enchanted," the bard had told him. "It will sing if any step on it during the night. A spell Arthus paid a great deal of money for."

Dark examined the possibilities. "Up, I suppose," he muttered.

He clutched the door's frame and peered up. If he leapt to hang from the railing that ran the length of the upper corridor, he could shimmy along it to the stairs and enter the study door from above. He'd be highly visible if anyone entered with a light, but that was a chance he would have to take. He thrived on such chances.

His heart danced a little with anticipation. This was what he was born to do.

His lips twisted in a wry smile. The last time he'd attempted such acrobatics had been in the Imperial Palace while attempting to do the very thing this young man was plotting. He'd learned a valuable lesson in humility that night and, strangely, in greatness.

Dark owed his rise in status and power to a man he'd tried to kill. It still didn't make sense to him, but he's accepted long ago that the emperor was a complex man who must've seen something in his would-be assassin, something that he could shape and use.

Banishing those memories, Dark placed a dining chair on his side of the door and stood on it to reach the banister above. He used the strength in his shoulders to pull himself up and then slowly worked his way hand-over-hand along the railing toward the stairs.

Once above the study door, he let himself down to a full stretch, his fingers aching with the effort of clinging to the banister and holding his weight. He pushed the door very gently with his foot. As expected, it was shut. Possibly locked.

His afternoon's discussion suggested the latter. Dark pulled himself back up to wrap his arms tightly around the banister. A throb began to spread across his shoulders, but Dark ignored it.

He kept one arm hooked round the rail, while with the other, he unwound the rope from his leg, leaving the end tied to his ankle. He looped the free end around the rail then slowly walked down the rope until he hung upside down. He ignored the protest in his leg as he put all his weight on the ankle he was suspended by. Using a bone hook retrieved from within his belt, Dark picked the study lock. He silently thanked his musical advisor of the afternoon—the bone remained undetected by the metal-sensing enchantment on the lock. Once it had clicked undone, he quietly twisted the handle and opened the door a crack.

From within came voices.

"You really think he can make it?" Arthus' voice was laden with sarcasm. "You're softer then I thought. I don't know why you came."

"He seemed confident."

"Hah!"

Dark pulled himself back up the rope and untied it from his ankle. Then he grabbed both ends and let himself plummet at speed. The momentum of the swing as he reached the end of the drop allowed him to crash his heels into the study door. As it swung wide he arrived feet first into the study, rising sharply from his initial crouch. For added impact, he let go of one end of the rope and pulled hard on the other. The free end whipped out and slapped hard across the hall floor, letting loose a deafening cacophony of sound. Deadly arcs of lightning flashed their way across the floor, sizzling and hissing, each fresh display letting out another rush of appalling noise.

Dark grinned at the stunned faces of brother and sister who had leapt to their feet at his flying entrance. "I hope you can shut that din off," he said conversationally.

Arthus frowned, pulled a small pipe from the desk drawer, and played a short melodic phrase.

Silence fell.

"I'm impressed." Arthus said. He sounded young and frightened.

Dark ignored a momentary stab of pity. "As you should be. I'm the best." He didn't even say it with arrogance these days. It was a simple fact.

"And the emperor wants you to protect me?"

Dark withdrew a beautifully honed dagger from a sheath beneath his leather vest. "No, the emperor wants me to kill you."

"Wh..." But Arthus was cut off when Dark's thrown dagger slammed into his neck.

"No!" Katya stared in horrified disbelief. "Why?"

"He plotted to kill Pileaus."

"You knew?"

Dark raised an eyebrow. "Pileaus knows. He watches every path and hears every breath." He'd discovered that for himself one dark night hanging upside down over the emperor's empty bed—a bed that should have contained an easy sleeping target. "Arthus had become dangerous rather than amusing."

"Why didn't you kill him earlier? You've been playing with him."

"I had to know he was committed to the plot. The Emperor does not waste men. And I had to get inside this room. Pileaus wants all the details."

"Bastard." Her gaze darted around the room, betraying all the papers he needed. "I suppose you wanted me here as a witness."

"I don't leave witnesses." He saw realization dawn in the beautiful eyes.

"No, please—didn't we mean—this morning—" Her voice tailed off in the face of his uncompromising stare.

"No, you're here to die." She hit the floor almost before he finished speaking. This time, the dagger split her heart. "No witnesses."

No one knew what Marcos Darkanian did with his nights—no one living, except one.

After collecting his weapons and the necessary papers, he turned back and knelt over the lady sprawled across the floor. Gently, he drew his hand across her face to close her wildly staring eyes.

Then, he surged to his feet and left without looking back. Regret was not a word Marcos Darkanian had ever understood.

— DOUBLE CROSS —

Scott Colby

Simonez didn't like the look of the crew that came in through his shop's back door. The twins came first, a burly pair of brutes with maybe a dozen teeth between them in their thick, blocky heads. Next came the obvious leader, a shifty weasel of a man who ran his eyes hungrily over every item in Simonez's stock room. Last came a man and a woman, an eerie pair in heavy cloaks who seemed somehow both learned and naïve—but they both moved like predatory cats, ready to pounce at the first sign of trouble.

"Rufello, I presume," Simonez said, his throat dry. "Had I known you were bringing a menagerie I would've set the table for dinner."

The little weasel wandered over toward a shelf laden with cans of nails and a few old boxes of bolts used in certain types of wagon wheels. He picked up one of the nails with a silk kerchief and eyed it disdainfully. "One must be careful when trading with new partners," the little man rasped. He dropped the nail back into the wrong can.

"Then let's make this transaction quick and to-the-point," Simonez replied, biting back his annoyance. "Did you bring it?"

Rufello briefly played with the jade earring that marked him as an experienced trader in Terre Haute. A journeyman, but not a master. He quickly unsnapped the gold clasps holding his jui leather coat shut and pulled the left side open. Hanging inside his jacket was an ancient ceramic tile streaked blue and black in a pattern vaguely reminiscent of some great beast's eye. The great orb in the center was a glittering diamond the size of a man's thumb.

Simonez bit down on his tongue to stifle a smile. That was it, all right, the last piece of the great fresco of Guil Kandhar's Hall of Epiphany. Legend spoke of a trio of brothers that first found the ruins of the mah'saiid empire's third greatest city. Time and the jungle and the great unknown disaster of the Purahd had reduced Guil Kandhar to a useless pile of rock and wood and metal, but the Hall of Epiphany somehow still stood, mostly untouched. In its great hall hung a beautiful piece of ceramic work, a fresco built of over a hundred different tiles inlaid with all manner of gold, gemstones, and precious metals. The brothers spent the next five years prying the tiles off the wall one-by-one. Each brother took an even share, with the oldest taking the one extra. The plan was to bring the tiles back to Priyati and find a jeweler who could extract the valuable bits—but no one to whom they brought the tiles could figure out how to do so. Neither heat nor cold nor applied force could pry the jewels and metals from the underlying ceramic. Knowing they were defeated, the brothers began to sell the tiles whole, and they were scattered to the winds over time.

But Simonez knew of a family that had spent generations piecing the entire fresco back together, one tile at a time. And now they were missing only one. Normally, Simonez was content to deal in the sundries and supplies the local relic hunters needed to travel the jungle, leaving the adventuring and the legend chasing to the young and the foolish. But when he'd caught wind of Rufello's find, he saw an opportunity he couldn't dare pass up.

"Put it on the scale behind you," he instructed. Rufello shrugged, gripped the tile with his kerchief, and set the tile on the clear plate. The scale tilted once, twice, three times…and then leveled out at the weight Simonez had left on the other side. Rufello's tile was the real thing; somehow, despite the differences in the materials laid into the tiles, each had the exact same mass.

Simonez reached into his vest to retrieve a hefty purse bulging with coins. "One thousand Imperial luma." He flipped one of the gold coins to Rufello for inspection.

The weasel didn't move to catch it, letting it bounce off his chest and clatter to the floor. "I'm perturbed by a curious thought, Simonez," he said slowly, tapping his pointed chin. "I find myself wondering why a simple shop keeper is so interested in the family good luck charm."

Simonez hadn't prepared for this. He'd been counting on Rufello's reputation as a greedy bastard to get this deal off smoothly, especially with the exchange rate on luma at an all-time high and climbing daily as Pileaus solidified his hold on the north.

His hesitation wasn't lost on Rufello. "You're not normally a relic dealer; all this crap makes that clear enough. I know you're not a collector because I broke into your apartment while you were out yesterday to check. So that means one thing: you're a middleman, and that little pile of coins is a fraction of what you can actually get for the tile."

"My purpose is of no consequence. The price I'm offering is more than fair."

"Who's the buyer?"

"Take it or leave it."

Rufello shook his weaselly little head. "Boys…"

The hulking twins were quicker than they looked. The one on the left feinted toward Simonez, distracting him so the one on the right could dart behind him and yank the merchant's arms behind his back. His brother followed up with a thunderous punch to the gut that sent the breath tearing out of Simonez and dropped the man to his knees. His captor threw him roughly to the floor, then each of the twins stepped on one of his hands to hold him down there.

"Who's the buyer?" Rufello repeated, a hint of annoyance in his tone.

"Eat shit," Simonez gasped, sucking wind as he tried to recover from the shot to his diaphragm. He wasn't about to let this slimy asshole get the best of him. If he could just free one of his hands…

Rufello trundled over to the shelves on the near wall and examined the cans of nails once again. His fingers still covered in a handkerchief, he reached into one and withdrew a long, sharp spike. With his other hand in his sleeve, he picked up a nearby hammer and hefted it, making a show of testing its weight so his captive would realize how heavy it was.

"Who's the buyer?"

"Emperor Pileaus," Simonez spat. "It's for the seat in the royal outhouse."

Rufello chuckled and shook his head as he came to loom above Simonez. "Clever. Mayhaps you'd like to try telling me you're an errand boy for the shuen and that they need my tile to make their taishu fly?"

He knelt down beside Simonez and pressed the business end of the spike into Simonez's kneecap, drawing blood that leeched up through his thin pants. "Last chance," he cooed, raising the hammer ominously.

"I doubt the merchant's council will see this little stunt as an acceptable negotiating tactic."

"Fine, we'll do this the hard way."

Simonez shut his eyes tight as Rufello raised the hammer. A new voice cut through the tension, a man's voice, deep and confident.

"You don't want to do that."

The spike left his knee and Simonez opened his eyes. Rufello's third man had stepped forward.

"You're right," Rufello said, standing up and presenting the hammer and the spike to his thug. "I'll get blood all over my nice jacket. Enjoy yourself, Boruin."

The man took the hammer and spike in his hands and examined them, looking from one to the other as if considering their use. Though the cloak hid his build, Simonez had no doubt that Boruin would be able to drive the spike clean through his leg with a single blow. The woman watched on from the far corner, nonplussed with the proceedings.

In a motion almost too quick to be real, Boruin flicked his forearm and sent the spike sailing across the room and clean into the left twin's eye. Simonez felt the man's weight leave his hand as he stumbled backward and screamed. In the same motion Boruin swung the hammer up and back, clipping Rufello across the jaw and sending him sprawling to the floor. The other twin stepped forward, taking the first few steps of a hard charge toward Boruin that seemed destined to end in a vicious tackle. But then the woman's hands flicked out of her cloak to fire a pair of throwing knives into his throat. He landed at Boruin's feet, blood bubbling up through his lips as he took his final breaths. Boruin was already on the other twin, slicing his jugular with a quick thrust of his sword. The body collapsed atop Simonez and the old merchant kicked it away in disgust.

Boruin offered Simonez a hand up, which he gladly accepted. "I'm too old for this shit," Simonez groaned.

"Aren't we all," Boruin replied with a smile. "But you've still got one of the best minds in Terre Haute. I tell ya, Sim, when you hired Wraethe and I to take jobs with Rufello, I thought you'd gone senile."

Simonez smiled back. "Lucky for me your reputation for being a man of your word turned out to be true. I owe you and Wraethe my life, Boruin. I won't soon forget it."

He turned to Wraethe. She'd knelt beside the man she'd killed, her head bowed over him as she mumbled a series of strange words he couldn't understand. It sounded vaguely like a prayer. "What's she doing?"

Boruin pursed his lips, as if considering how much to say. "Paying her respects to the dead."

A heavy knock on the front door of the shop, three rooms away, interrupted Simonez's next thought. "Hail in there!" came a familiar voice. "You at home, Mr. Simonez? I thought I heard a crash."

Simonez swore under his breath. "Constable Brais. His patrol brought him through the neighborhood early tonight."

Boruin nodded. "We'll head out through the back. Can you handle him?"

"He's young and naïve and civic-minded enough to be a pain in the ass, but yeah, he won't be a problem."

Wraethe was already on her feet and heading out through the back. Boruin turned to follow, but Simonez grabbed his forearm. "I mean it, Boruin. If you ever need anything, you know where to come."

The old mercenary smiled. "I'll take you up on that day, Sim. Though I worry that the kind of trouble that follows me might make you regret it."

"Mr. Simonez!"

The men shook hands and then Boruin disappeared out the backdoor and into the night. Deep in his gut, Simonez knew he'd see the man again. When he did, he'd break his own back to repay a debt he knew could never be repaid.

— NAMING PLACE —

Emma Melville

The city shone in the bright sun, spread out before him as he descended from the heights of Vision. The soft Diun light he travelled through pushed forwards, the sharp line where sun and moon met rolling toward Maeda Criacao's outer walls.

Bramble paused to watch Diun claim the city boundary, a wry regret catching his heart. No shades of gray here in the Dreaming Lands, no shadows of uncertainties. He missed the borders, the half lights of his valley, the times between times.

He'd probably spent too long on the edges of the Dying Lands, lit by dusks and dawns, but he'd grown to enjoy the twilights, neither one thing nor another. In a way it suited the life he'd made. The Valley of Munier hung between, neither of the Dreaming Lands nor the Dying.

Bramble shook his head and took a deep breath of Aiemer-rich air before descending, following the stark line of light into the city.

He wondered, briefly, what that made him; neither one thing nor another, perhaps. A pertinent question when on his way to a naming. His own had been somewhat unique, which he supposed fit.

Other Fae were entering the city, some no doubt also interested in the fate of the Lean'Aghan. He caught glimpses of them arriving from the circling talamhs. Some he'd already passed on his journey, exchanging greetings and news before their separate paths spun them off through the ever-changing landscape of the Dreaming Lands.

The path dropped suddenly, dipping through a gateway carved in stone, carrying Bramble forward without volition until he found himself standing still on a paved path. Behind him was the gate, the opening to the Dreaming Lands. If he looked back he knew he'd see merely a haze of multi-colored light. The path he'd entered by was there somewhere and, if he stretched out his awareness and grasped at the Aiemer strands, he would find it. Even just standing still he could feel the vague pull of the valley, of home. Content that it was where he expected and could be found at will, Bramble set off into the heart of the city.

The streets were paved in golden stone which glowed softly even after the sunlight had passed. Buildings were few and irregular, interspersed with the wide expanses of nature which were as much home to the Fae as the carved stone. An array of colors assaulted the eye, the Aiemer flows deepening and brightening everything even under Diun's gentler light.

Bramble wandered slowly around the outer city, drinking in the familiar sights. Nothing ever changed in Maeda Criacao, a constant hub in the continual flux of the Dreaming Lands—a necessary paradox. He meandered clockwise through the golden streets and lush parks, ignoring the impossible palaces ringing the center of the city, the sacred heart. The sky-touching spires and columns, twisted trees, and flaming waterfalls of the Nai'Oigher had never held much attraction for him, monuments to the immortal arrogance of the courts. He preferred the gentler places, the natural, still pools and elegant swoops of land when left to its own devices.

The noise around Bramble gradually grew, bringing him out of his reverie. His feet had finally led him to his destination: the Delledeir market.

He stopped, letting the riot of color and noise wash over him. It brought a smile to his lips. Here you could buy or sell anything, trade even your soul if you owned one. Stalls were set up haphazardly in a giant wheel with wares of every conceivable make strewn across them. Each one had its attendant Delledeir, either buying and selling or merely observing and arbitrating, maintaining the balance so important to the Fae.

Their distinctive features—thin faces, long noses, beady eyes, twitching fingers—marked the Delledeir, the ferret caste.

Bramble nodded to a couple he recognized and headed for the market's heart. Here was a clear central space containing a single table spread with a velvet cloth of shimmering hues. On it was placed a single set of golden scales and a giant book. Behind the table stood two Fae, ancient and unchanging. Cadwyn, First of the Delledeir, barely came to Bramble's shoulder. His short hair was white, his eyes nearly black. His lips and fingers were never still, as if eternally counting invisible profits and losses. His companion was much taller and upright, his face having the high, sloping forehead and faraway gaze of the Riddari. Harvlyn, Keeper of Names, rested his hand lightly on the book in front of him while his dark eyes scanned the crowd. He showed no signs of recognition, though Bramble knew those long fingers had recorded the name of every one of them.

Bramble remembered his own trip to the stall so many, many years ago, Cadwyn's probing questions and Harvlyn's scratching pen after their initial consternation at his singular appearance and lack of mentors.

Bramble smiled to himself; he had never fit any mold. He walked across the empty space, exchanging the barest dip of the head—equal to equal—with Harvlyn.

"I thought perhaps you'd decided not to bother this time," Cadwyn said. "I know of only three to come."

"But any may be in need of refuge," Bramble said mildly. Naming was not always a time for celebration.

He found he was scanning the crowd as Harvlyn was, looking for the telltale sign of the Lean'Aghan: the slightly waxy look to features not yet settled to a caste.

It didn't take long to spot one. A slight, dark Fae already sporting the thin features and bright clothing of the Delledeir. Bramble relaxed; this was a Lean'Aghan already settled to a role, and the naming would be a mere formality. There would be no questions this young one couldn't answer. Bramble gave himself a mental tap—'young' indeed, the Lean'Aghan was well formed and may even be considered late for a naming.

He watched the new Fae approach, accompanied by other Delledeir, obviously approving. Their clash of colors lit up the Diuntyne market, but there was no answering clash of opinions.

Cadwyn barely paused to allow the Fae to present themselves. "Your name for the forming."

"Taihal."

Cadwyn wrote the name on a piece of parchment and placed it on one of the scale pans. He waved his hand slowly above the other pan, and Bramble could feel the Aiemer shifting and changing. Gradually a small form took shape in the air above the pan: a miniature set of scales. They grew and solidified until a set of Delledeir scales—Liam's weights—sat in the pan. They perfectly balanced the parchment scrap.

"Delledeir Taihal," Cadwyn said, "take your weights."

"Agreed." Harvlyn opened his huge ledger and wrote the name and caste in elegant flowing script.

The newly named Delledeir hovered a moment longer, but the two Fae showed no further interest.

"Congratulations," Bramble said. "May all roads be profitable." An old greeting for those who traded.

"Thanks." Taihal gave a fleeting smile, scooped up the new set of scales, and turned away.

Bramble watched him vanish into the crowd and was about to turn away when he spotted a second Lean'Aghan. This creature looked almost carved, its polished skin a rich mahogany, limbs long and flowing and its hair of emerald green. The Lean'Aghan moved with a flowing grace across the market to reach Cadwyn.

"Your name for the forming?" Cadwyn said again, pulling another piece of parchment forward.

"Rowan of Kamutu's talamh." The voice was a deep baritone as he named the talamh of creation and craft.

Cadwyn wrote the name and placed it on the scales as Bramble attempted to guess the caste. This was obviously a land shepherd; they were the most likely to cite their talamh as part of their name. The variety was less clear, as each talamh left its own distinctive mark on the Dreaming Lands and those who cared for them.

A small crook took shape in the second pan, growing slowly until a six-foot staff of wood lay across the pan, balancing the name.

"Fiernann," Cadwyn said confirming Bramble's guess. "Tree Shepherd." The newly named Fae bowed gracefully while Harvlyn wrote in his book and then moved off without another word.

"I think you had a wasted journey, my friend," Cadwyn said. "These are happy with their choices in life."

"Is that all?" Bramble was tempted to agree with Cadwyn's assessment.

"I heard rumor of a third," Cadwyn said, "but only that. Nothing definite."

"I'll wait then, see them all now I'm here."

"There," Harvlyn said, startling them with the sudden vehemence of the word.

A crowd had gathered around the open space following a small group of travellers. There were three figures, as mismatched a bunch as Bramble had ever seen, and he stood straighter. He had been right to come; this naming would not be so simple.

On one side of the Lean'Aghan scurried a Delledeir, its bright garb of oddments and precariously balanced hat as eccentric as its movements. On the other side, in stark contrast, strode a Riddari, tall and slim and clothed in deepest black.

But it was the features of the Lean'Aghan which had drawn the crowd and now held Bramble's eye. They had twisted and run like hot wax, misshapen and malformed. The eyes were odd, one blue and one gold, and its hair was a matted mess. The deformed creature walked with a limp, as if one leg hung shorter than the other, and its back hunched to one side, making it perilously lopsided as it moved.

"Your name for the forming," Cadwyn said as the three lurched to a stop before the table.

"Chalia," the Delledeir said promptly.

"Penris," the Riddari was just as fast.

"The Lean'Aghan's name," Cadwyn corrected.

"Yes, Chalia."

"Penris."

The Lean'Aghan laid a long, slim hand on the sleeve of each. "We cannot agree on my name." Her voice, unlike the rest, was pure, soft and silken. The disputing Fae smiled at her and nodded.

"I'm sorry," the Delledeir said. "We cannot agree. Chalia is a natural trader, born to the craft. Why, I've made better deals since Chalia travelled with me than ever before."

"Nonsense," the Riddari said. "You confuse her skill with yours. Penris keeps excellent records and together we found—"

"You found? Chalia merely traded the information you required to—"

"Penris—"

"Please." The Lean'Aghan reached out to them a second time, her voice gentle, "we came here so these good people could settle our argument."

"Of course, yes." The two turned expectantly, their choler immediately forgotten.

Bramble watched the Lean'Aghan sharply; her features seemed to move and fall even as she spoke. The flawless voice issued from lips twisted and cracked.

"Put both names down," he suggested. "Let the scales decide." They could give her a name, at least; her caste was beyond doubt and—whatever her mentors argued—she would be neither trader nor keeper.

Cadwyn carefully wrote both names and then paused in the act of placing the parchment on the scales.

"Are you ready for a naming?"

"Of course she—" the Riddari began.

"I spoke to the Lean'Aghan."

"Of course," she said. "I want to be..." she hesitated over the choice of word and then said, "I want to be whole. I love both of my friends, but I always feel torn and holding the balance is...I just thought the naming would give me a path once and for all."

"The scales merely confirm. You have chosen the path."

"Oh, but I haven't. I really can't decide."

"The scales will confirm your path. Will you accept your name?" Cadwyn spoke firmly but without anger.

"Of course." She sounded worried now, thrown by Cadwyn's serious tone. "Why? Is it a problem because I don't know which—"

"I know your path," Cadwyn said, finally dropping the two names onto the scale. "I am surprised those you travel with cannot divine it." A murmur from the watching crowd suggested agreement.

Gradually, a form took shape on the second scale pan. It was a silver dagger, beautifully crafted with a set of scales carved into the handle. Cadwyn lifted it and turned it over. Down the blade ran a name.

"Ainghid Fas," he said, "I name you Charis."

A ripple of applause ran round the watching Fae, and many bowed low while the newly named Charis stared at Cadwyn in slack-mouthed amazement.

"Agreed," Harvlyn said as his pen scratched across the parchment in strong strokes.

The Fae found her voice. "But—"

"Agreed," Harvlyn repeated, shutting the huge book with finality. He nodded to Bramble and Cadwyn, picked up the ledger, and strode off towards the court palaces.

Cadwyn began to dismantle his scales, handing the dagger to the bewildered Charis.

"What do I do?" she said, turning the blade over and over in her hands.

"What you will. The scales provide a name, not a future."

"You can continue as you were," Bramble said gently. "You may not be Delledeir, but it is true that your skills aid the trade. You diffuse discord."

"I provide a different sort of balance," her voice was bitter. She looked to her two companions, who hovered expectantly on either side. "I think I will take a break from travel."

Two Fae with a single voice: "Oh, but you—"

"No." Almost without volition, Charis reached out towards both as if to lay a hand on each sleeve. Then her eyes widened and she snatched her hands back, clasping them together.

Her troubled gaze met Bramble's. "That's what I did, wasn't it? Forever calming, touching, taking their anger and passions. Ainghid Fas." She spat the last word and threw the dagger to the ground. She turned abruptly and headed away, moving as fast as her misshapen form would allow.

"Leave her," Bramble ordered the two who would follow. Ignoring his own advice, he picked up the knife and set off after her.

She couldn't move fast, so Bramble caught her easily and fell into step beside her. He kept quiet, simply moving with her while she stamped the anger from her system. Eventually her twisted gait forced her to stop and rest in a grassy area. Bramble pulled several Aiemer strands together to provide a carved chair for her to sit upon.

She collapsed, breathing heavily while Bramble fashioned himself a second seat and relaxed into it.

"Who are you?"

"Bramble."

Her eyes widened slightly. "Old Bramble?"

"I have heard it said so."

"You train champions."

"Indeed."

"What do you want with me?"

"I have been known to teach other things on occasion."

"Like what? How to die?"

Bramble sighed. "No, child. Acceptance."

"Accept this?"

"Ainghid Fas maintain the balance of the Dreaming Lands, Charis. You know this, you said so yourself. You own great honor for your gifts."

"Gifts? To warp and twist and die while Fae live forever?"

"Not forever," Bramble said mildly, "and dying does not have to be a foregone conclusion."

"How so?"

"Restraint and care can be learned. Solitude can be provided. Chants and charms can be said."

"Loneliness does not sound like an attractive life."

Bramble nodded, his heart heavy with pity. "I cannot promise your life will be easy. I can provide a space to rest, where you can learn to accept your future."

"Why?"

There were answers he could give to do with loss and loneliness and the life he had made on the borders, but he gave the reply he'd laid before the Courts half a lifetime ago.

"Balance," he said. "The Lean'Aghan are left to be formed by fate and to bring that form to a naming, but if we are to maintain who we are as Fae then that neglect to allow nature to take its course must sometimes be balanced by nurture, by the care and guidance of one who can light a path that remains dark."

Charis nodded, much as the princes of the court had done. Balance was an argument all Fae understood, inbred into a psyche that couldn't quite grasp the shades of gray Bramble had come to value.

"I only set one limit on my company," Bramble said. "Until you learn control, you do not touch me, and you never use your gifts on me. My passions are hard won and my own." He smiled to take the sting from his words. "Will you journey with me, Charis, and spend a little time in the Valley of Munier?"

She took a deep breath, and then her face contorted in its best approximation of a smile. "I think I would like that," she said.

He held out the dagger to her, but she shook her head. "Not yet. I think that would be too solid a truth."

"I'll keep it for you until you're ready." He slipped it through his belt and stood. "Let me show you my home."

Sometimes, he thought, after the stark realities of a naming, a chance to hide in the shadows was a blessing.

— A DAY OF STRANGERS —

Dylan Birtolo

Marc stood as tall as he could manage and stretched to reach the glass bottles on the top shelf without having to fetch the ladder from the opposite side of the room. The tips of his fingers lightly grazed the wider storage jars as he turned them just enough to read the labels. Finding the one he was looking for, he grabbed a shelf halfway up and used it to pull himself to the tips of his toes. Rolling the glass jar on the shelf, he worked it to the edge. When he could see the lip of it hanging over empty space, he placed a finger underneath it and slid it off. With a smooth motion, he caught the falling jar in his other hand, absorbing the impact with his whole body to protect the fragile contents.

"I do wish you'd be more careful," a voice said from behind him. Marc didn't need to turn around to know the look his master wore.

"I know, Master Garbas, but does it matter if the contents are still intact?" Marc turned around and presented the glass jar of roots floating in a small pool of water.

The older man shook his head, making the earring dangling from his right ear sway back and forth. He took the jar with both hands and held it between his fingertips. He turned and looked at the ladder. "Next time you could spend five seconds doing it properly."

Marc only half-heard the words. He was staring past his master at the woman who entered the alchemist's shop. She had black hair, worn long and straight, and was dressed plainly—she wore a simple dress with no ornamentation and had no jewelry—but her beauty shone through in a way that made Marc lose track of everything. Her lure was natural and not based on the trappings of her status. She was Sabina, the woman with rare herbs for sale. Marc had asked about her, but no one in his village knew much. She showed up every two weeks, sold some herbs to the alchemist, bought some food and occasionally a tool from the blacksmith, and then returned to the nearby woods.

That fact alone made some talk about Sabina in hushed whispers. The woods were rumored to be haunted, and no one from Antionne had gone there for as long as Marc had been alive. They didn't dare use the trees on the edge for firewood, since a curse was supposed to fall upon the house of any who dared trespass on the unholy ground.

Garbas noticed his apprentice's lost stare and grunted as he walked into the front room carrying the jar. He spoke to Sabina, working out the details of their transaction. Marc watched over his shoulder as he walked around the back room, making a minimal effort to appear hard at work.

Sabina looked up as she finished her transaction and caught Marc's eye. She smiled at him and a slight blush rose in her cheeks; it was small enough that he couldn't be sure if he imagined it or not. Then, she turned and walked from the shop. Marc stood for several seconds, watching the door. It wasn't until Garbas cleared his throat and thrust a jar into his chest that Marc was shaken from his daydream.

Several hours later, Marc and Garbas had their second unusual guest of the day. Shortly after the train arrived, a large man entered their shop dressed in flowing silks, the likes of which Marc had never seen. He had a presence which drew the attention in the room directly to him. Something in his small dark eyes sent a shiver down Marc's spine when he matched the man's gaze. The stranger walked straight to Marc and managed to look down at the apprentice despite being only a few inches taller.

"Where is your master?" his voice was thick and sounded strange. He rolled his R's in a way that made his conversation sound like a growl.

"In the back, brewing some potions. Shall I fetch him?"

The stranger said nothing but nodded his head. Marc retreated to the back room to summon Master Garbas. As his master came forward, Marc stood around the corner and leaned as close as he dared to eavesdrop on the two men. He only caught pieces of the conversation.

"...a young woman...sells rare herbs..."

"...Sabina...woods to the east..."

Marc didn't need to hear any more. He grabbed his jui leather jacket and bolted to the back door of the shop, knocking over a table in his haste. He heard it slam to the ground, followed by the crash of several bottles and jars as they shattered against the floor. He glanced over his shoulder, but no one emerged from the back of the shop. He saw two more strangers standing in front of the shop and holding the bridles of three horses. Marc could only hope they'd be slow enough getting started that he could reach Sabina first.

He moved as fast as his legs would carry him, stopping when his lungs were burning. He caught his breath in the fields between the village and the woods. The closest trees were only a few hundred yards away. Taking several deep breaths, he forced himself to a jog. Up ahead, he could see a path leading into the woods. It was a trail barely large enough for a person to walk, but it had been well traversed and all the low vegetation was flattened. Marc hesitated for a moment at the edge of the woods, glancing uneasily at the forbidding trees. He reached up and pulled his jacket tighter around him.

"Sabina!" he called out into the woods. He waited and listened for a response. "Sabina!" he called out again, and again he was met with silence.

With a final glance behind him, Marc turned back to the woods, took a deep breath, and plunged down the path. The branches reached at him as he stumbled forward, and for a moment he thought they were alive and reaching down to tear him apart. He swatted them away and twisted as he ran down the path, their wooden fingers clutching at his clothes and trying to inhibit his progress.

Marc stumbled in his panic, landing face-first in a bed of small tan flowers. He rolled over to stare at the trees, half-expecting them to be grasping for him. It took him a few seconds before he realized the trees were standing still save for a gentle swaying in the breeze. Chuckling at his foolishness, Marc stood up and dusted himself off. He continued down the path, this time moving at a brisk walk.

It wasn't long before his throat began to itch. Marc reached up and rubbed at his neck, but it provided a limited relief at best. Soon, he was rubbing his neck constantly as he walked. He opened his mouth to call out for Sabina, but found that his throat refused to respond to his will.

"Help! Intruder! Intruder!" Marc felt himself calling out. He tried to quell the shouting, but he continued to screech out a warning. Clamping his hands over his own mouth barely muffled the sound.

Marc heard a crack from the woods ahead of him. He tried to be still but shouted out "Help! Come quick! Interloper!"

Sabina stepped out of the growth in front of Marc and looked at him, her head cocked slightly to the side. She had a rag tied over her nose and mouth, but he recognized her. Unfortunately, her appearance did little to quell his shouting. Sabina rushed forward and shoved a rag into his mouth. He could still breathe through his nose, but his shouts were muffled.

"You should not be here," she whispered, turning around and walking deeper into the woods. She held a hand out behind her to help guide Marc. He took it, following her deeper into the forest.

As they walked, she turned to talk over her shoulder. "You have been infected and your voice is not your own."

He wanted to stop shouting, to tell her about the men coming who were looking for her, but he continued to try and scream around the gag in his mouth.

Up ahead, the path widened into a clearing. A small wooden shack stood in the center of it, with a fire pit dug out in front of the door. Sabina guided him into the clearing, half-dragging him towards her hut. Marc looked down at the ground and saw hoof prints, three sets of them. He jerked back on Sabina's wrist, almost pulling her to the ground. When she whipped her head around, a fire burned in her eyes. Marc ignored it and pointed frantically at the ground.

"Hoof prints?" Sabina narrowed her eyes as she bent towards the marks and touched them with her outstretched fingers. "Who would come up here?"

"We came looking for you, Sabina." The voice was thick and dark. Marc recognized it instantly.

Both Marc and Sabina turned to face the man in the silk robe. The other two foreigners stood behind him near the edge of the clearing, holding three horses. Marc rushed forward, putting himself between the stranger and Sabina. He charged at the man, dropping his shoulder in an attempt to buy Sabina time to escape. The man saw the move and twisted to avoid the mad rush. Marc stumbled and the stranger elbowed him in the back, sending Marc sprawling.

The pain in his back combined with his continuous shouting made it difficult for Marc to get air. He rolled onto his back and propped himself up to a sitting position, breathing as deeply as he could through his nose. His throat continued to scream of its own volition, depriving him of the air he needed to recuperate. The man in silks looked down at Marc with a frightening grin. He turned back to face Sabina. She was standing tall in front of him, but the sweat on her brow was clearly visible.

"We wish you no harm, Sabina," the man gave a bow. "I would like to present you with a proposition."

"Who are you, and what do you want?" Sabina asked, raising her chin as she did so.

"We are Mana'Olai, and we have traveled here to seek your expertise."

"Expertise with what?"

The man held out his hand and gestured towards Marc. "With the gruw. You are clearly familiar with this," he hesitated as he searched for the right word, "creature. You can walk among their fields and not be infected. Your knowledge would prove most useful."

Sabina's shoulders softened, but her legs remained tense. "What for?"

"We find that we need to expand the creature's functionality. We are attempting to breed a more useful gruw, a gruw-makken. With your knowledge, we would be closer to success."

"Why should I help you?"

"We offer glory, gold," he paused watching for the effect these terms had. Sabina didn't even blink. He gestured towards Marc again. "Perhaps this young boy's dwindling life."

Marc's eyes went wide as he heard those words. He shook his head, but the effort made his vision spin. If he kept shouting, it would not be long before he passed into unconsciousness. From the man's comment, that would not relieve him from his curse.

"What you propose is impossible. The gruw infection cannot be cured."

"And if I prove you wrong, do you agree to come with me and share your knowledge with others who are fascinated by this creature?"

For several agonizing seconds the two bargainers stood there, until Sabina nodded her assent. The stranger snapped his fingers and one of the two men with the horses pulled a bottle out of his silks. He rushed over to Marc and removed the gag.

Everyone winced as his shouting filled the clearing. The foreigner put the bottle cap in his teeth and pulled, opening the vessel. He poured the contents into Marc's throat and clamped the young man's mouth shut. Marc tried to swallow the liquid, but it went into his lungs instead. He began to cough violently, leaning over as he did so. He felt a huge sense of relief as he coughed up what looked like a four-inch long tan flower. Before he had a chance to do anything, the man behind him crushed the parasite under the heel of his boot.

The stranger spoke to the wide-eyed Sabina. "We could learn much from each other. Would you like to assist us in the creation of a new species?"

Sabina looked from Marc up to the stranger. She regained as much of her composure as she could before she nodded.

"Good. Then may the god-kings smile upon our agreement."

— IMBER'S OCEAN OF GLASS —

Scott Colby

There once was a man named Imber.

Imber lived alone in a tiny hut at the tip of a tiny sliver of a cliff jutting out above the sea. He lived off the land, hunting and scavenging in the nearby jungle for food and materials, but never taking more than he needed.

One day, Imber found himself deeper in the jungle than he'd ever been. The Mana'Olai, who'd moved into the area a few months prior, had eaten all the local game. Normally, he never would've tracked a boar so far into the forest, but Imber was tired of living on fruit and fish.

The steady trail of hoof prints brought Imber to a small clearing. The soft soil and clinging scrub of the jungle floor suddenly became barren, black and hard, crisscrossed with cracks and fissures. Imber didn't like the heavy, oppressive feel of the place, but he'd come too far to give up and go home empty-handed. He let his spear lead the way, clenched in white-knuckled hands.

The tracks ended abruptly at a small pile of ash in the center of the clearing. The remains of a campfire, perhaps, judging by the size of it. Imber kicked the ash with his bare foot in frustration. He was not an educated man in the usual sense, able neither to read nor write, but Imber knew that boars didn't just spontaneously combust. The animal had to have gone somewhere.

"Good afternoon," a small soft voice said hesitantly.

His nerves on end, Imber whirled to face the speaker with his spear at the ready. The voice belonged to a tiny old woman standing in front of a pair of charred trees at the edge of the clearing that bent together in a way strangely reminiscent of a door. She leaned heavily on a twisted walking stick, clothed in layer after layer of blackened tattered rags despite the heat and humidity. Bushy gray hair sprang upward in thick patches from her high sloping skull. She seemed somehow even warmer than her surroundings, the warmth radiating from her body in waves that distorted the jungle behind her.

"G-good afternoon," Imber stuttered, lowering his spear and bowing politely. "What are you doing out here all alone?"

"I come here sometimes to ponder life," she replied slowly. "It's a beautiful spot, don't you think?"

Honest to a fault, Imber shook his head. "It's very dreary."

The woman shifted, a subtle movement that conveyed a world of displeasure. The gesture was lost on Imber. "And what type of place do you prefer?"

Imber answered without hesitation. "My home, for one." And with that, Imber launched into a monologue about the only topic in the world that could make him speak that passionately for that long.

"My grandmother was the first to tell me about the sunset. She would sit me on her lap and hold my hands in hers and tell me about the D'battu, about the great exodus across the ocean from slavery at the hands of the terrible God Kings. Food was scarce, potable water even more so. The days were long and hot, the ramshackle rafts offering no protection from the elements. She insisted that the nights were the worst. In the dark she couldn't see the other sailors, or the raft beneath her feet, or even the sea itself. In the dark you didn't know if you were still really alive. That moment when the sky turned orange and pink and red, when the sun first peeked above the horizon—that was what kept her going, what reminded her that she was on her way to a better life.

"I made my grandmother tell me that story every day until the day she died. After the funeral, I set out on my own, determined to see the sunrise with my own two eyes. I had never seen one—we lived in a deep valley surrounded by treacherous mountains that blocked the view, and the forest beyond was no help. I still don't remember how long I walked, or even how I knew I was going in the right direction. But eventually I saw the sea, and with my heart soaring, I walked all the way to the cliff where I would build my home. That first sunrise was even more glorious than my grandmother had told me.

"My home only has three walls. Nothing blocks my view of the horizon. Those first tendrils of sunrise wake me every morning, as gentle as my mother used to when I was a child. I roll out of bed and sit on the edge of the cliff to greet the sun and I know that I am still alive."

The old woman stood stock still as Imber spoke, then yawned when he finished. "So, you're the one that lives on the cliff," she said mischievously. "How would you like to get an even closer look at the sunrise?"

"I'd like nothing better!"

The old woman smiled and tottered off into the forest, disappearing through the charred arch and leaving Imber alone with his thoughts. Though he loved his home and its location, he'd only ended his journey because going further would've been impossible. Imber was no sailor. Occasionally he'd lay awake at night, wondering if he should pick up and follow the coast north or south until it once again turned eastward.

But what if he'd already found the point closest to the sun? Then he could walk forever and never find a better view, and he was sure that someone would take the spot on the cliff in his absence. If there truly was a point closer to the sunrise, it was a place he could never reach on his own—but somehow he knew this strange woman could get him there.

She returned a few moments later bearing a small leather satchel. The warmth of her made Imber's skin break out in a thick sweat, and he almost took a step back as she reached up to drape the satchel around his bare shoulder. "Bury the contents of this bag on the beach within reach of the tide at midnight during Nurom Misuer's next full night," she explained. "Light a fire atop the sand and cast three bluestars into the flames. Allow the tide to consume the fire. When you wake the next morning, your wish will be granted."

Imber smiled at her, testing the bag's weight. It was light enough that he wondered if perhaps it was empty, but he could see its contents bulging against the sides. "Th-thank you," Imber replied. "How can I repay you?"

She winked. "Don't worry about that, my dear. Kindness is its own reward."

Imber didn't get much sleep the next five nights as he waited for Nurom Misuer to wax full. He couldn't remember ever being more excited. Those next few sunrises lost their luster a bit; they were beautiful enough, but Imber knew that his future sunrises would be even better. He left the satchel on his little table, unopened, afraid that examining its contents prior to burying them would somehow ruin the magic.

On that fateful night, Imber ran down to the beach alone, smiling up at crimson Nurom Misuer watching him from among the stars. He dug a small hole in the sand with his bare hands and then carefully placed the contents of the satchel inside. Three small stones, black as the surrounding night. A tuft of feathers dipped in blood. The beating heart of some strange beast, warm and viscous in his hands. He replaced the sand carefully, as if burying a beloved family member, and then he arranged a small pile of driftwood atop it all and set the whole thing ablaze with flint and a bit of moss that all the locals used as kindling. When the heat from the flames was enough to make Imber back away, he retrieved the three bluestar flowers from his pocket and tossed them into the fire. The flames flared suddenly upward and turned briefly purple, then returned to normal.

Imber wanted to stay and watch the magic, but the crone had insisted he get a good night's sleep while it did its thing. His rest was surprisingly gentle, awash with pleasant dreams of bright sunrises bigger and brighter than any he'd ever seen. Sometimes he was alone, but more often than not, his grandmother was by his side.

He woke slowly with morning's first light, stretching and yawning and scratching himself as he made his way outside to the edge of the cliff to take in the sunrise. His mind was still clouded with sleep, and he'd almost forgotten the previous night's events until the site before him jarred his memory back into place. There were two sunrises now, one seemingly in the ocean. The water was strangely still and flat. He'd never seen the ocean so calm. He leaned out over the edge of the cliff to look straight down and found another Imber staring back up at him.

Realization came slowly to Imber, but when it did his heart leapt up into his chest. The old woman's spell had worked! She'd turned the sea solid!

He grabbed what little food and potable water he had, stashed it in the old woman's satchel, and ran down to the beach. The tide had frozen in place on the beach just beyond where he'd lit his fire the night before. He bent down and knocked his knuckle against the sea. It was just as hard and sturdy as it looked. Imber took one tentative step onto the ocean, then another and another until he was gone from the distant horizon.

A few days later, the sea was back to normal, lapping at the shore as it always had before. No one knows what happened to Imber, but many claim to have seen an old woman puttering about the charred remains of his house, often sitting at the edge of the cliff to watch the sunrise.

— SHADIVENGEN —

Mark Adams

He watches the lone figure as she surveys the carnage of the valley spreading out below the bluff where they stand. The once lush meadowland has been churned into a muddy sludge by the two days of battle. She looks on impassively as the monks and servants from both sides move about the valley, counting the dead and collecting the wounded. Scores of oxen-drawn wagons busily ply away in the Necrosian Garden.

Her long raven hair clings heavily to her forehead and face, damp from hours beneath her helmet. Her fine hauberk of chainmail lays in a heap to her right and her leather vest hangs open to the waist, the linen shirt beneath soaked with sweat. Her face, normally a picture of confidence with porcelain skin contrasting her ebon hair, looks haggard and weary, streaked with the grime of battle. Only her eyes, crystal blue and sharp, do not show the strain of the day as she registers the activity below.

A slight gust brings the chill of early Feralis with it, and the wind makes her uncharacteristically shiver. Her eyes turn flinty, and her hand drops to rest on her long sword. She turns away from the scene below, her knuckles going white as she tightens her grip around the hilt.

As he watches, the tiredness in her face washes away, replaced by resolve. Losa, daughter of Emperor Pileaus and pride of the Northern Army. Her hair, her personal colors, her status in her father's eyes, and her legendary wrath—there were many reasons why the men in her service whisper another name.

The Black Queen.

She turns away from the bluff. "Calib," she commands, softly.

He shifts, allowing himself to be seen, and bows.

Her eyes focus on him. "Bring General Ayet here. Now."

Calib nods. "As you wish."

Walking toward the beach, he sees tents of all sizes stretch away into the haze. Ayet's tent is easily recognizable, bright red and huge, its pennant a white stallion on a sable field. Calib shifts in the shadows, slips behind the pair of soldiers guarding the entrance to Ayet's pavilion, and steps inside.

The general sits on a mound of cushions, a silver goblet in his hand. Five others, all in uniform, share the pavilion with him. They are laughing about something and clearly at the end of a meal when Calib shifts out of the shadows.

"Gods!" chokes the man closest to him, having seen the small, heavily armed man all in black leather suddenly appear out of thin air. The man awkwardly springs to his feet and scrabbles backwards, kicking over a decanter of wine and crashing into a second man, sending both of them sprawling to the floor. A third man, already standing, draws the dagger at his waist and drops into a crouch, quickly moving from shock to defense.

Calib ignores them all, his attention focused on Ayet. "You are summoned," he says.

The room explodes into turmoil. The two fallen men strive to untangle themselves while the others gain their feet, pulling out what weapons they have and facing this sudden threat. Only Ayet and his aide, Commander Higalen, make no move to rise.

"Enough!" roars Ayet. "Put your weapons away!" He glares at the men in the room, but it takes several heartbeats for the command to register. Ayet frowns at the blossoming wine stain on his expensive rug. "Damn you, Calib! You dare to enter my quarters unannounced?" The general rises from his cushion, red anger creeping up his face. "I should throw you in the stockade!"

Ayet, a huge, muscular veteran of countless campaigns, towers over the small, darkly clad Calib, who stands immobile as the general approaches. "I do not answer to you, general," he says, his tone indifferent. "Nor am I bound by you. You are summoned."

The officer with the dagger senses a confrontation and steps between Calib and the general. "Who is this man?" he questions.

Commander Higalen answers. "Calib. A Shadivengen."

The officer blanches, a look of disbelief on his face, and quickly takes a step back. "Shadivengen!" he stammers, colliding with Ayet and knocking the silver goblet from his grasp.

"Curse you, Rogen!" Ayet bellows, slapping the side of the officer's head with the flat of his massive hand. "He's just a man, nothing more."

Rogen stumbles aside, barely sparing himself the indignity of falling to the ground.

"Royal Shadows are a myth!" declares another officer.

"No," rumbles Ayet. "They are real enough. One for each royal." He casts a sharp glance at the other men in the room. "Control yourselves! They are not magical, just...tricky."

"You are summoned," Calib states again, patiently. "Mine is not the wrath you risk with delay."

The anger in Ayet's face waivers. A flicker of worry crosses his brow. He masks it quickly, unnoticed by the men in the room. He grinds his teeth, knowing that the little bodyguard knows his fear. "Fine," he hisses, his jaw clenched. "Lead on, lapdog."

Her vest has been refastened—the only indication that she has moved at all from her spot on the bluff. Calib leads Ayet and his officers, all of who insisted on attending the general, up the hill. Hearing them approach, Losa turns to faces the small group of men. She alone notices Calib shift out of view.

"I see you have brought your council," she says, fixing Ayet with her crystal blue eyes. "Good. This will be educational for all."

The general nods his head toward Losa. "Why have I been summoned?"

Catching everyone by surprise, Losa steps forward and strikes the general across the face. "You will address me as 'my lady,'" she snaps.

Ayet takes a step back, the force of the slap far less than the sting of humiliation. "As you wish, my lady." He straightens, rising to his full height. "Now, my lady, for what have I been summoned?"

She looks at him for a long moment, and then turns away to gaze out on the valley below. She motions for Ayet to step beside her. A hint of nervousness settles in his eyes as he joins her.

"I have to wonder," she begins, motioning towards the valley, "just why there is so much activity here."

Calib, now closer to his royal charge, sees the look of poorly feigned puzzlement on Ayet's face. "There was a battle here, my lady. What else would you expect?"

Her eyes flash dangerously. "Do not be dense, Ayet. Why is there activity here?" She again indicates the valley below with her hand.

Ayet clears his throat, his anxiety clearly building. "This area represented a credible threat, Losa." He points to the far end of the valley, perhaps a mile distant. "The Oran reserves were camped there, awaiting orders to join the enemy's front. This was a flanking maneuver."

She rounds on him, her voice trembling, an iceberg of anger. "Three thousand men, Ayet. Three thousand of my men died here for no reason!"

"No reason?" he barks back at her. "We destroyed more than twice that many Orani! How can that be 'no reason?'"

"I gave you a direct order to bring these men to support the shield wall on the north flank! Those reserves were nothing but green boys. No threat! Oran would have never brought them up, as supporting the north flank would have routed the Oran army. You wasted these men!"

"You are but a girl, Losa, not even twenty. I have three decades of–"

Losa moves so quickly that only Calib sees her in detail. In a single motion, she pivots, draws her sword, and strikes Ayet. The blade catches his throat, and his words die in a choking gurgle. Her sword is sheathed before the other men even realize Ayet has been attacked. Ayet's hands fly to his neck in a vain attempt to check the flow of blood. He stares at Losa blankly as the crimson cravat grows on his white tunic. Slowly, he drops to his knees, and then pitches forward onto his face.

"Ayet!" shouts Rogen, his shock quickly turning to fury. He pulls out his dagger, his eyes burning. "Die, witch!" He springs forward with reckless abandon.

With speed honed by a lifetime of training for no other purpose than to protect, Calib draws his matched set of single-edged swords from across his back and steps between the crazed officer and his ward. Suddenly aware of the Shadivengen, Rogen tries to correct his approach, but too late. One of Calib's blades hits high, the man's momentum driving it through his chest. The other hangs at the ready. Watching impassively, Calib holds him upright as the life leaves his eyes. With a tug, he frees his weapon, letting the man collapse on top of Ayet.

"No one," he says, watching the others, "touches the Mardente."

"Enough, Calib," comes Losa's voice, surprisingly soft. "It is over. They understand."

"Aye, my lady," agrees Higalen. His voice sounds tight. "We are yours."

In only three weeks the Great Northern Army, under the command of the Black Queen, has brought Oran to its knees. Before Feralis is over, the king of Oran kneels before Losa and offers his fealty. Losa establishes her capitol in the great fortress of Tivalis and brings the rule of Pileaus to Oran, folding the small nation into the Empire.

Calib is constantly on his guard, remaining ever diligent. Unlike a Shadivengen in the great city of Deos, where often there is little to do for days at a time, duty on the front is pressing. Threats to Losa are constant, Calib having slain three Orani assassins and one mercenary sent by the shuen in their short stay. More disturbing still is the rumbling of the officers. While Losa firmly owns the hearts of the men, some of the veteran officers are chaffing under her command.

Upon moving into the solid walls of Tivalis, Calib finds he can relax. He follows Losa down the smoky, torch-lit hall, reflecting that having four solid walls around Losa is far better than the canvas pavilion death trap in which she slept in at the front. He doesn't bother shadow walking here, deciding to show any assassin (or would-be assassin) his vigilance.

He makes sure to enter her chambers before her, checks her bed and wardrobe, and ensures his seal on her window is unbroken. Satisfied, he motions for her to come in. She closes the door behind her and moves to the bed, shrugging out of her clothing as she does so. Calib watches her impassively. He has been her royal shadow since the day she was born, and any pretense of modesty in front of him had been shed long ago.

He watches her as he has a thousand times before. Her six-foot slender frame is well-muscled and lithe. Aware that her father's approval is dependent entirely upon her gender and she is as likely to gain one as change the other, she pushes herself always to be more. More than he thinks she can be. She knows nothing will be enough.

Though flawless of skin, porcelain-smooth and alabaster-white, she is no beauty. Striking to look upon due to her self-confident charisma, only her eyes are considered truly beautiful. He could lose himself in those eyes.

Calib would die for Losa, regardless of any order-specific oaths. He would kill Pileaus himself, should the Emperor ever raise his hand in anger against his daughter.

Losa slides beneath the heavy wool comforter with a grateful sigh. "Wake me in five hours, Calib."

He watches her until her breathing becomes rhythmic, a soft whistle coming with each breath. He quietly steals from her room, locking the door behind him. The chamber across from hers belongs to her personal guards, and he raps on the door, instructing two of them to stand guard until he returns.

He arrives in the kitchens to find only a few others eating. Gathering a loaf of bread, still hot from the ovens, and a bowl of thin soup, he sits at one of the far tables alone. Surveying the room, he focuses on the other men. A group of three young officers are laughing and seem oblivious to him. Another group eat in relative silence, broken by an occasional whisper.

A lone commander enters. He slowly surveys the room, eyes stopping on Calib. The man smiles, but not in pleasure.

The hairs at the base of Calib's neck rise in warning as the man approaches, but Calib's thoughts are strangely clouded. His senses tell him he should return to Losa's quarters, but he cannot make his legs obey. He sits, mutely watching the commander take the seat across from him.

"Hello, Shadivengen," the commander says, his tone mocking. "Enjoy your soup?"

The words are like a shock through Calib's system. In a daze, he looks at the empty bowl, realization slowly dawning on him. His fingers fumble at the edge of the bowl, turning it over and shoving it away from him. The bowl rolls in lazy circles to the edge of the table, where it tumbles off and shatters on the floor.

"War...sh," Calib stammers. "Warsh hash you…"

"Save your breath," the commander says softly. "Don't fight it."

Knowing his options are now few, Calib takes the wooden spoon he somehow still clutches in his left hand and pushes the handle down his throat. He leans to his side, vaguely aware that he loses his seat as he does so, crashing to the floor. As he begins to wretch, a pair of strong hands fasten about his shoulders.

"Stop him!" shouts a strong, deep voice. He does not think it belongs to the commander.

"I still say we should kill him now!" says another. "With him out of the way we can deal with the Black Queen easily."

"No," says a third voice, raspy and harsh. "We stick to Higalen's plan."

"No names!" shouts the voice Calib knows belongs to the commander. Failing to regurgitate the soup, he is lifted from the floor and roughly shoved into a chair. A hand takes his chin in an iron grip and a face draws close to his. Though the speaker's face is too blurry to identify, he couldn't mistake the commander's voice.

"Now listen to me very carefully, Shadivengen. This is what you shall do..."

Calib blinks. The bowl of thin soup sits half empty before him and the loaf of bread is untouched. Dipping his spoon in the bowl, he pauses. Hadn't he finished the soup? He frowns, disgusted at being so lost in his own thoughts that he allowed his perception to be clouded, even for something as simple as his meal. Deciding that he is not hungry any longer, he stands and walks past the two groups of soldiers who pay him little heed.

He makes his way directly to Losa's hallway, the two guards still standing on either side of her door. They snap to attention. Calib nods, ready to send them back to their posts in the guardroom, when inspiration strikes him.

"It has been a long month since leaving Deos," he says to them. "Her highness will be asleep for another three hours or so. I release you from service for the rest of the night. There is a band of troubadours in town, I am told. I recommend you see if they live up to their reputation."

The two glanced at each other warily. "Sir Calib," one says, "we dare not leave our post."

Calib waves his hand dismissively. "Do not concern yourself. I will attend to the Mardente for the rest of the night."

The two look at each other again, then shrug nervously. "Aye, as you say, Shadivengen."

Calib watches them go, his mind struggling with something just out of reach. He nearly calls them back, but the moment has passed. He shakes his head, frowning. What was he thinking? Brow furrowed, he turns away from the retreating guardsmen and pulls the small key from a pouch at this belt. Sliding the key into the lock, he quietly pushes the door open.

Losa still lies beneath the heavy comforter, her breathing slow and steady. Calib closes the door softly but returns the key to his pouch without relocking it. Taking up his customary position in the corner of the room, he settles back on his heels to wait until it is time to wake his ward. Time crawls by and Calib finds his thoughts in turmoil. He has spent decades conditioning his mind to remain clear and rested, ever vigilant in protecting Losa. Now, however, he cannot get past the bowl of soup.

The door swings slowly open, the light from the flickering hall sconces casting three wavering shadows into the room. The men enter, shrouded in hooded cloaks, and cross to Losa's bed, each drawing a dagger in turn. Calib's mind screams, but he cannot make his body react. He watches them surround her bed.

"Soup," he croaks, the word like a thunderclap in the quiet bedchamber. The three turn to him in unison, their stares burning him. "Soup!" he croaks again, his voice stronger.

"Damn him," hisses one. "I told you this would not work. We should have killed him."

"Kill him now. I will deal with the girl," says another. The voice is familiar, but it is beyond his clouded thoughts. Two of the men break away from the bed and move toward him, their daggers slowly rising.

"SOUP!" Calib bellows, the word like a mantra fixed in his mind. His head suddenly clears, and he is filled with the horror of the situation.

The Shadivengen sprints into motion, dropping to a crouch and sweeping his right leg across the floor, kicking the legs out from under one of his attackers. The second figure manages to dance back and keep his stance. Calib pivots on his left heel, bringing the full strength of his leg beneath him, and pushes hard against the floor.

Leaping high into the air, he pulls his swords free of their sheaths and rakes them across the standing man, splitting him from shoulder to stomach. The fatality of the blow vibrates up to his wrists. He twists at the apex of his leap, spinning the swords as he does so. Putting his weight behind the blades, he drives them into the chest of the first man, still dazed at having his feet kicked out from under him.

Calib rolls past the dead man, one of his blades refusing to come free of his chest and tearing away from Calib's grip. Coming up in a crouch, he instantly surveys the scene. The third man stands on the far side of the bed, his dagger poised above Losa. She's desperately clutching his wrist, but the attacker has strength and leverage on his side. Without hesitation, Calib hurls his remaining blade. It flies straight and true, striking the man high in the chest and knocking him back against the wall.

He slides slowly to the floor, fixing the Shadivengen with his dying stare. To Calib's surprise, he begins to laugh. "Soup!" he says, and then the laughter turns to choked coughs. "Damn soup," he wheezes, and then says no more.

Calib rises to his feet and slowly turns to face the bed, finding Losa sitting up. Her icy stare fixes on him, and for the first time in his life he cannot maintain her gaze. He lowers his eyes, his cheeks blossoming crimson with shame.

The assembly hall is filled to capacity with officers and soldiers of the Northern Army. Five bound men stand on the steps of the dais. It took Calib two days to track them down, but four of them, along with the three he slew, were the men present when he was poisoned. The fifth is Commander Higalen.

Losa, sitting in the high seat upon the dais, raises her hand and silences the hall. She stands, glaring at the condemned men before her. For a long moment she is silent and finally looks out upon the assembled soldiers.

"These men," she begins, "are accused of conspiring to kill the Supreme Commander of the Northern Army, the Mardente du Deos." She draws her long sword and points it at Higalen. "That, Commander, would be me."

The hall erupts in anger, the outrage of the men resounding against its stone walls. It takes several minutes to restore silence.

"Higalen," she continues, "you know firsthand what punishment awaits you. Have you anything to say?"

The commander drops to his knees, his head bowed, but says nothing.

"I thought not," she says, her voice cold. She steps forward, and with a single stroke, strikes his head from his shoulders. It takes less than a minute for the heads to total five.

Losa returns to her chair, but she does not sit. She wavers for a moment, and then seems to steel herself. She turns to face the hall. "Calib!" she commands, her voice strong and firm.

Calib shifts from the shadow and steps out from behind her chair, moving next to her.

"You are Shadivengen. Your only duty is to protect." She stares at him, but he can see the battle waging behind her eyes.

"I have failed you, my lady," he says quietly, dropping to his knees. His eyes do not leave hers.

"Yes. You failed."

He can see her fighting to do what she must, but her resolve is failing. She cannot afford to show any weakness. Not now. Calib knows he must help her, one last time. He lowers his head, missing the single tear welling in the royal eye. He hears the soft whisper of her sword...

／— ACKNOWLEDGMENTS —

Pileaus has long been a project near and dear to my heart. Fifteen-ish years ago (holy crap) I answered a post on a writing message board. Suddenly I was up to my eyeballs in what was then known as *Baeg Tobar.* It was the first setting I wrote for that wasn't exclusively my own. Working with the legion of talented creators who've contributed has undoubtedly made me a better writer and editor, and it's certainly opened doors I might not have found otherwise. I will always be eternally grateful to everyone who has ever been involved.

I'd like to start by giving a special shoutout to the amazing Max Gladstone for both his awesome introduction and the fiction he's contributed. Thank you also to Alana Joli Abbott and Gwendolyn Nix for their stories and their editing prowess. And of course, thanks to all the other authors whose fabulous work graces these pages: Mark Adams, Jeff Limke, Emma Melville, Robert Lee Beers, Andrew Schneider, and Dylan Birtolo.

They say you shouldn't judge a book by its cover, but in this case the cover image Chris Yarbrough provided is so freakin' amazing that I'd encourage you to make an exception.

Thanks to Daniel Tyler Gooden, author of *The Unmade Man,* the very first *Pileaus* novel. Although his work doesn't appear in this book, Dan and I spent untold hours brainstorming and setting the scene for a lot of what's in here. I'll always look back fondly on my work with him—and that time he came to visit and I barbecued for him in the aftermath of a huge snowstorm.

And last but absolutely not least, I'd like to express my biggest thanks to Jeremy Mohler and the team at Outland Entertainment. Without Jeremy's persistent belief in the setting, *Pileaus* and this collection wouldn't be a thing. Thanks for encouraging me to stick with it!

Til the next one!

—Scott Colby, Editor